GETTING IT ON WITH GARGOYLES

HAVEN EVER AFTER - BOOK ONE

HAZEL MACK

COPYRIGHT

Editing - Indie Edits by Jeanine

Cover - Anna Fury Author

Cover Art - Linda Noeran (@linda.noeran)

❀ Created with Vellum

THIS BOOK WAS WRITTEN BY A HUMAN · **HUMAN GENERATED** · **I DON'T SUPPORT AI BOOKS OR ART**

AUTHORS ARE NOW FACING AN UNPRECEDENTED CHALLENGE - ARTIFICIAL INTELLIGENCE (AI).

AI-based "books" , which are computer written, rather than human, are flooding the market and reducing our ability to earn a living wage writing books for you, our amazing readers.

The problem with AI as it stands today? It's not capable of thinking on its own. It ingests data and mimics someone else's style, often plagiarizing art and books without the original creator or author's consent.

There's a very real chance human authors will be forced out of the market as AI-written works take over. Yet your favorite authors bring magical worlds, experiences and emotions to life in a way that a computer can't. If you want to save that, then we need your help.

LEARN MORE ABOUT THE HARMFUL EFFECTS OF AI-WRITTEN BOOKS AND AI-GENERATED ART ON MY WEBSITE AT WWW.ANNAFURY.COM/AI

SYNOPSIS

**The small town of Ever, Massachusetts is idyllic and quaint.
It's also chock-full of monsters.**
When my sister thrifts an aged map with iridescent lettering
leading to a town called Ever, I roll my eyes. According to a
quick internet search, the town doesn't exist. We only manage
to find it with the help of a sexy gas station owner who offers to
come for me if I call him. *Swoon.*

I quickly learn that Shepherd isn't actually human, nobody in
town is. News flash—he's a gargoyle—a dominant, possessive,
crème-brûlée-loving monster. That should terrify me, but
something about him keeps me coming back. Maybe it's the
snark. Maybe it's the delicious snacks. Maybe it's his wingspan,
which leads me to wondering about the size of *other* things. I
digress.

No one realized that when I came through the town's protective
wards, something happened to them. Now the town—and my
sisters—are in danger from a soul-sucking evil that's constantly
trying to burrow its way in. Can Shepherd and I save the town
and our shot at love, or will evil ruin our happily ever after?

CHAPTER ONE

THEA

"I swear to God, if this is another wild-goose chase I'm gonna slap you." Wren glares at our sister Morgan from the back seat, arms crossed.

Normally I'm the peacekeeper between us triplets, but I'm inclined to side with Wren at the moment. "Morgan, honey, this is starting to feel a lot like that time you said we should go find that great hiking trail, and we drove around for hours, never found it, and ran out of gas. Remember that?"

Morgan glowers at me from the passenger seat, tossing her long red braid over her shoulder. "You two love to bring that up, but I swear this is different. I mean, look at this map!"

On cue, she shakes the map in my face. It's odd, for sure. It looks a million years old, all faded parchment and dark ink. But in low light, the darkest ink has an almost iridescent sheen.

Morgan turns to Wren and hands her the map. "Come on, *Mary*, isn't this just the adventure we need?"

"I don't know, *Winifred*," Wren counters.

When we start using the Sanderson sister nicknames, I know Wren's ire has faded—for now at least. It's almost laughable how like the *Hocus Pocus* triplets we are. Morgan's tall and

1

red-haired. Wren is buxom and curvaceous with dark hair like Mary, and I'm the petite blond with no boobs to speak of.

Thank God I'm not a ding dong though. Shudder.

"Let's make a deal." I fall easily into mediator mode. "If we drive another half hour, and we can't find the town of Ever, we'll agree your map is bullshit and go home. This was supposed to be a girls'-slash-birthday-prep weekend, not the road trip from hell."

Morgan frowns, but in the rearview, I watch Wren give her an irritated look.

Finally, Morgan sighs. "Fine, but I'm telling you, this place is real. This map is amazing. It can't be a fake."

Wren's dark eyes meet mine in the rearview. She's thinking what I'm thinking, which is that the gorgeous map of Ever, Massachusetts, is total bullshit. Morgan thrifted it from a little antique store and came home talking about a visit to Ever. A quick internet search suggested no such town exists.

Still, it was intriguing and we're definitely due for a getaway weekend, so Wren and I went along with Morgan's desire to find Ever. When she gets an idea in her mind, she's a damn bull in a china shop until she gets what she wants. She's such a fucking Leo.

My beat-up Honda pings, the gas light blinking on.

I give Morgan a pointed look. "Seriously, dude. We need gas or else we'll be stuck out here and it won't matter if we ever find Ever."

Morgan and Wren both groan at my terrible joke, but then Morgan squeals with excitement. "Look! A sign! It says Gas Up Ahead."

I follow her pointer finger, and sure enough, a faded sign mentions gas just a few miles away.

Relief fills my chest. Frankly, I am not cut out for car camping. Not even in the summer, and sure as shit not in early October. And definitely not in Massachusetts, where the winter wind is practically a weapon when it whips past you.

"The map says we're close to Ever, right?" Wren questions from the back seat. "Maybe we'll be able to get directions when we stop for gas."

We're silent the next two miles, but I breathe a sigh of relief when we round a corner and see an old-timey gas station. It's itty bitty, just a small, retro-looking store with one pump.

I pull up and hop out, but Morgan beats me to the machine. "I'll grab the gas. You wanna see about directions?"

I know she's being helpful because she doesn't want me to put the kibosh on this girls' weekend. I pinch her side, then hand her my credit card. Turning toward the store, I pull my coat tight around my frame and hunch my shoulders against the bone-deep New England chill.

When I push open the door to enter the store, a tinkling bell announces my arrival. No one's at the cashier's station, but a slight movement catches my eye. A massive man ducks out from a back room, grinning at me.

He's really fucking tall, well over six feet. Dark chocolate waves fall over both ears as even darker eyes meet mine. They crinkle in the corners when he smiles. His features are so sharp they seem chiseled from stone. An angular jawline leads to a perfectly dimpled chin, complete with a five-o'clock shadow.

Did this fine specimen walk right out of a damn *Vogue* magazine? What in the hell . . .

"You look lost," he states, his voice husky and low. He leans over the counter, his eyes level with mine. "Need directions?"

The smile he gives me is genuine, friendly, and way sexier than it should be. What is this hottie doing working at a gas station in the middle of nowhere? Somebody slap him on a romance cover, stat.

"Directions are exactly what I need." I laugh, wishing I'd done something with my hair. I point to my sisters outside and shrug. "We're looking for a town called Ever, but we've been lost for a while."

His smile broadens as he gestures with two fingers for me to come close. Something about the way he crooks those fingers sends heat curling through my belly and right to my clit.

"Happen to have a map on you?"

I resist the urge to clench my thighs as I glance back out at my sisters. Wren catches my eye, and I wave for her to join me, mouthing the word map. She seems to get it and grabs the map from the front seat.

The man speaks again. His voice is so gravelly that I cross my legs, praying for the ache between them to dissipate.

"GPS never can seem to find our town, no matter how many times we request the map companies to update it. We're more than a little remote here, which you've probably surmised."

"I gathered that," I deadpan.

Wren swings the door open, shuddering at the chill with the map in her hand.

"Damn, it's colder than a witch's tit outside," she complains before I cough helpfully and gesture to the attendant.

"I hear you're lost," he repeats. "Got a map? I'll give you directions."

Wren grins and shoots him an elated, flirty look, which instantly infuriates me. "I do happen to have a map. We'd love directions. We were supposed to get there hours ago. God, I hope there's a hotel or something."

He gives her a pleasant neutral smile. I feel a victorious thrill that it's not as sexy when directed at her. I got the sexy smile. The point goes to Thea!

She hands him the map. He grabs a permanent marker, and I resist the urge to ask him not to use it. I shudder when I think about that ink on Morgan's fancy-as-fuck thrifted map, but she can deal.

"Could you point out a hotel as well? I'm not sleeping in

Lucille," I manage, turning to beam at Mister Extremely Good-Looking. "Lucille's my Honda. Ever has a hotel, right?"

I glance over hopefully, but he shakes his head and shrugs impossibly broad shoulders.

"The motel just outside Ever is a gateway to hell. You're better off checking in late at the Annabelle Inn, our bed-and-breakfast. I'll call Catherine to let her know you're on your way."

Gateway to hell? The first things I imagine are bed bugs and strange stains on the blanket. The shudder I was holding back skates down my arms in the form of goose bumps.

"Shit, we don't want to be a bother." I hate the idea of waking up some poor hotel worker to help us when it's way past business hours.

The attendant smiles and draws on the map, circling a spot in the middle.

"Catherine won't mind one bit. You'll love her. She's very inviting and knows an incredible amount about Ever. She's a wonderful tour guide. I'm Shepherd, by the way. I live near the inn, so you're just as likely to see me there as here."

He reaches over the counter to shake my hand. I resist the urge to preen as I grip it and shake. He's got a strong handshake, something I can appreciate. It makes for a great first impression.

I can practically feel Wren gawk at us.

I studiously ignore her.

Being the twiggy sister has often led men to ogle her lusciousness first. Wren is all plump curves with amazing tits and ass.

But something about the way this man stares at me makes me feel special. His dark eyes never leave mine. His thumb rubs gently at the back of my hand as he shakes it.

I'm fucking entranced by this interaction.

I do manage to get out an introduction, though. "I'm Thea,

and this is my sister Wren. The one outside is Morgan."

"Lovely to meet you," he murmurs, directing the words at me.

He still hasn't looked at Wren.

When I glance at her, she's scowling at him with a curious, deflated expression.

I hold his hand a beat longer than necessary, clearing my throat when he releases it and stands tall, handing me the map. He reaches behind the cash register and grabs a business card, handing it to me.

"Follow where I indicated and you'll get to Catherine's. That's my cell on the card. If you get lost, call me and I'll come for you." Dark eyes focus intensely, a hint of a smile on his face.

I take the card with a nod of thanks.

I'll come for you.

Fuck. Those words shouldn't light me up from the inside out; they're not inherently sexual, but the way he delivered them makes me want to hop up into his arms and bite that chiseled jawline.

A slow smirk pulls his smile upward at one corner. Oh, he knows exactly what he did, sneaky, devilish man.

I need to get out of here before I embarrass myself by doing something crazy, like saying the words in my head out loud.

"Thea?" Wren's voice breaks through my thoughts.

I tuck my pale hair behind my ear. I know I'm blushing, but I can't help it, having such light skin.

He knows what the blush means, too, based on the self-satisfied look on his gorgeous face.

"See you around, Shepherd," I say, dredging up my confidence from somewhere.

I give him a big smile as I open the door and follow my sister out into the bitter weather. As I go, I sense his gaze on my back, and I resist the urge to turn and see if he's watching me like I think he is.

CHAPTER TWO
THEA

Wren grabs my arm the second we head out the door. "Ohmygawd, Thea, what the hell was that?"

"Oh no," I deadpan. "Hell's at the motel, remember?"

We both snort as she slaps my shoulder. "Seriously. He was practically salivating over you, and he lives in town! We might get you laid for the first time in a hot minute. This weekend is looking up, sis."

The good thing about Wren is that even though she thought he was hot, she'd never go after a guy she knew I was into.

And I am into Shepherd.

It's dumb, because we're only here for a weekend. For a girls' weekend, no less.

But still.

My cheeks are still pink when we get to the car. Morgan looks up from pumping gas.

"What's got you two so smirky?"

Wren waggles her dark brows, opens the back door, and slides in. "The dude inside was hot and hitting on Thea. He lives in town. He offered to *come* for her . . ."

Morgan snorts and replaces the gas handle. "He offered to come for you? Do tell."

I mutter something about how it didn't sound exactly like that when he said it, except that it fucking did. Now my brain is full of visions of him naked, hovering above me. I bet he'd be great in bed. Any man that good at eye contact must know how to fuck.

Morgan grabs the map while I attempt to compose my filthy thoughts. She opens it and gasps.

My hands fly up in the air. "I didn't do it! He just grabbed the marker and wrote!"

She turns the map so I can see it. Where Shepherd wrote in black permanent ink, there's now a golden line from the gas station to the circled spot in the middle of the paper.

I blink twice and frown. "He wrote in black, I'm confused."

She shrugs. "This map is weird. But I told you, it's real."

I have no idea how she made that leap, but like a lot of things when it comes to Morgan, I shrug it off. Color-changing ink is the least of my concerns. All I want right now is my bed and my vibrator because the heat between my thighs has not gone away. If anything, it's—

A horrifically loud sound cracks through the crisp air. Morgan and I spin around to face the shadowy country highway. The noise comes again, something between an owl screech and a wolf howl. All the hair on my neck stands. A low growl is followed by a third shriek. Morgan grips my arm so tight that I worry she'll break a bone.

"Get in the car, Morgan," I whisper-hiss.

Shepherd appears out of the gas station with a shotgun propped on his muscular shoulder. He's no longer giving me the sexy smile. Instead, he looks intensely focused and ready for trouble.

"You ladies should get out of here. We've got a wild animal

problem, and they bug me from time to time out here. I promise you'll be fine in town."

Without another word, he stalks into the road with the shotgun in his hands.

That's all I need to hear to get my ass in gear. I zip around the front of the car and hop into the driver's seat. Morgan grabs the map and examines Shepherd's directions. In the rearview, I see Wren turn to watch him.

The horrible shriek echoes a fourth time. In the mirror, I see Shepherd standing in the road, his back to us as he looks toward the deserted highway.

"Well, that's not fucking creepy," Morgan mutters before turning. "What do you think that was, wolves?"

"It was so loud, it sounded like they were right there," Wren murmurs, glancing behind us as we drive away from the gas station.

I'm a bundle of nerves, wondering if we barely missed being attacked by an animal in the middle of nowhere. My eyes stray to the rearview, where Shepherd's figure fades into darkness. God, I hope he's okay. It sounded like the animals are a somewhat regular occurrence, and he didn't seem worried, but damn.

We're able to follow his directions easily, and after about twenty minutes of dark forest, we round a bend and look down into a beautiful picturesque valley. Even at night, it's lit up with lights. Where I expected a sleepy little country town, it appears almost busy.

There's something white ahead. When we get closer, I see an ancient-looking wooden sign with hand-painted letters.

Welcome to Ever, Mass. Where Ever-yone is welcome! Population 853.

"Well shit, that's cute as hell," Wren chirps from the back seat.

I huff out an irritated breath. "You'd think being a detective and all, I would have been able to find a whole-ass town."

"Touché," Wren acknowledges with a sage nod. "It's the middle of the night though. Your detective skills aren't on point, and that's okay."

I cringe, my heart clenching in my chest. My detective skills haven't been on point since we lost our parents in a freak accident six months ago. I don't know if my skills will ever be on point again. Every time I go down to the precinct, I see my father's empty desk and I can't think.

Wren must sense my sad turn of thought.

"It's okay to not be okay, honey."

I nod, but I focus on the two-lane road ahead of me to avoid tears that threaten to spill. Both sisters fall silent. I'm sure they're lost in sad thoughts just like me.

After five more minutes, we wind our way into the valley. Then we discover a main street I can only describe as darling. There's a vintage-style red and black movie theater, a brick building marked town hall with a large gazebo in front, a general store, a flower shop, and a few more spots. There's even an adorable ice cream store, and next to that, a coffee shop called Higher Grounds. It's late at night and dark out, but a fair amount of people walk down the street and wave as we pass. It's every girl's small-town dream come to life.

"Take the next left at Sycamore," Morgan murmurs, focused on the map. I haven't seen a cross street yet, but I keep my eyes open.

We pass through downtown, with orderly streets of charming small cottages visible ahead. This place is a gingerbread wonderland. It's fucking cute. I can't wait to spend a weekend exploring.

A street sign announces Sycamore ahead. I make the turn, and a bright sign for the Annabelle Inn greets us. I let out a sigh of relief as Wren and Morgan high-five.

"Not gonna lie, *Winifred*," Wren jokes. "I thought you were full of shit. But this is so beautiful."

I laugh at how they fall back into their Sanderson sister personas as I park the car in front of the beautiful two-story home. Pale pink siding and white gingerbread trim cover the front. Wide windows line the first and second floors, lights on in a few. When I hop out and open the trunk, a figure appears on the front porch with a big smile.

The first thing I notice is how elegant the woman is. She's short, maybe my height, but impeccably put together with lovely gray hair, perfect makeup, and a hint of mischief in the way she looks at us. Even this late at night, she wears a flowing wrap dress that accentuates her plump frame.

I like her immediately.

"Catherine?" I confirm as I hop up the two steps from the car to the walkway.

She nods and clasps her hands together. "That's right. Shepherd called to let me know you'd be along. It's always a bit of a journey to get to Ever, but I'm thrilled you made it!"

"Us too!" shouts Wren from the car. "We thought we were about to get eaten by wolves at the gas station."

Catherine's smile falls a little, and she shakes her head. "We do have a bit of a wild animal issue now and again, but as long as you stick close to town it's not an issue."

I smile at her. "We're so glad to be here and sorry to show up so late. We'll be excellent guests, I promise!"

Catherine's smile returns. "Don't even worry about that, girls. Let's get you checked in."

We grab our bags and make our way up the long, concrete pathway. That's when I realize it's much warmer here than outside the valley. It must be at least sixty-five degrees.

"God," Wren gasps, noticing the weather at the same time. "How the hell is it so warm here?"

Our hostess laughs, and it's a friendly tinkle that sets me at ease. "We're in a funky little microclimate here in the valley. It's like this all the time, almost like we're isolated from the rest of the world."

Must be nice. I sure as shit wouldn't miss New York's winter weather. The wind through the buildings is sharp enough to cut you.

We make our way up the front steps of the gorgeous pink Victorian and through paned glass double doors.

The inn is beautiful inside. The floor is an intricate parquet of light and dark woods. Soaring archways lead into rooms on the left and right, and the check-in desk is just inside the foyer. A hallway behind check-in leads toward the back of the house. Stairs swoop at an angle above the desk. When I look up, the ceiling is painted with a gorgeous, detailed monster mural. Gargoyles, fairies, and werewolves cover the space. There's even a gryphon in one corner.

"Stunning, isn't it?" Catherine follows my gaze as she steps behind the desk, jiggling a mouse to activate her computer screen.

"Stunning," I agree as my sisters make a fuss over the house's design details.

Catherine looks at us. "How long would you like to stay?"

Morgan grins. "We haven't done a sisters' getaway in a while, so we figure a weekend should be good."

God, we could use it. We've had a rough six months.

A series of creaks and groans punctuate the silence. Catherine glances up with a half smile. "Ancient plumbing," she whispers with a conspiratorial wink. There's another creak as she grins and checks us in.

Morgan hands her a credit card for incidentals as I stare at the incredible beauty of the Annabelle Inn.

Wren drifts to the bottom of the staircase, trailing her fingers along a gargoyle carved into the banister.

"This place is incredible," she whispers, dropping to one knee to look closer.

Catherine glances over and smiles. "The Annabelle has a rich history that I'd love to share with you, but I know it's late. If you like, I can give you a tour of the town tomorrow morning. Why don't we head upstairs, and you can pick rooms."

Despite how cute the inn is, I know we're all fading fast. Now that I'm not focused on finding Ever, my eyelids feel like ten-pound weights.

Our hostess leads us up creaky wooden stairs. They dump us into a hallway that splits in both directions.

She turns with a smile. "Feel free to pick any room, I've got all the keys here. I find that certain rooms speak to certain individuals, and you're my only guests at the moment."

Morgan looks at the very first door. Carved into its face are four gargoyles frozen in a circle. She turns the knob and pushes through, gasping once she's inside. Wren and I follow her.

"It's so pretty," Wren whispers as we look around.

A king-sized bed sits to one side with all-white sheets and blankets. The room's exterior wall is curved, with a bench seat that runs underneath tall windows. We cross the simple room, admiring the detailed woodwork. When I look up, the ceiling here is painted too.

Gargoyles cover every inch of it. Their skins are every shade of black and white and gray and purple. Devious, angry expressions stare down at me.

Morgan shudders. "Creepy."

"I think it's beautiful," I murmur, in awe of the art.

Creepy is more my style anyway. Macabre, dark things have never bothered me. I'd never have followed Dad into the force if they did.

Wren tugs at my long braid. "Guess we know who wants this room."

I wrap my arms around myself and sigh. "It's perfect."

Catherine pulls a key off a giant ring at her belt. "Here you go."

Morgan walks to the window seat and peers out. "More gargoyles." She turns to Catherine. "Do all the rooms have a theme?"

"Oh yes," our hostess chirps. "Next door is the rose room because it's got a lovely view of the garden out back. Next to that is the lagoon room. That one is mermaid themed."

"I'll take that last one." Morgan grins. "Give me beachy vibes all day."

"That tracks," I snark at my three-minutes-older sister. "Miss beach volleyball."

Morgan shrugs, but I see her pleased smile. Of the three of us, she's the athlete.

"Happy to go with roses," Wren finishes.

Our hostess takes two more keys off her ring and hands them to my sisters with a kind smile.

"If I'm not at the front desk but you need something, simply ring the bell and I'll come. I serve breakfast from eight to ten, but there's a twenty-four-hour diner tucked behind the sweet shop. Please take me up on the offer of a tour, as well."

"We'd love that," Morgan smiles. "And we're sorry for arriving so late. We're thrilled to be in your beautiful home."

"To that end," Catherine says, "I live on the top floor. It's off-limits to guests, but there's a bell at the bottom of the staircase at the end of the hall. I'm not a great sleeper, so ring me if something comes up."

"I'm Thea," I say, realizing we haven't introduced ourselves. "These are my sisters, Wren and Morgan."

Catherine clasps her hands together with another motherly smile. "So lovely to meet you three. I'm going to hit the hay, but I hope you get some rest. Don't hesitate to let me know if you need something."

She takes her leave, and then we sink into the window seat and stare outside. This room has an amazing view of a lush garden with strategic uplighting. The beams highlight rose bushes and a myriad of fauna that definitely shouldn't be blooming in October.

Microclimate my ass. This place is paradise.

In the middle of the garden, perched on an intricately scrolled pedestal, stands an enormous gargoyle. It's seated on its haunches, a long tail curled around clawed feet. Its mouth is open in a sneer, fangs poking out from top and bottom jaws. Pointed ears curl back like horns, its wings tucked behind its back. Even from up here, it's clear the statue is massive.

"Damn, that's hot," snarks Wren, elbowing me in the side. "Nice view."

Morgan looks over and shoots me a smile. "I don't know about you two, but I'm toast. I'm about to hit up my mermaid lagoon room. Don't plan on me for *anything* before ten tomorrow."

Wren gives me a knowing look. Morgan is just like our mom —not a morning person. Wren and I are a lot more like our dad. Early birds unite.

"Nightly hug!" Morgan shouts, opening her arms.

Wren and I fold into them the way we started doing when we moved back into our parents' home. The nightly hugs last a long time these days. Even though our folks are gone from the house, it's a comfort to live where so many memories were made. Plus, for me, it's closer to my work in the city.

I breathe in Morgan's shampoo and Wren's subtle French perfume, and when we part, I smile. "I can't wait to explore Ever with you two tomorrow. Up bright and early?" I give Morgan a hopeful grin.

She returns with a shake of her head. "I told you no and I meant it. A weekend away from the hospital is the best possible medicine. I need it."

Wren snorts and looks at me. "You know I'm your girl for early adventures. I'll take the next room over, the rose one. Just knock on the wall for a half-hour warning."

When we break the hug, Morgan reaches out to twist my long blond hair around her finger. "I'm glad you didn't give up on my map. Thank you."

I return her smile and shoo her out of my room.

"I was this close, Morgan. Two more minutes and it would have been straight back to New York."

She sticks her tongue out but follows Wren up the hall to the room two doors over, letting herself in with a wave goodnight. Wren unlocks her room and gives me a quick wink before disappearing inside.

I close my door, and my mind drifts back to Shepherd. I pull his business card out of my back pocket, nibbling at my lower lip.

Call me and I'll come for you.

Rummaging around in my suitcase, I find my rose vibe and fall into the bed with it.

I think about Shepherd's gravelly voice as my hands slip between my thighs. Looks like I'm going to be the one coming tonight.

CHAPTER THREE

THEA

I wake up at 7 a.m. like always. I swear my body is on a timer. I've never had to set an alarm.

The snarling gargoyle faces on my room's ceiling are the first thing I see. "Good morning, boys," I salute.

I know Morgan thought this room was creepy, but I've always thought gargoyles were strong and beautiful. I love them.

Then again, I'm a fan of creepy things. I love haunted houses and Halloween and everything spooky.

I hop out of bed and dress. At the last minute, I remember Shepherd said he lives close to the inn, so I braid my hair and wrap it around my head like a crown on the off chance I run into him. Wren always calls it my "pixie look," but I'll admit, it's pretty cute.

We missed dinner last night because it took so long to find this place, and my stomach rumbles loudly to remind me. Wren's always up for early adventures, but when I dress and go next door to her room, light snoring is the only sound I hear. She could probably use the sleep, so I decide to walk to the diner Catherine mentioned and grab some breakfast. Maybe Wren will be up by the time I get back.

I creep down to the lobby, not sure if our hostess is up yet either. When I get to the front door, I find it unlocked. Hopefully that means Catherine's already awake, or maybe this place is just so safe they don't lock doors. Either way, I don't have the conundrum of wondering how to lock up behind myself.

Balmy, cool air brushes against my cheeks. There's a slight breeze today, but it's still far warmer here than it was on our way into town.

So weird.

I unzip my coat and head down the walkway, taking a left toward the main street. I haven't made it twenty feet before a giggle from behind a hedge makes me pause. An answering snort follows, and when I peer around the bushes, I blink twice. A small boy stands there, facing off with another. Gray batlike wings fan out on either side of his back.

He doesn't seem to notice me and darts into the shrubs with a teasing laugh. Then he and another child tumble out together, tickling one other as they cackle.

I rub my eyes and blink.

No wings.

I'm crazy and seeing things. Or maybe he was just wearing a little costume set that fell off.

Either way, I—

"Ignatius Zion, get up right now." A loud voice scares me and the kids.

One darts off into the shrubs, but the first one I saw stands tall, arms zipped to his sides. A hulk of a man comes out of the small cottage next to the Annabelle.

For a moment, I think he's Shepherd, but I quickly realize he's not. They've got the same wavy dark hair, but this man's a little taller, a little beefier, and the thunderous look on his face is the farthest thing from friendly. No sexy smile here.

I freeze as he storms across the lawn and stops in front of the child parked right in front of me.

"What are you doing out here?" the man barks, crossing his arms as he glowers at the boy.

"I wasn't alone, I was with Kev—"

"But where were you supposed to be?"

The boy blanches and looks over at me.

I'm intruding on their conversation, but it felt rude to walk away.

The man's pitch-black eyes flick to me, and his frown deepens. He opens his mouth to say something when someone interrupts us.

"Morning, Iggy."

The kid and I whip around to see Shepherd crossing the street. Relief surges through me at not being the only one to watch the kid get in trouble.

He's wearing tight-ass jeans and a black jean shirt rolled up to reveal massive, muscled forearms. Jesus, I'd like to rip the whole thing off his shoulders. If God took the time to sculpt the perfect man, it would be the man strolling toward me right now. I hold back an appreciative sigh.

The little boy sprints past me and leaps into Shepherd's arms, throwing his tiny self around Shepherd's neck.

"Uncle Shepherd, Dad's mad, but I just came out because I heard the pretty lady. And then I got distracted because Kevin tackled me. Make him *not* mad, okay?"

I try, and fail, to hold back a laugh as Shepherd joins us. The boy turns and crosses his arms, a mirror of the big, angry jerk to my left. The tiny child glares at the man I assume is his dad.

Shepherd grins at me. "Morning, Thea. This is my nephew Ignatius, or Iggy. And that scowly asshole is my older brother, Aloitius."

Aloitius? Ignatius?

Okay then.

"Nice to meet you," I say, reaching my hand out for Aloitius's.

He looks at it but doesn't uncross his arms. Instead, he looks over at his brother. "I need to speak with you later." Dark eyes flick over to me dismissively, then back at his brother. "Privately."

"No problem, Alo," Shepherd agrees in an even, friendly tone. "I'll come by at lunch."

"Fine. Come on, Iggy," the man demands.

Shepherd drops the child gently to the ground, watching as he scampers to his father and crawls up into the man's arms.

For a moment, I see a softer side of the hulking father. He closes his eyes as his son burrows his face in his neck.

"Sorry, Papa. I'll do better, 'kay?"

"We don't always make the perfect choices, but we strive to, right?"

Seems kinda intense to me, and I wonder where his mother is, or if he has one in his life.

The two hug tenderly, and then Shepherd's brother turns without a word and heads for the cottage.

I plaster a smile on my face as I turn to Shepherd.

"Well, your brother seems . . . "

"Alo's a big ole sourpuss. He's had a rough few years. He's not as bad as he seems."

Shepherd's voice is as deep as I remember. My nipples pebble in response to it. I'm grateful when he doesn't look down to see the headlights.

"I half expected you to call me last night," he murmurs, stepping closer.

He smells like fresh soap and some sort of deliciously spicy aftershave. God, I'm dying. He's overwhelming this close to me.

My mind spins back to my rose vibrator, and I sputter, losing any ability to form coherent words.

"In case you got lost, I mean," he clarifies.

But the grin on his face tells me he meant his comment sexually, and that flusters me. The downside of being so pale is that my cheeks heat, so I'm sure they're red.

"I like the blush," he teases before grabbing my hand and pulling it through his arm to rest in the crook of his elbow. "Come on, I heard your belly rumble from across the street. You need breakfast. And by the time I'm done feeding you, Catherine will be ready to give you and your sisters a tour."

"Are you not a good tour guide?" I joke as I grip his forearm.

His forearm is hard as a damn rock. I wonder about the rest of him. I don't mean to glance down at his crotch, but there's an obvious bulge at the front. This man is filling out those jeans to the point of bursting.

I struggle to swallow and force myself to look up. Shepherd grins and leads me along the sidewalk toward Main Street.

"Catherine always does tours. She's lived here longer than most of the other residents. Plus, she's an amazing storyteller. She'll make you laugh, cry, and swoon the whole time."

I don't think I'll have any trouble swooning this weekend, based on the current soaked state of my panties. But still.

We make small talk the remaining few blocks to Main Street. He looks both ways before we cross. To my surprise, the street isn't empty even though it's early. To our right, a group of children plays hopscotch on the sidewalk. Across from us, two elderly women sip coffee in front of a shop bursting at the seams with flowers. Wren will die when she sees those flowers.

"God, this is the cutest town," I murmur.

Candy-striped red and white awnings punctuate each store, giving the whole street a retro vibe.

Shepherd laughs, a rugged rumble that makes my core clench tightly.

"I've lived here most of my life. It's a wonderful place to grow up and raise a family."

The mention of family sends a stabbing sensation through

my heart. I picture my parents the last time I saw them. I hugged Dad before he packed all of Mom's suitcases in his beat-up Honda—now my beat-up Honda. They promised to call when they got to their destination, but that call never came.

Shoving that shit aside, I smile at Shepherd. "Where'd you live before Ever?"

He grins, a dimple popping on the right side of his smile.

God, I'm a sucker for dimples. But then again, who isn't?

"My folks are in Switzerland year-round, and I grew up there. Hence the ever-so-slight accent. Once it was time to venture out on my own, I knew I wanted to come to Ever. I had friends here, and this town is everything I wanted in a permanent place to live."

That sounds so nice.

"Did Alo follow you?"

Shepherd's smile falls, but we've reached the diner. A tall metal pole is topped with a big neon sign that reads the Galloping Green Bean. Shepherd opens the door, his other hand coming to my back.

Once we're inside the small lobby, he continues. "Alo had a rough breakup with Iggy's mother when Iggy was a year old. It's been hard for him without a partner. He came to Ever to be close to me so I could help him. I do what I can to support them, but I think he still feels overwhelmed, to be honest."

I feel for him, I do. I'm not ready for kids, I'm only twenty-eight. But I sure as shit wouldn't want to be forced to go it alone.

"He's lucky to have you."

Inside, the smell of coffee and bacon slaps me so hard that I groan.

Shepherd looks around, waving at a white-haired waitress behind a long bar. "We'll take my usual spot, Alba. Okay?"

She looks up and waves, blue eyes the color of the sky sparking with mischief when she sees me.

"Shepherd, you brought a woman to breakfast?"

I swear, the whole fucking diner stops on a dime, every head swiveling to look at us. It's something out of a movie.

Shepherd seems to take it in stride. "Alba, this is Thea. She and her sisters are in town for the weekend, so I expect you'll see them a time or two."

"Expect I will." The woman grins, pointing toward the far end of the retro diner. "Seat yourselves, I'll bring coffee."

I know my cheeks are pink as hell from the attention, but I try to focus. Shepherd rubs my back, ushering me down a long bar to a booth in one of the front windows. We slip into a red and turquoise pleather booth. The diner has the perfect retro vibe going on. There's even a '70s-style cheeseburger with arms and legs winking playfully from the front of the menu. I suppose all diners must strive for the same feel.

Shepherd slides into one side, hunching over as I laugh and pull the table closer to give him more room.

"I think you might be the biggest man I've ever met," I chuckle, leveling him with a conspiratorial wink.

Oh fuck. Did I say that out loud? It's like we're in a war of double entendres, and my cheeks are so hot I might combust.

He lounges back against the booth and stretches one muscular arm along the back. His other forearm rests lightly on the table, his hand clenched into a loose fist.

"Oh, I bet I am, Thea." His lips curl into a big grin.

Everything this man says sounds incredibly sensual.

I regret what I just said because I can't deliver that sort of sauce without blushing.

"I'm not normally this awkward," I blurt out, making things more awkward by the second.

"Oh, I hope like hell you are," he snorts. He grabs a menu and hands it to me. "I know it's seven in the morning, but Alba's chef makes the best cheeseburger you've had in your life. If you're into breakfast food, the blueberry pancakes are perfection."

I open my mouth to respond because I live for breakfast food, but Alba shows up. The smirky cheeseburger mascot is printed on her frilly turquoise half-apron.

She sets two black coffees down and pulls creamer packets out of her apron pocket. "Ready to order?" She pushes a set of pink horn-rimmed glasses high onto her head and looks from Shepherd to me expectantly.

"You know we aren't," he counters. "You're being nosy, per usual. Give us five minutes, please."

I throw my hand over my mouth to avoid laughing aloud.

Alba purses her lips and puts both hands on her broad hips. "Prompt service isn't being nosy, young man."

"It's never been quite *this* prompt before," he counters with a grin.

A chuckle comes from the table behind us, and Alba sashays away, grumbling under her breath.

"Are all small towns like this?" I laugh. "Everybody up in your business?"

Shepherd laughs. "I can't say much about other small towns, but most residents don't leave Ever. Once you settle here, this is it. Being in everybody's business is commonplace. Case in point, Alba's likely to show back up in three, two—"

On cue, Alba sways back into view, her lips still pursed in feigned indignation.

"Well, are you ready?"

Shepherd shrugs. "Has it been five minutes?"

"I'm ready," I say, even though I haven't looked at the menu. Diners are the same everywhere. "Can I have a stack of chocolate chip pancakes with a side of smothered eggs and bacon?"

"Smothered eggs? Does this look like a Waffle House to you?" Alba gives me a disapproving look, blue eyes sparking with fire.

"No," I snort. "But you knew what I meant, didn't you?" I give her a saucy little wink as Shepherd shakes with laughter.

Half an hour later, I listen raptly as he talks about growing up in Switzerland and moving to Ever. His life sounds idyllic, and even though my childhood was full of love, I find myself a little bit jealous. Plus, his parents are still in Switzerland. He gets to visit a few times a year.

I'm a jelly donut. I want family in cool locations. My Aunt Lou lives in Jersey, and that's about all I've got left of close relations.

Shepherd smiles at me. "Tell me about your family and your sisters."

I know he doesn't mean to ask a prying question, and normally I wouldn't blurt out the whole sordid tale. But there's something about this man that makes him easy to talk to, so I tell him the whole thing—how I followed in my father's footsteps and became a detective. How he and mom left to go on a trip and never came back.

He listens quietly, and when I'm done, he reaches across the table and grabs one of my hands. "I'm so sorry, Thea." Dark eyes stare at me with an expression I've seen a lot lately—pity.

I hate that. I need to move on from this damn topic.

Pulling my hand from his, I grab my coffee and sip at the dregs. "Is there anything at all that sucks about living here? You make it sound so idyllic and wonderful."

It's almost like the entire diner freezes again. Behind Shepherd, the people in that booth tense up enough for me to notice it before they relax and carry on.

He gives me a neutral look. "What you saw last night, the noises? That's the worst we get around here. They're a pain, though."

"I had forgotten all about that," I murmur, remembering how he stalked into the street like a predator.

"They don't come into town, but they like to mess with the gas station, probably because it's remote and I have snacks." He shrugs and glances out the window.

"Tell me more about this gas station," I press. "You live in town and work there? Did you take it over from someone when you moved to Ever?"

He nods. "An elderly gentleman ran it before me. He was happy enough to sell it and retire somewhere tropical. It's the only gas station for miles, so it keeps me busy. Plus, I serve on Ever's Town Council. Those jobs keep my schedule pretty tight."

"Ooh," I snigger. "Town Council. Is that as bad as an HOA? I've heard those things are a bitch to run."

"*So* much worse," he chuckles. "The Town Council is all-consuming. Still, I'm happy to give back. I love it here." He looks down at my empty plate. "It's after eight. Think your sisters will be up?"

I glance down at my watch, but it seems to be stuck at two a.m. Outside the diner's window, Main Street bustles with activity.

"Yeah, let's head back. I'm anxious to hear if you've oversold Catherine's tour abilities or not."

His dimpled grin grows wider.

Alba returns with a friendly wave, shoving her glasses down onto the very tip of her nose. "Am I putting this on your tab, Shepherd?"

He inclines his head, but I grab my credit card from my phone.

"I'm happy to pay for mine."

Shepherd scoffs. "I don't know how they do things where you're from, but here in Ever, when a man takes you to break-fast, he intends to pay for it. Put the card away, woman." His voice is rough and commanding.

When I look up, there's a fiery intensity to his gaze. Just like at the gas station, I swallow hard around a desperate need to crawl over this table and throw myself into his big arms.

Is this a date? He brought me here and he wants to pay. Even though he didn't specifically call it a date, it feels like one.

When I don't fight about it, he nods at Alba. She snorts derisively and leaves us. Shepherd manages to fold up out of the booth and extends his hand to me.

Am I about to hold hands with a man I just met last night?

Looking at his beautiful, thick outstretched fingers, I decide that yes, yes I fucking am.

CHAPTER FOUR

THEA

"Girl, where have you be—" Wren's voice cuts off when she notices Shepherd at my side, my fingers through his as we cross Main Street toward Catherine's inn. She plasters a sweet smile on her face and waves at Shepherd. "Nice to see you again. Have I missed the tour?"

As he pulls his fingers from mine, the loss of contact sends a wave of longing crashing through my chest.

He smiles at my sister. "Not at all." He turns and gives me his sexy grin, slipping one big hand into the front pockets of his jeans. "I've got to run some errands for a friend, but I'll see you soon?"

With his free hand, he reaches out and brushes his thumb across my upper lip, grinning as he brings it to his mouth and sucks softly.

"You had chocolate stuck to you," he murmurs, black eyes flashing.

My cheeks go pink.

He smirks and turns back to Wren. "Catherine is the best tour guide in town. You're in good hands. Have fun, ladies."

After another soft smile, he heads up the street in the other direction.

Wren comes to my side and grabs my hand as we watch him go.

"Jesus, that man fills out a pair of jeans." She grips my chin hard and turns me to face her. "Tell me everything. You were supposed to get me up, you hussy."

"You were snoring when I got up," I grit out between squished cheeks.

She drops the grip and drags me back toward the inn. Even so, I crane my head backward to get one last look at Shepherd as he walks away, and damn, I'm glad I did. His jeans hug the thick curves of his ass and legs. I've never seen legs that muscular or an ass that round. Who even makes jeans to fit a man like that?

Drool slips out of my mouth.

Wren laughs. "Oh girl, you've got it bad."

I let out a dramatic, Scarlet-O'Hara-worthy sigh. "Wrennie, he was so sweet at breakfast. He told me all about how much he loves this town and how nosy everybody is. It was adorable."

She bumps my shoulder with hers, and we giggle all the way back to the Annabelle. When we get there, Catherine and Morgan stand on the front porch, sipping coffee and chatting.

Even though my watch seems to have frozen, I know it's still early. Despite that, our hostess is dressed in beautiful black slacks and a billowy white shirt that accentuates her curves. Her hair is curled so perfectly she looks like a Parisian fashionista.

Pale gray eyes twinkle at me. "I heard you already grabbed breakfast. Shall we do a quick tour of downtown and then come back for the buffet here?"

"You heard I had breakfast, huh?" I tease.

Something about Catherine makes it easy to say what I'm thinking. She gives off such an open, comfortable vibe.

Her eyes twinkle again. "Oh, the news that you showed up to

the diner with Shepherd spread like wildfire. Everybody knows by now. Welcome to Ever," she laughs with a shrug.

Morgan's nostrils flare, but she grins and gives me that sisterly tell-me-everything look.

"Let's walk and talk," Catherine encourages.

We turn to follow her.

I point at the tall hedge that lines her property, separating it from Shepherd's brother's house. "I met your neighbor this morning, and his son."

Catherine's smile falls as she folds her arms across her ample chest.

"Poor Alo has had a hard time of things since his partner left. Now he's raising Iggy all alone. They're great comfort to me, though. They come over quite a bit, so don't be surprised if you see Iggy running around the Annabelle. He lets himself in, and Alo usually follows."

"I'm glad to hear there's more to him than being kinda rude," I admit.

Her eyes sparkle as she turns to me. "Oh, there's a lot to know about Alo, and nearly all of it is good. He just takes some time to get to know. He tends to think he needs to do the single-parent role alone, but the reality is being in Ever means he has help from our community when he's willing to accept it."

I get lost in thought then, thinking about how we're just here for the weekend. I can admit that my breakfast with Shepherd has me wishing I lived a helluva lot closer. I wonder how long it would take me to get here from New York if I didn't drive around in circles for hours first?

Shaking that thought off, I gesture toward Main Street. "Tell us everything, Catherine. We are ready for the tour!"

She smiles again. "Well, Ever has a long and complicated history, but it's the friendliest place I've ever lived. I came here as a young woman and settled after meeting my partner."

"And where is he now? Or she?" Wren clarifies.

"Gone," Catherine sighs. "Long gone, but not forgotten."

Her voice is sad, but she brightens up as we head down the front steps and toward Main Street.

For the next half hour, she walks us up and down both sides of Main. We learn the rich history of the sweets shop, ice cream parlor, movie theater, and general store. There are other adorable spots too, and I think all three of us are in love by the time she's done. Ever's downtown is quaint and beautiful, and I can tell my sisters are just as excited to be here as I am.

"God, Ever seems like the perfect place to live," Wren sighs. "That flower shop? I could spend all day there."

Catherine turns to us with a smile as we near the inn once more. "It is wonderful. But"—she turns to us, her expression still happy—"it's also chock-full of monsters."

~

For a long moment, none of us say anything.

Wren coughs politely, clearing her throat. "You mean, there are jerks here like anywhere else?"

Catherine's tinkling laughter sounds far more lighthearted than I'm suddenly feeling. A rock sinks in my gut when she shakes her head.

"No, Wren. I mean what I said in the literal sense. Ever is chock-full of monsters. Actual monsters."

Morgan grabs Wren's arm and mine and pulls us close. She's stiff as a damn board. "Okay, then . . . we're going to just be on our way. We'll grab some breakfast or some—"

Catherine sighs. "I do find it far easier to simply rip the Band-Aid off, and you seem like such nice girls. Ignatius!" she calls out, and the kid from this morning barrels out of the house next to the inn, followed closely by his hulking father.

"Hello, Alo," Catherine greets the man, who scowls as he descends his front steps and gives her a curt nod.

My hands are blocks of ice as Iggy joins us, looking expectantly up at Catherine. His blue eyes are wide and friendly.

She smiles down at the plucky child. "Ignatius, my sweet. Would you be so kind as to let down your glamour?"

My throat dries up like a fucking desert. His *what*?

Next to me, my sisters are stock-still. I think we're all in shock. Is this about to turn into some sort of horror movie where we have to fight our way out? I like creepy, but I don't want to be in the middle of an actual murder scene. Well, not as the victim.

Iggy looks at us, then over at his father, who nods in assent.

The child looks up hesitantly. Then his body shimmers into a smoky black wisp and reforms, and what stands in front of us is undoubtedly a tiny gargoyle. He's blocky and muscular with an angular face topped with spiky horns. Leathery wings open wide behind his back. He has fucking claws on every goddamn finger and toe. Only three fingers are on each of his tiny hands.

Fuck me. I blink my eyes, trying to understand what I see, but my brain's CPU utilization is too far over a hundred percent to compute.

Wren screams, Morgan hisses, and I blink rapidly as I drop to a knee and stare, a hysterical cackle leaving my lips.

Iggy's face is all angular, rough-hewn lines, but the eyes are the same. Still blue, still joyous. He unfolds his tiny wings again, unfurling them as my sisters back up. Wren starts asking a million questions, I think, but all I can do is stare at Iggy, who flaps his wings and lifts off the ground in front of me, hovering at eye level.

I stand and back up so I'm touching my sisters. I need grounding. I need to be grounded. I'm hallucinating a fucking gargoyle child. This can't be real. I must have lost my mind due to an overwhelm of Shepherd's hotness. Jesus, was this morning even real?

I pinch myself to check, but as I do, Alo stalks close enough to join our group.

Catherine looks up and smiles in what looks like encouragement. Alo disappears into a puff of smoke, and when his body reforms, he's easily seven feet tall and a massive, terrifying version of his son. He looks like a damn demon, or a . . . oh shit.

He looks exactly like the gargoyles painted on my bedroom ceiling. My breath constricts until all I can do is suck in short gasps of air and pray my heart doesn't explode out of sheer terror.

Alo scowls, and a bead of sweat rolls down my face.

Then he opens his mouth, revealing sharp fangs, and lets out an ungodly roar.

That's when the screaming starts. I don't know who it is—me or Wren, probably not Morgan.

Everything starts to go black as I fall to the ground.

Lights out.

Goodbye, world.

CHAPTER FIVE

SHEPHERD

I hear the screams before I round the corner from Main toward the Annabelle Inn.

Mine. Mate. Protect.

The words flash through my mind, reinforcing my need to get to her fast.

Alo let out a battle cry, but there was no urgency in our family bond. So, he's making a fucking point, I guess. Meeting Alo usually means a rough initiation into town because he's such a grump. I wanted it to be gentler for Thea and her sisters. That's why I encouraged them back to Catherine's for a tour. I didn't think Alo would be home this morning.

I sprint around the corner. Thea's on the ground. Her sisters hug one another as Alo looks smugly down at her prone form. Iggy flutters around her face, peppering her with a million questions even though she's passed out. Moving fast, I drop to a knee by her side and lift her carefully into my arms, snarling at my older brother.

"You had to roar? It scares the shit out of everyone, Alo!"

His smirk broadens, and Catherine crosses her arms with a heavy sigh.

Thea's sisters seem to snap out of their shock then.

"Put her down this instant," barks the redhead, Morgan.

The other sister claws at Thea and almost pulls her from my arms. I hold back a growl as I clutch her tighter to my chest.

I jerk my head toward the Annabelle.

"Let's get Thea inside until she comes to. I'm worried she might have hit her head when she fell." I give my brother another glare.

He makes a point of looking in the other direction.

Catherine gestures to the inn. "Girls, I promise there's nothing to be afraid of. We are all friends here."

"I knew there was something fucked up about that map," Morgan shouts, hovering beside me as I start for the door.

I make it up the Annabelle's front steps far faster than the triplets. All gargoyles are fast, not that Thea knows I am one yet. I bet she'll make the leap quickly when she sees me standing next to my brother and nephew.

In my arms, her beautiful blue eyes begin to flutter. Pink bow lips part into a sexy smile, even though she struggles to open her eyes all the way.

"God, you're hot," she whispers. "Are you a gargoyle too? Your wings must be like, really big, right?"

She lets out a hysterical cackle, and that's when I start to worry about a concussion. Flirting with me after assuming I'm a literal monster seems the wrong response for this particular moment.

The Annabelle creaks and groans when I let myself inside.

I glare up at the ceiling. "Pipe down," I warn her.

There's another irritated squeak, and then the inn is silent.

The group piles in behind me. I lay Thea down on the living room sofa and drop to both knees beside her, stroking blond hair away from her heart-shaped face.

Gods above, she's fucking stunning. She looks like an angel laid out on the sofa in front of me.

"Thea!" Wren, the brunette, shouts.

She shakes her sister, and I resist the urge to shove her away. I'd love nothing better than to shift and take Thea to my nest, to bundle her up in the pillows and blankets, and snuggle her until she's ready to open those pretty blue eyes for me.

I try to remember these girls just saw Alo in gargoyle form. The monster revelation is always a shock for new, non-monster residents.

Catherine and Iggy join us, and Iggy hands Morgan a cold, wet towel.

She takes it like it's a red-hot poker but gently places the towel on Thea's forehead.

"She'll be fine, she didn't hit her head very hard," Iggy offers, hovering slowly above her.

When I give him a warning look, he darts to the back of the sofa and lands. He gives me an apologetic shrug as he tucks his tiny wings behind his back. Wide blue eyes are filled with worry.

I sense Alo come in the front door. He stops at the end of the sofa and crosses both arms, now helpfully back in his human form. "New resident orientation starts in fifteen. Better get her up fast. The Keeper'll be pissed if we're late."

"Alo," I snarl, "the Keeper can wait. Maybe if you hadn't surprised her, she wouldn't have hit her head in the first place."

He gives me a look, *the* look. The older brother why-do-you-care-anyhow look.

I shoot him back my best impression of our father, but he rolls his eyes and reaches over to grab Iggy, slinging my nephew onto his shoulder. "I'm headed for the gazebo. I'll let the Keeper know you're delayed."

"Thank you, Alo," Catherine says, dropping to both knees beside me.

She brushes Thea's bangs to the side. A tiny dribble of blood is just above her ear, but thankfully, it doesn't look serious.

Catherine tsks. "Oh, I think she'll be alright. It was just a little scare."

"A little scare?" Morgan barks out. "A little scare? Just what in the frosty fuck is happening? Are we seeing things? Are you both . . . whatever Alo is? Which was what, by the way?" Her voice rises to near hysterical by the time she voices the last question.

Catherine stands and turns. The sisters hold onto one another as they watch me dab carefully at Thea's forehead.

"I'm not a gargoyle, no. I'm a succubus. We're not a danger to you, no one in town is. Girls, I promise all will be explained at the new resident orientation."

"Resident?" Wren's tone is worried and urgent. "Are we prisoners?"

The house creaks and groans a little, laughing at Wren's question.

"Oh no, not at all." Catherine is quick to clarify. "You may leave whenever you want to. The reality is that nobody ever does."

"That's ominous as fuck," Morgan snaps.

I open my mouth to explain, but Thea bolts upright, flinging herself to the back of the sofa. Her blue eyes are wide and terrified, but the moment her sisters sink next to her, she visibly relaxes.

"Thea," I murmur, using a tone I've never used with another woman.

Those sky-blue eyes turn to me, and long lashes flutter as her lips part.

"You're alright, sweet girl," I croon. "You're safe, alright?"

"Shepherd?" she croaks, leaning out of her sisters' embrace to throw both arms around my neck. "What the hell is going on? Am I dreaming?"

I feel her sisters watching us, but I wrap both arms around her anyhow and tuck her head under my chin. I love how, despite seeing Iggy and Alo drop their glamours, she's drawn to me. She's mine, she just doesn't know it yet. I'd preen about it if I didn't know she was in pain.

"No, angel. This isn't a dream. You're safe, your sisters are safe. And I promise I'll protect you."

Because you're mine, I don't say aloud. *And I knew it the moment I clapped eyes on you at the gas station.*

I didn't call the triplets to Ever with the map, but I'm sure as shit glad someone did because Thea is definitely my mate.

CHAPTER SIX

THEA

I 'm in an alternate reality.

That's it.

That's the only possible explanation for Iggy and Alo turning into winged monsters and Alo roaring at us. Waking up to a concerned Shepherd whispering sweet nothings while I hugged his neck like a life buoy just cements my theory—alternate reality.

In the distance, a bell rings. Or maybe it's all in my head. Maybe this whole *thing* is in my head, and I've finally lost my marbles. I don't know what was in those pancakes this morning at the diner.

Shepherd stares at me, dark brows furrowed in concern. I reach out and touch his face. Still handsome. Still rough and manly.

"Still tan," I murmur. "Still human. Am I crazy?"

His dark eyes sparkle, but Morgan butts in and grabs my arm, pulling me away from him.

"What in the hell is going on here?" she hisses.

Wren wraps an arm around us, and I'm in a sister pile as we stare at Shepherd and Catherine.

Catherine smiles up at him and gestures at his big frame. "Friend, it might be helpful to let down your glamour too. I've said it before and I'll say it again. Ripping off the Band-Aid is really for the best."

I clench up. Wren hisses in a breath. Next to me, Morgan's chest rises and falls so fast I worry she's experiencing heart failure.

Shepherd's focus is still on me, and when he smiles, it's just like the night we met—dazzling.

"I won't hurt you, any of you. I know this is shocking, but we're all friendly here."

When none of us respond, his smile falls a little. A swirl of smoke clouds the air, and the tan fades from his skin. Dark purple-gray horns slide out of his forehead, curving up and away from his face. They look sharp as hell. His hair goes darker, pitch black, but it still falls in soft waves around his ears.

One of my sisters makes a strangled noise. Behind Shepherd, a long tail that ends in a flat spade shape lashes from side to side like an angry cat. My eyes widen, and the tail stills.

"You're still wearing clothes," I blurt out.

It's the only thing I seem able to focus on. He was wearing that sexy fucking jean shirt this morning, and he's . . . still wearing the sexy jean shirt.

Shepherd laughs. "We don't lose clothing during a glamour drop, thankfully."

"Are you gonna eat us?" That's Wren, blurting out a more useful question.

Catherine's smile grows bigger.

Shepherd shakes his head. "We're not cannibals, honey. We're just monsters. Everyone in town is. When you arrived yesterday, the town and its inhabitants, whom we call Evertons, were all cloaked in a glamour to make us appear human to you."

His words bang around in my brain, but I can't form them into any sort of coherent thought. A man stands in front of me with purple skin, horns, and, oh my god, I didn't even notice at first but giant wings are tucked behind his back. They end in black dagger-like claws.

The sound of a bell ringing breaks through my shock. Catherine cocks her head to the side and gives Shepherd a look. "We really should get to orientation. Thea seems alright, other than a bit shocked."

"Definitely," Shepherd murmurs, not taking his eyes from mine.

"We're not residents," Wren barks. "We came here for a damn girls' weekend, not to do . . . whatever this is."

"You don't have to stay," Shepherd croons gently, dropping to a knee, which brings his purple-gray face level with the three of us.

His eyes are nearly black like this, such a dark brown I can't distinguish the iris from the pupil.

"We always do orientation when someone non-monster joins us. Ever isn't a normal town, and we'd like to give you an overview before you spend your weekend here."

I stare at him, trying to decide if I sense anything sketchy about this situation, apart from him not being a goddamn human. I don't, though. He seems genuine.

"So we're not in danger?" I clarify. "And we can leave whenever we want."

"Of course," he agrees. "Catherine is still your hostess, and the Annabelle is still your home for the weekend. Although, I hope you'll decide to stay longer. Ever is an amazing place to explore."

I think we're all too shell-shocked to agree or disagree, but when Shepherd holds his hand out for mine, I allow him to pull me upright.

The bell rings again, and Catherine smiles down at us. "That bell calls the town's residents to Town Hall, where you'll meet the Keeper. He's the monster version of a mayor. Let's go, I promise you're safe with us. If you go to orientation and decide you'd like to leave, we won't hold you back from doing so. I give you my word."

As if on command, the whole inn seems to shudder around us.

Catherine's grin broadens, and she gestures toward the door. "Come on, girls."

Somehow, we manage to make it out the door and back to Main Street. Shepherd pulls my hand through his elbow again, but I'm still in too much shock to stop him. Wren and Morgan hover next to me, linking our arms all together.

The only thing keeping me going are Shepherd's fingers stroking mine where my hand rests in the crook of his arm. If he lets go, I might sink into a heap on the pavement. When I glance down at his hand, I see it only has three fingers. Three *huge* fingers tipped in sharp black claws like his wings.

I pull my arm away from him and wrap it around my middle. My heart feels like it might burst out of my chest like that alien movie.

Up ahead, I see a white wooden gazebo. Townspeople crowd underneath it, maybe a few hundred in total. Are they all monsters? Oh god, oh god, oh god.

I stop in my tracks, yanking my sisters to a halt, when a couple enters the packed building, and the entire structure creaks and groans. As we stand, gobsmacked, the entire structure shifts and expands, adding another ten feet or so to its overall width.

"Did that building just grow?" Wren's voice is high as fuck, a sure sign she's about to lose her cool. Which is really saying something because Wren is a goddamn rock.

She's the chill one, and if she's freaking out, it's time for me to lose it too.

"Does the inn do this? Is that what all those noises were?" Morgan questions.

Wren and I swivel our heads in her direction.

Catherine beams and claps her hands together. She seems pleased with Morgan's question. "Something like that, dear. The Annabelle is thrilled you're here. We'll discuss this at orientation, of course, but I can give you a more in-depth tour of the inn once orientation is over."

I blink my eyes rapidly, trying to take in the incredibly overwhelming information that continues to batter me. Looking up at Shepherd, I narrow my gaze on those beautiful, dark eyes.

"So everyone from the diner is a monster? Even Alba?"

"Mhm," he confirms.

When he nods, I can see the tips of his horns. God, they look sharp as hell.

"She's . . . what?" I straighten my spine because now that the shocks are coming in a nonstop wave, I'm fucking concerned.

"Centaur," he says in an apologetic tone, running both hands through perfect, wavy locks.

"And you, Alo, and Iggy are gargoyles? Catherine's a succubus. What other monsters are there?"

For a brief moment, there's a flash of worry on his handsome face. He nips at the edge of his lip, and despite my current discomfort, the move sends heat through my lower stomach to pool in my clit.

Catherine pats me gently on the back. "Girls, let's get to orientation, and I promise we'll answer all your questions."

We walk the last half block in complete silence, and when we step into the gazebo in front of Town Hall, the building creaks and groans again, widening even farther. It's something out of a horror movie, the way every person turns to look at us. I haven't felt this much the center of attention since our parents' funeral. It's a horrible feeling.

The bell that was ringing stops abruptly. Then all I hear are the shuffles of feet against aged plank flooring.

"Nothing to see here, people!" shouts Morgan.

But of course, there is something to see, because this new resident orientation? It feels like it's for us with how everyone is examining us like dogs at a show.

That's when I notice the tall figure standing at the far side of the gazebo. He looks human enough. In fact, everybody in here does. Dirty blond hair swoops up and away from his forehead, his features angular and elegant. Dark eyes that seem to shine from within look our way, and that's my first clue he's not human. His eyes almost glow. He's dressed in a long-sleeved black turtleneck and dark jeans.

A pale scar travels from his hairline down to his jaw. I wonder how monsters heal. Is it different from humans, or the same? That thought dissipates when I realize there aren't any more seats. My sisters and I lean against the railing. I'm thankful when Shepherd and Catherine stand with us on either side.

"Now that everyone is *here*," the blond male begins, his tone dismissive and arrogant, "let us begin. Everyone, if you'll please let down your glamours." He raises his hands, and a rush of noise fills the gazebo.

Some are gentle, like the wisp of clothing falling to the ground, and others are the break and crack of bones being loosed from joints and resetting. I've never heard noises like this.

I press myself harder against the railing, rubbing my eyes in disbelief at the scene unfolding in front of us.

Mr. Turtleneck looks over and smiles, although it looks more predatory than anything. He still appears human though, so maybe he is? "Evertons, meet our newest residents—Morgan, Wren, and Althea Hector."

How the fuck does he know our names? Oh god, I hope we're not getting adultnapped into some weird, hidden monster sex ring. I can't deal with that right now. Normally, I'd be all for busting up a sex ring. Today is not that day.

Every head swivels again, but this time I'm looking at a host of humanoid and non-human faces. The woman seated closest to me has feathers that sprout off her head like an owl. Feathered wings are tucked up behind her back, and she's got chicken feet. Next to her, a man who looks like a garden gnome sits with his feet barely hanging off the edge of the chair.

All around, every face is focused on us. I don't even recognize most of the types of monsters I see in front of me. Gulping hard, I look down at the plank floor and try to recenter my focus. My brain is working on overdrive, but I'm out of space to keep processing.

A high-pitched, squeaky voice rings out from somewhere in the audience. "Who called them?"

"What does that mean?" Morgan whisper-hisses at Catherine. "We had a map."

Before I can follow that train of thought, the man at the front speaks.

"I did," he says simply.

That's all. He did it. He called us, whatever the fuck that means. A hush falls over the crowd. Then a buzz rises, and everyone begins to whisper.

He allows it for a moment before his voice booms over the crowd. "Silence, please. I'd like to get through orientation quickly so you may all welcome our new residents."

Everyone shuts up, which makes me wonder who this asshat is and what kind of hold he has on the town. Is this the mayor Catherine referenced? Questions begin to filter through the overwhelm.

Next to me, Shepherd leans against the railing, looking at the male with a slight frown.

I cross my arms as I wait for the man to continue. The shock is wearing off, and my detective skills are pinging. I know one thing for certain—if I or my sisters are in danger here, there's nothing I won't do to get the hell out of Ever.

SHEPHERD

Thea's shock and frustration are almost tangible. Her sisters seem equally out of sorts. I can see they're about to start peppering the Keeper with questions. His style is brusque as hell, but he's kept Ever safe for ages; that's his job.

And it's my job to make sure he's able to do his well. He, Alo, Ohken, and I are this town's leadership, something I'm anxious to explain to the triplets. We aren't a danger to them.

Turning to the girls, I give them a heartfelt look, one I hope feels calming and not too alpha-dominant. All three pairs of eyes drift to my claw-tipped wings. Shit. Welcoming new non-human residents is always dicey, but I've never been this invested in the process.

Orientation was never for my *mate* before. I'm in uncharted territory, and I can't even tell her that right now.

I opt to explain what I can, despite the whole town as my audience.

"The Keeper's going to do a brief overview of Ever, and then my friend Ohken will answer questions. After that, you're free to explore, okay? You're not prisoners here. Catherine and I will say it again and again, but on my honor, it's the truth."

Thea looks up at me, eyes wide and blue as she nods, nipping at her lower lip.

A soft growl rises unbidden from my throat because I want to be the one nipping that plump lip. There's a lot I want to do with her. Gargoyles tend to mate fast and rough.

Only one male in my family tree has ever mated a non-gargoyle, and I'm not close enough with him to ask how it went for him.

Thea's human. I've got to approach this differently with her. We've had other human residents; it's not unheard of for monsters to mate with humans. I just never thought I'd fall into that category.

The entire town waits silently to see how this will go with human residents. Usually, there's shock, then screaming, and finally, a mixture of awe and panic. It's been a long time since we got a human resident. Nearly a hundred Ever-years, I think.

This is a big deal.

The Keeper gives me a look that screams he's ready to get the show on the road. I nod, letting him know the triplets are as good to go as they can be. Then I step closer to Thea, making my intentions clear to my friends and neighbors, even though she isn't aware.

I get a few knowing smiles.

The Keeper grits his jaw tightly as he brings his arms wide.

"Ever is one of hundreds of safe towns for monsters all over the world. We call these towns havens, and each haven is protected by a Keeper like myself. Keeper is both my title and name, and you may address me as such. The human equivalent would be something like the mayor and police force wrapped together."

Thea bristles at his mention of police. I wonder if it's

because of what she shared with me about her father being a detective.

Morgan scoffs and crosses her arms, but the Keeper continues, addressing the girls directly.

"Each haven is different, but *Ever* is comprised of a wide variety of monsters. In many ways, we're just like a regular small town."

"Is that right?" Morgan barks, dark red brows raised. "Maybe a vampire runs the coffee shop, and the werewolf biker gang will fix my car. Is that what you mean? Just regular old small-town America? How'd we get here, dude? How and why did you 'call us,' and what the fuck does that mean?"

The Keeper frowns at her direct line of questioning, but I, for one, appreciate it. It's easy to share Ever's history and cultural makeup at a later date. She wants the specifics now, and she deserves to know.

The Keeper crosses his arms over his chest and scowls. "You're not human, none of you. You probably haven't ever realized it, but you three belong in Ever. You're monsters, just like the rest of us."

Shit. Color me shocked.

The triplets blanch, but Morgan presses on. I watch Thea's pink lips fall open in shock. She looks hurt and confused, and without really meaning to, I wrap one hand around her side and rub slowly. I don't think she realizes she sinks into my touch until she looks up and those blue eyes flutter.

Morgan practically snarls. "So, somehow you decided we're not human, which by the way, is a pile of horse shit, and you called us here? Again, why? And it was the map, wasn't it?"

The Keeper smiles, but it's not friendly. It never is. His job is serious and difficult, and his austere personality matches the weight of it. He steps forward, his smirk pulling the pale scar that bisects his lips.

"I called you with the map, Miss Hector, because you're my mate."

Every head in the place, including mine, turns from the Keeper to Morgan.

"Oh hell no," she shouts. "I'm nobody's mate."

A surprised murmur works its way through the crowd.

I glance at the Keeper in surprise. I know him better than most Evertons, but he's never mentioned a word of this to me. I'm a little surprised since he, Ohken, Alo, and I work together every day.

"What about the wolves?" Thea's voice echoes over the shocked crowd.

I see she's moving past the mate comment.

The Keeper cocks his head to the side. "Wolves?"

Thea lifts her chin and crosses her arms, matching his stance. "The wolves, or whatever we heard on the way into Ever. Some kind of an animal chased us, and Shepherd suggested we'd be safe in town versus out by the gas station. What were we really in danger from, and are we in danger here?"

The Keeper smiles again, a sinister smile. "Monsters are in danger everywhere, Althea. That is why Ever, and the other havens, exist in the first place."

With that cryptic statement, he lets his arms fall to the side and nods at Ohken, who usually takes over the second part of orientation as our official town Question Master. The Keeper doesn't wait around and stalks out of the gazebo, heading toward Main Street without a backward glance.

The girls watch him go with expressions ranging from fury to outright disbelief.

In the front row, a giant figure stands—Ohken the troll. One of the triplets gasps as he rises and walks quietly to the front of the gazebo.

I try to see him like the girls might. Ohken's a full head taller than me, but then most trolls are. He's about twice as wide and muscular too, and I'm a big male. His skin is a pale green, and two sharp white tusks jut out from his lower lip. He probably looks horribly imposing to them.

"Quiet, friends." His deep voice booms out over the gathered Evertons.

Even Morgan falls silent at the weighty command in his tone.

He smiles at the triplets, opening his arms wide. "As the Keeper mentioned, we are thrilled to welcome you to Ever. Catherine is your appointed welcome partner, and she can answer any additional questions that come up post-orientation. As you can see, nearly all of Ever is gathered here. We make it a point to show up for new residents." He smiles before looping his thumbs through his belt and continuing.

"My name is Ohken Stonesmith. I'm a bridge troll and part of the Town Council. I also own both the General Store and Fleur."

One of the triplets lets out a terrified squeak.

Ohken slips his hands into his pockets and continues on, looking like a university professor.

"Ever has a rich history of monster and human residents. You aren't the first humans here. I'd encourage you to spend some time in the garden and along Main Street. Catherine will provide you with a detailed welcome packet, but for now, what questions do you have?"

I risk a glance at my brother. His jaw is tightly gritted as he watches Ohken and studiously avoids my gaze.

Be nicer to the triplets, I snap into our family bond. *No more unnecessary roaring.*

You've been telling me to have more fun, he returns.

I roll my eyes. He knows that's not what I mean.

"We want to leave," Morgan barks. "Will you stop us if we try to go?"

Ohken's russet eyes flick from Morgan to Thea and Wren. He looks amused.

My heart gallops in my chest because I know exactly what he'll say.

"Of course not, Miss Hector. But we can't have you remembering us, for your safety and ours. If you opt to leave, you'll need to stop by the gas station so Shepherd can wipe us from your mind."

"And if we just don't do that?" Morgan snaps. "You'll what, force us?"

Ohken's smile falls, but instead of looking mad, he looks intensely sad.

"No, Miss Hector. We're not in the habit of forcing anyone into anything here in Ever. But it would be safer for you."

"Why?"

Her question is valid. Thea tucks even closer to my side. I don't want this to get out of hand, and we're headed there fast.

I reach around Thea to tap Morgan on the shoulder.

"Hey, remember the sounds you heard that I called wolves? It's not wolves, Morgan. It's other monsters. Most monsters who live outside of havens aren't good, they're not kind. If you had info about Ever's defenses, they'd want to use that to hurt people. That's why it's safer for you if we wipe your memory before you leave." I barrel on after seeing how shocked all three of the girls look.

"I'll make it clear. We don't *want* you to go. We'd love for you to stay and have a lovely girls' weekend. Ever is the perfect place to do that, and you're safe here." I refuse to say I won't stop them if they try to go because the reality is, I don't know what I'll do if Thea tells me she doesn't want to stay.

Ohken's voice echoes around the gazebo. "I imagine it's hard to drum up questions in a situation like this. Orientation is always hard, but please know we're here to answer questions. Let's call it a day, and Catherine can go through the welcome packet with you. You're always welcome to come find me, too."

A rustle rushes through the gazebo, and the residents begin to rise.

Thea presses herself harder to my side as a centaur clops to a stop in front of us.

He smiles down at the triplets, his hands folded carefully in front of his bare waist. "So lovely to meet you three. I'm Taylor. I live in the forest with the other centaurs. You'll learn all about that in the welcome packet, of course, but do swing by for a visit!" He keeps his voice light and friendly.

I expect the girls to be either suspicious or terrified, so I'm shocked when Thea reaches out to shake his hand.

Taylor looks down at her with an equally surprised expression, but it morphs into a huge grin as he takes her small hand in both of his and pumps it vigorously.

"Nice to meet you, Taylor," Thea says, her voice clear and strong.

I don't know where this confidence came from. Maybe she's just faking it while she schemes how to get the hell out of town. But there's a sense of knowing about her that lives smack in the middle of my chest, and it bursts into glorious fireworks as I watch her interact with my friends. I love Ever, and I want her to love it too. At least until I get a chance to make her fall for me.

～

After twenty minutes of greeting new friends, I sense the triplets are beginning to lose their cool. Morgan looks like she's holding back a million questions and taps her foot anxiously against the gazebo's plank floor. Wren is silent and watchful. Thea just looks exhausted.

I reach for her chin and guide her face so I can look into

those beautiful blue eyes. "Let's get you three back to the inn. We can go over the welcome packet and answer your questions. Plus, Wren looks like she could use a drink."

We look over at Wren, who frowns up at me. "I'm in full-on shock mode. Tequila, please. Big ass margarita. Need booze." She runs one hand through her chocolate waves just as Ohken steps up, the last in line.

I watch her cheeks flush pink when he holds his hand out to shake hers. She grips it, and he gives her that same smile that makes most of our residents swoon. I'd call him something of a heartbreaker around here if I didn't know for a fact that he's never hooked up with anyone in town.

I nearly laugh as she opens her mouth to speak but zips it quickly closed.

"Nice to meet you three," Ohken rumbles, meeting each of the girls' gaze. "I know this is a lot to take in. Please find me at the General Store or Fleur if you have any questions. I'm here for you, we all are." His lips curve into a big smirk as Wren nods, pulling her hand slowly out of his.

I look over at Catherine. She's holding back a smile.

And so it begins. Three new residents show up, and monsters are already showing interest. If Ohken has his eyes on Wren, nobody else will go near her. I wonder if he plans to formally announce his intention . . . I cast that thought aside, though, because the girls aren't fresh meat to be picked over. They're living, breathing people, and they've had the shock of the century.

Next to Wren, Morgan's got her arms crossed as she watches the last few residents leave and head toward Main. Ohken gives the girls one last smile and then follows the rest of the crowd.

The girls are silent for a minute until Morgan throws her hands above her head like she gives up.

"I mean, what in the fucking hell?!" she shouts, scowling over at her sisters. "We've gotta get out of here."

Catherine and I watch silently. Wren doesn't say anything but stares off into the distance.

Thea looks at me, then Catherine, and then her sister. "Let's just get back to the inn and we'll talk, Mor, okay?"

Morgan huffs but leads the way out of the gazebo and up Main. We hitch a left at Scoops and head for the Annabelle. The moment we arrive, the inn shimmies a little. The rafters holding the front porch roof creak as the home exhibits her excitement. She seems thrilled that the secret's out. I imagine she's tried to be fairly quiet until now.

I open the beautiful glass front doors for the girls, smiling as they go through. Thea's the only one who says thank you, patting me once on the forearm as she follows her sisters into the living room to the left of the entryway.

All three sisters fall onto the pink frilled Victorian-style sofa and speak at once. I resist the urge to pull Thea into my lap in one of the room's oversized armchairs. She's had a shock, and despite appearing to come to terms quickly, I can't imagine this is easy for her.

Catherine disappears to the check-in area and comes back with three thick manila envelopes, containing the usual welcome packet. Morgan takes hers with trembling hands, and Wren grabs the other two, handing one to Thea.

I watch all three girls as Catherine hovers by my side. Iggy zips through the front door, and Alo joins just behind him.

"Be nice," Catherine croons over her shoulder.

The triplets freeze, except for Morgan, who throws one long arm protectively across her sisters' fronts.

An ache takes up residence in my heart over that move. Gargoyles are protectors. We protect everyone. To see someone afraid of us makes my chest physically hurt. I rub at it with the back of my hand to ease the tension.

"Sorry about earlier," Alo grumbles. "I was just playing around, but it was rude."

Still, the snicker he lets out in our family bond tells me he doesn't mean the apology. I mentally slap him before returning my attention to the triplets.

Catherine smiles at the girls. "The Keeper is always very short on details, and I know it's hard to come up with questions on the spot. What can we answer for you now?"

"Well Jesus, I don't even know where to start!" huffs Morgan. "We came here for a girls' weekend. We can't just become residents and start mating monsters. We have lives outside of this. And we're human. This makes no sense!"

"Wren?" I look to the middle sister, who's been so quiet and seemingly lost in thought during Morgan's outburst.

She blinks a few times, then looks at Iggy and Alo in gargoyle form. Finally, she shrugs. "I don't know what to even ask, so maybe fill in the details of what that guy, the Keeper, didn't tell us. He didn't say all that much. Worst orientation ever. I give his delivery skills zero out of ten."

I try not to laugh at that. She's not wrong. Popping down to my knees, I fold my tail around my waist and focus on the girls.

Catherine gives me a gentle look when I reach out to rub the back of Thea's hands where they sit on her knees. I can't stop touching her or focusing on her soft skin. I'd like nothing better than to pull her to my chest and fly away. I always thought I'd mate a gargoyle from another haven when the time was right. My mind is a scattered mess of emotion as I look at Thea and resist the urge to touch her more than I am. I'm sure I'm feeling the pull of attraction more strongly than she is right now. I know I am.

Alo sits in the chair next to me, sensing my focus in our bond as he realizes what this girl is to me. He's not peppering me with questions yet, but I'm sure he will the moment he gets the chance to.

Catherine places a hand on my shoulder, careful not to touch my wings. "Well, let's start with the basics, which includes time. Time and weather work differently in Ever. You could stay here for a year and it would equate to about twelve days outside our wards. So, your girls' weekend could be several months long, and your friends and family back home would be none the wiser. And the weather is always like it is right now."

"What about calling or texting our family, will that work?" Wren is quick to ask the question, her eyes narrowed.

Catherine shakes her head. "The town was glamoured when you arrived yesterday, so your phones worked for that short while. Now that the glamour is down, they're no longer functional. However, you can always call or text from the gas station. We use another system in town, the comm system. Small leather watches are in your welcome packet. You can speak into the comm watch and call or message anyone. That's how we communicate within the town when the town glamour is down, which is all the time unless we have a new non-monster resident."

There's a creaking noise, and then the floor under the sofa ripples, jolting the welcome packet in Morgan's hands.

"The inn communicates, doesn't it?" her voice is soft and curious.

When I look at her, she's looking up at the monster mural on the ceiling. I'm shocked she picked that detail up so quickly. On cue, the windows behind the sofa slide open and shut on repeat. The house is laughing.

Catherine laughs along with the Annabelle. "Every home and building in Ever is bound to its owner. The inn is bound to me, and my living here is a relationship, a partnership of sorts. It's the same for Alo, Iggy, and their cottage. The same for every building on Main Street, too. Every home has a personality, some more pleasant than others."

"The movie theater makes me spill my drink when I go in," Iggy suggests helpfully. He hops across the carpet and up onto the sofa next to Thea. He leans close to her, whispering loudly in her ear. "That's because it knows Dad doesn't like me drinking soda, so it enforces the rules for him." He crosses his arms and scowls. "It's literally *so* rude."

Thea's lips curl into a smile, and she looks up at me. I nod in confirmation. I know the human world doesn't work like this. She's taking it in with surprising ease. She still hasn't opened the welcome packet, though.

"Talk to me about how we're not human," she murmurs, her focus moving from me to Catherine and, finally, over to Alo.

"That was a surprise to me too," I offer. "The Keeper has a unique ability, because of his role, to sense those with monster blood. If you were gargoyles, you'd already know it and shift, so you're not that. He can help us figure out what you are if you want that. Chances are you have a bloodline farther back in your family tree. That's why you didn't know you're not fully human."

"And the danger?" Wren presses. "The wolves? Or whatever? If we left, you said we'd be in danger if you don't wipe our memories or whatever."

"Not wolves," Alo begins, his voice sorrowful as he pulls Iggy onto his lap and slings one arm around his son. "Thralls. Not all monsters want to live in havens. They don't all agree with monsters hiding from humans. There's a divide in our world between those who abide by the treaty that created the havens centuries ago and those that don't. It's a war that's gone on forever. Thralls want to destroy the havens, turn monsters to their side, and rule over the humans who have no idea they even exist."

"Why do they have to destroy havens to do that?" Thea's voice is soft but curious.

Alo continues. "The way haven ward magic works creates a sort of multiplicative effect. The power in the wards acts as a network that protects us from the outside world for the most part. If haven wards fell all across our world, it would have a catastrophic effect. Our governing body, the Hearth, works with the Keepers to maintain security among the havens."

Morgan rubs at her temples. "Okay, time out. I'm trying to be cool about this, but I'm at the very limit of what I can absorb. Everybody's a monster, we're possibly not human, more monsters want in, there's something called the Hearth. I just can't right now. Can we take a pause?"

"And maybe get that margarita?" Wren gives me a pleading look. "I am in desperate need of that margarita."

I slap Alo again through our family bond. He takes the hint, setting Iggy down. He disappears out the front door to head to his cottage and grab margarita ingredients.

Iggy flaps over to Wren, alighting on her thigh and holding his hand out. He waits until she tentatively wraps her fingers in his before speaking. "Dad lets me hold his hand when I'm nervous, so you can hold mine. I promise we're super nice, plus you live next door to me and Dad. We're cool neighbors! I'll come over whenever you feel scared, okay? That's what gargoyles do. I'll protect you."

If my heart wasn't solid stone, it would burst at my nephew's compassion. He's right. A gargoyle's role is to protect, and when I look down at Thea, I know I will protect her with every fiber of who I am.

CHAPTER EIGHT

THEA

I have no idea what I'm feeling right now. Some weird mix of anxiety and shock and curiosity. That last one is the detective in me. Dad used to say it was a detective's job to be curious. Maybe that's why my sisters are still sitting in stunned silence, but I look down at the thick welcome packet in my lap.

Catherine catches on quickly and gestures toward the manila envelopes my sisters hold.

"Okay, girls, if you open the packets, you'll find the comm watches I mentioned. However, there's also a quick brochure on the history of Ever, a map of the town and the broader haven, a welcome letter from the Hearth, and an explanation about their role as our governing body. I know you're overwhelmed, but if you take a peek at those things and have questions, I'm right here, okay?"

Morgan sits in complete silence, looking down at the welcome packet like it's a viper about to strike.

Wren looks over at me, and I can almost see panic rising in her green eyes.

"I really, *really* need that margarita," she says, gripping the welcome packet to her chest like it's her lifeline.

The front door opens, and Alo strides through with a canvas bag full of what I hope are margarita ingredients. Shepherd stands and smiles at us.

"I've got you, Wren. Be right back, okay?" Dark eyes flick to me. "Wanna help me in the kitchen?"

He holds his hand out, his three-fucking-fingered hand, and I take it like this whole thing is normal. I set the welcome packet down and give Wren a reassuring look.

"Be back with drinks, okay, Wrennie?"

She nods and looks over at Morgan, who's still staring at the manila envelope. Catherine regards them both with a kind but unsurprised look.

Shepherd tugs my hand gently. We leave the living room and round the check-in desk, heading down a long hallway, which I suppose must lead to the kitchen.

When we enter the bright, sunny space, Alo is squeezing limes into a blender with a scowl on his handsome face. He doesn't smile when he looks up at us.

I'm starting to get the feeling this guy is gonna be a pain in my pucker.

Shepherd notices his brother's sourpuss look and swoops his left wing out, clocking Alo on the back of the head. He follows the swipe with a warning look.

Alo snarls as he swats the claw-tipped wing away with one hand. "What was that for?"

Shepherd's voice is a deeply disappointed rumble as he pulls out a barstool and tucks my hair over my shoulder. "You're being fucking rude! We have new residents."

His fingers—all three of them, oh my god—aren't warm to the touch. They're not cold either, they're just . . . neutral. Is he even warm-blooded? Would that be rude to ask? Maybe he's like a lizard, a gigantic, handsome lizard.

"Sit, please, I'm still worried about your head," he murmurs to me.

Alo scowls up at us both before unfurrowing his black brows. "Sorry, Thea."

"Whatever," I mumble.

I'm sure I've got a concussion because a gargoyle just whacked another gargoyle in front of me. But instead of running like a normal person or clinging tightly to my sisters in the other room, I'm sitting here. Watching them make margaritas.

It occurs to me that I said I'd help.

Shepherd shoos Alo away from the blender. "I'm better at this and your five year-old is doing a better job of hosting than you are. Go make nice with the humies, please."

Alo rolls his dark eyes but disappears quietly out of the kitchen.

I turn to Shepherd with a look. "The humies? As in humans?" I don't know whether to snort in indignation or because it's funny.

"Well," he laughs, grinning big enough for dimples to pop on either side of his smile. "Not one-hundred-percent humans, according to the Keeper. Not sure what you are, but humies is our word for not-really-all-the-way human. Once we know what you are, you'll get called that. If you decide you want to know," he tacks on, pouring juice into the blender.

I blink once, slowly, as if doing so will force clarity into my brain. It's shell-shocked. I'm certain of it now. That's the predominant emotion I can name. Because there's no other way I could sit in this kitchen, *humie* that I am, and just talk about being not human like it's no big deal.

"Hey, everything is gonna be fine, Thea," Shepherd says as he turns the blender on.

Ice crackles and breaks in the blender as he leans over the big white kitchen island. He's so big that he could reach out and touch me. When he slides one hand across the marble counter-top, I reach for him without even thinking.

His dark eyes bore into mine as the blender rattles away in the background. He takes my hand carefully in his far larger one, shifting farther over the island. He brings my knuckles to his lips and brushes his mouth across them. His skin isn't as warm as mine, but his breath is. And the way he's focused on my eyes is lascivious.

Heat blooms in my core, and my mouth falls open. There's a monster kissing my hand.

He presses a feather-light kiss to my knuckles, and then another, and another.

Iggy flaps into the kitchen, letting out an earsplitting shriek. "Oh my gods, Uncle Shepherd! Are you kissing a girl? I'm telling Dad!"

Shepherd lets out a huge belly laugh, and I yank my hand out of his.

Iggy gives his uncle a withering look and flits through the air on tiny wings, grabbing my shirt and pulling me off the barstool and to the door. "Listen, he should know better than to share cooties like that. Ignore him. Come with me, I'll keep you safe."

"I can keep her safe, Ignatius," Shepherd chides from behind us.

Next to me, Iggy gives me a look that screams "Yeah right!" and drags me back to the front of the inn.

Shepherd joins us a moment later with three margaritas, giving Wren hers first. She takes it and gulps it down fast, throwing herself against the back of the sofa with a palm smashed to her forehead.

I look at Iggy.

"Brain freeze," he says with a knowing expression.

I hold back a hysterical laugh. I guess some things are universal.

Shepherd grabs his nephew by the tail and pulls him close,

patting his shoulder. I watch Iggy tuck himself onto Shepherd's muscular shoulder and settle in, almost like he's going to shift into the stone version of a gargoyle. Do they do that? Are they ever stone? Suddenly, I have questions.

Shepherd smiles at me, then my sisters. "I suppose it might be good to take a full step back for a minute."

My sisters stare blankly up at him, but he continues, placing one big hand on his chest.

"Shepherd Xavier Rygold, of house Rygold based in the Swiss haven of Vizelle. You've met my nephew, Iggy, and my brother Alo. Alo and I work with the Keeper to protect and bolster the wards that protect us from the outside world. That work includes a variety of responsibilities. But the three of us and Ohken form Ever's Town Council."

He gives me a quick wink before continuing. "Technically, I have an office in Town Hall, but I haven't been to it in ten Ever-years. Working closely with the council are Catherine and Doc Slade, who spend a fair amount of time in meetings, making sure we have the right programs and plans in place for our haven."

He gives us a kind look. "I know it's a lot, but take a look through your welcome packets. Catherine is a masterful question-answerer. I'll be with the Keeper this afternoon, but I'll check in later. Don't forget the comm watches in your orientation packets. Just speak any of our names into the face, and if we're available, we'll answer." He points to a leather strip on his wrist.

On cue, Iggy holds his hand up too. Sure enough, a thin blue leather strip is fitted around his stony gray arm.

Shepherd smiles at me. "Any last questions before I go?"

I've honestly got too many rattling around in my head to put them in any sort of priority order, so I shake my head.

He makes a point to visually check in with Morgan and Wren too, but they're both mute.

"Okay then, see you later," he announces, heading for the door with Iggy still perched high on his shoulder. He shoots me a final smile as he pushes the door open. Alo trails them both outside, and then we're alone with Catherine.

Who. Is. A. Succubus.

Wren reaches for me, pulling me down onto the sofa next to her and Morgan. I hold my margarita high to avoid spilling it. I'm gonna need this booze for sure.

Catherine is seated in a chair just in front of us, and she smiles. "I know you have questions. They probably can't all be answered in a day, but where shall we begin?"

"How and why did the Keeper call us?" Morgan asks the obvious question, although I'd completely forgotten about the whole "calling us" thing in light of the "not human" bit. I was planning to grill Catherine about what kind of monster she is, but Morgan's question makes a lot more sense.

Thinking back, the Keeper did make it sound like he pulled us here purposefully.

Catherine cocks her head to the side. "That answer is a little convoluted, but the short version is that now and again, a resident will feel a pull to someone outside of their haven. Each haven has a magical artifact that acts as a homing beacon to guide people in. I didn't know this, but it seems the Keeper found you, Morgan. And he used the map to pull all three of you here."

"To be his mate," Morgan clarifies.

Catherine sighs. "That's a better question for him. As far as I know, we are the only haven without a mated Keeper. It's time he took a mate, but he didn't seem to be courting you with the way he blurted that out earlier. That was a surprise to me."

"Ya think?" Morgan seems disgruntled, and I get it.

The Keeper seemed less than friendly, and when I think about how Shepherd behaved when we met, there's a huge difference in behavior.

Not that he's my mate. He's just crazy hot.

"Ever pulled the wrong ones in?" Wren asks.

I perk up. I've got questions about the danger we might be in, assuming we stay and don't pack the car in the next ten minutes.

"Just once," Catherine murmurs. "My mate, Wesley. He was a very powerful warlock. He never fit in here, and he slipped out of our bedroom window one night and disappeared. I regret calling him here, but I cannot undo that." She looks so sad, her cheeks pale as she looks down into her lap.

Wren clears her throat politely. "And the thrall issue? Even if we decided to stay, it seems Ever isn't safe?"

Catherine nods slowly, seeming to decide how much she should really tell us.

"Tell us everything," I say. "We have to make an informed decision about sticking around this weekend. Or not." I say that last quickly, glancing at my sisters to make sure we're a united front.

We haven't run for the hills yet, but based on their expressions, I could still see it going that way. This is turning into the girls' weekend from hell. God, there might even be demons here!

When her pale gray eyes meet us, there's a sadness in them that makes my heart hurt. "The thralls work on instinct alone. They're attracted to both ward magic and protective magic. Their only goal is to feed on the monsters there, to take their souls and convert them. But they're mindless and disorganized. The Keeper's job, along with Alo and Shepherd, is to maintain the wards and ensure Ever is safe. It is incredibly rare for a thrall to manage their way through."

"How rare?" Morgan pushes.

"It has only happened once in my lifetime." Catherine looks at us in earnest. "I know the Keeper seems unfriendly. He is responsible for more than you can imagine. He's kept us safe for nearly a hundred Ever-years. He is excellent at his job, so I can tell you with absolute truth in my heart—I have never felt unsafe here."

I will my cheeks not to heat as I ask the question that's burning in my mind. "If nobody ever gets in, why does it take a whole crew of people, err, monsters, to keep Ever safe?"

Catherine gives me an understanding smile. "Alo and Shepherd are the town's gargoyle guardians. They keep an eye on the town itself, looking for anything amiss. Shepherd is also responsible for the gas station, where we guide new residents in. He is the first friendly face we want new residents to meet. Thralls don't get in because our protector team is so very excellent."

I know my cheeks are pink because they're flushed as I tug at my shirt collar and take a sip of the margarita. Damn, it's good. Bitter but sweet. That man can make a drink.

"This is like the most elaborate Truman show ever," Morgan mutters, setting the margarita down as she slumps into the plush, velvet sofa.

Catherine gestures to the manila packet in Morgan's lap. "Open it. Let's try out your comm watches to make sure they work. It's the best way to get a hold of anyone in town, including me!"

Morgan pauses for a moment, then opens the envelope, taking out a stack of paper neatly paperclipped together. A blue leather band falls out from between the pages. Wren and I do the same, and a moment later, we've each got matching bands on our wrists.

"I'll try a message now," Catherine says, lifting her wrist to her mouth. "Send a message to Thea Hector."

At first glance, there doesn't appear to be any sort of screen, but then my band begins to glow, and the words Catherine said hover just above the leather band like a hologram.

"Holy fuck," Wren murmurs, leaning over to stare. She grips

my wrist tight and then looks at Catherine. "What other functions does it have?"

"Calling as well!" Catherine is quick to answer, bringing her watch to her face. "Watch, call Wren Hector, please."

Moments later, the band on Wren's arm begins to vibrate, and Catherine's name pops up hologram-style.

"What if you don't want to have a conversation aloud," Morgan says.

"Unfortunately, there's nothing like a cell phone here, so if you want to talk to someone, you can message them or ask them to come over. It's sort of nice." She chuckles. "Ever might seem old-fashioned in some ways, but it's a very tightly-knit community."

Wren takes a deep swig of her margarita, crunching the ice as she eyes the blue leather band. When we're all silent for a few awkward moments, Catherine clasps her hands together.

"Listen, girls, why don't you wander over to the Galloping Green Bean and get some early lunch? Alba will take good care of you, and you'll have some time to talk through what you've learned."

"Who owns that, the centaur?" Morgan's tone tells me she's struggling to keep it together under the wealth of information that's been piled on us.

"Precisely!" Catherine chirps. "That would be Alba. She is absolutely lovely." Catherine stands, clasping her hands together in front of her trim waist. "I just want to remind each of you that we are thrilled you're here, and we hope you'll stick around for your weekend. Ever is a wonderful community. I know you'll love it if you give us a chance."

The word shell-shocked flits through my brain again. I think that's what we all are because Wren and Morgan are silent as a grave, and all I can muster is a half-assed "thank you."

The inn shifts and moves, creaking as Catherine looks up

toward the ceiling. "Alright, I'm coming! Cool your heels, Annabelle."

Another angry-sounding creak follows, and Catherine disappears in the direction of the front desk.

"So . . ." Morgan's lips form an O as she drags the vowel out. "How are we feeling about this?" She taps her foot on the ground again, something she does when she's disconcerted. Which is the perfect word for what I assume we're all feeling.

"I want to stay," I blurt out without even thinking.

Where did that come from?

Wren gives me a slightly surprised look. "Would this have anything to do with a certain hot gargoyle?" She pauses and runs one hand through her hair. "I can't believe I just said that sentence aloud. What in the fuckety fuck?"

"Okay, hear me out," I start. "I'm admittedly curious about the not-human thing. Aren't you two the least bit curious about that? Plus, I don't see why we couldn't still do our weekend here and leave with some wild memories."

Wren looks thoughtful, and Morgan looks disgruntled. "Remember how curiosity killed the cat?"

She's not wrong. My curiosity has gotten us in hot water a time or two. Although, the same could be said for her desire to find a town on a random thrifted map. Still, it sounds like there's a lot more to it than what we originally thought.

Morgan huffs. "You might not feel that way if a creep called you his mate in front of the entire town and then took off as if he was simply commenting on the weather. What does that even mean anyways? I don't even live here!"

"That was a little bit weird," I admit. "But you don't have to go anywhere near him if you don't want to. I assume."

Morgan nods her head slowly.

"Listen," I start. "Why don't we go get some lunch? When we get back, I'll call Shepherd to see about verifying the time-passing bit because that's hard to believe. The last thing I want to do is disappear for a while and freak Lou out. She would kill us if we dropped off the face of the earth, especially after—" I still can't say the words about what happened to our parents, how we lost them so suddenly and in such a freakish way.

"Lou would freak. She'd probably manage to find her way here and bust through the impassable wards or whatever," Wren says. "I can just see it now, to be honest. So yeah, let's verify the time-passing conundrum because I frankly don't believe that."

I look at my sisters, one brow curled up in what I hope is a happily suggestive expression. "So, we're staying?"

Neither one of them answer. But it's not a no, and somehow, that makes me feel relieved.

CHAPTER NINE

SHEPHERD

I stalk the wards near the gas station, the Keeper by my side.

He eyes the nearly-invisible film with a thoughtful expression. "You said the thralls congregated here after the girls came in?"

"Yeah, eight or ten, maybe a few more." I plant both hands on my hips as I turn to look at him. "They don't usually work together like that."

"We've seen it once or twice in the last few months," he responds, his voice flat. His tone has always been like that, or at least since he became Ever's Keeper. I knew him before, and it still shocks me how different he is since taking up the Keeper's mantle. I'd always heard it changes the being who accepts that responsibility, but seeing it happen is disconcerting. We lived here together for decades before he was called to the role. He was always charming and joyous, before.

"Grab my dust, would you?" He waves a hand toward his vintage Indian motorcycle without taking his eyes off the wards.

I trot to his bag, grabbing a leather satchel from one of the side pockets. Pixie dust glows green, lighting the bag from within.

"You're running low. Need me to go to the general store?"

"Ohken plans to swing by the castle later. The pixies are a little behind this week. Someone's been distracted."

Ah. He means Miriam. The diminutive pixie has had a thing for Alo for years, but she was always on the sidelines while he was mated. Now that he's not, I know she has high hopes. And that means distraction for her job helping the pixies make dust. Honestly, I think Alo is oblivious.

The Keeper turns to me with a wry look. "I can almost hear the wheels of your mind spinning. Are you considering giving Alo a push?" One blond brow trails upward in what must be skepticism.

I shrug. "Alo's focused on Iggy, but we're all here to help him. I'd like to see him happy. He's getting grouchier by the moment."

The Keeper nods once but doesn't respond. He paces quickly to me and grabs the pixie dust bag, reaching in to retrieve a handful of the brilliant, green powder. His hand practically glows as he tosses it on the ground at the base of the wards.

As always, I watch in awe at the way the barrier seems to soak up the dust, glowing green for a moment before it fades to a filmy, paper-thin white again.

The Keeper is quiet as I trail him along the ward edge behind the gas station, pondering what happened the night the triplets arrived. I'm about to ask him another question when my comm watch pings and the name I most want to see pops up.

Thea Hector.

Grinning like an idiot, I speak into the watch. "Answer Thea."

Moments later, there's an adorable harrumph. "Is this thing working? Hello? Shepherd, are you there?" A muffled sound comes from the background, probably one of the sisters. "Yeah, Wren, I get it, bu—"

"Hey, Thea." My voice dips an octave. The Keeper turns around and gives me a snide, knowing look. I flip him the bird and speak again. "You girls alright?"

Thea's voice is tinny through the watch. "Yeah, we're at the Galloping Green Bean eating lunch. We'd like to verify the whole time-passing situation. I hope this doesn't seem rude, but we're struggling to believe it."

The Keeper turns around again, pausing as he crosses his arms.

"Not rude and not a problem. Do any of you have your cell phones with you?"

There's another muffled scramble, then Thea comes back on. "We didn't bring them because Catherine said they wouldn't work. Want us to grab them?"

"Yeah, grab one, and I'll swing by and pick you up. We can chat about how time passes here, it's a little tricky."

"We have my Honda. Can we meet you?"

I scowl at that. I'm a protector species. It doesn't sit well with me not to pick her up. When I look at the Keeper, he's full-on scowling too.

Join the club, buddy. Although, where I'm fully intent on pursuing Thea, he seems more reticent about her sister.

I knew Thea Hector was mine the moment she stepped into my gas station. While it's obvious she's attracted to me too, I need to rein in my natural emotions. If she had grown up with monsters, I'd have whisked her to my nest by now and claimed her.

Instead, I need to win her over by courting her—and her sisters to a degree. They seem close, and I want them all to love Ever so they'll stay beyond a girls' weekend. Scratch that, I need it because if Thea decides to leave, I don't know what the hell I'll do.

"Shepherd, you there?" Thea's voice brings me crashing back to the present.

"That's fine," I lie. "The Keeper and I will be dusting the wards so just wait at the gas station if you don't see me."

She's silent for a moment. "And we'll be safe?"

"Absolutely," I confirm. *I'll protect you with my life.* That's the part I don't say.

She thanks me and hangs up. I turn to the Keeper, but his face is a mask of irritation.

Well, two can play that game. "You want to talk about the whole mate announcement and then not saying another word to her thing?"

I didn't think his scowl could grow any deeper, but it does.

He shrugs as he turns from me, reaching into the pixie dust bag to continue his work along the wards.

Like I often do, I trail him and keep an eye out for thralls and holes in the wards. It's a unique ability of gargoyles to work alongside a Keeper like this, identifying inconsistencies in the ward's surface and sensing thralls. There aren't any around now, but if they came close, I'd know.

"I don't want to talk about her." The Keeper's voice surprises me with its soft intensity. It's almost like he can't get the words out, so they fall from his mouth in a rush.

The mantle of Keeper weighs heavily on his shoulders, and the charming, carefree mischief-maker of our younger years is gone. Now he's stubborn, serious, and consumed with protecting Ever.

I'm not one to push him to talk about a topic he'd rather avoid, but I feel compelled to say something.

"I'm here if you ever do want to talk about it, okay? We've been friends for a long time."

He looks at me, his mouth open like he might speak. After a few quiet moments, he zips his lips shut and shakes his head, turning and walking away from me.

Setting the topic of Morgan aside, I lengthen my strides to walk alongside my longtime friend. "Do you ever regret this job?"

He's silent for a moment, appearing thoughtful as he tosses pixie dust at the base of the wards, watching it soak in and revitalize the thin film that protects our town and our friends.

Eventually, he stops and faces me. "Being Keeper strips one of nearly every choice, Shepherd. You know that better than most since you and Alo are my closest partners. I don't regret becoming a Keeper once I was identified as having the potential to do it, but I regret the loss of choice."

"Like with Morgan?" I can't help but ask, knowing vampires like him believe in fated mates the same as gargoyles do.

If he calls Morgan his, it's because he believes beyond a shadow of a doubt that she's meant for him. I'd love nothing more than to see him happy and not such a shell of a person.

His blond brows form a V, and he looks down at the ground, seeming to hunt for his words. When his gaze meets mine again, it's focused and harsh, the same mask he puts on for the whole town. I know I won't get the real, emotion-backed answer. I'm about to hear the political version of things.

"I have no intention of pursuing Morgan Hector," he states in a neutral, official tone. "Having identified her existence is sufficient to get the Hearth off my back about my mating status."

Snorting out a laugh, I clap him on the shoulder. "I hope you've considered that if she is indeed your mate, perhaps not being courted won't sit well with her."

He shrugs my hand off. "Then I'll just have to ensure I am thoroughly unpleasant. I don't have time for a mate, Shepherd."

Oof. Doesn't seem like "unpleasant" will be too difficult. But I don't say the words aloud. For whatever reason, he's not ready.

We pace the wards for a while, reinforcing them. Eventually, I hear the sound of tires.

"The girls are here."

The Keeper shoots me a look. "I'll continue along the wards."

Without waiting for a response, he takes the bag of pixie dust and disappears into the darkness of the forest.

I sigh, but even as I wonder about his behavior, my thoughts turn to Thea and the fact that she's close.

Bunching my muscles, I press off the soft earth and beat my wings. I sail through the dense forest and land in the middle of the road just as the triplets pull up in Thea's old Honda. It lets out a mechanical wail when she puts it in park. I'll need to have the wolves take a peek at it. It's clearly in need of a tune-up.

Thea's eyes are huge as I flare my wings out wide, then tuck them behind my back. I considered pulling my glamour back on, but it does nobody any good for me to pretend I'm anything but a monster. Wren and Morgan get out of the car slowly, looking at me cautiously.

The look on Thea's face is different as she approaches. Blue eyes are nearly overtaken by the dark pupil. When she stops in front of me, I reach out and place a hand on her side. I don't know if it's too much, too fast, but she let me hold her hand earlier. I'd rather apologize later than ask for permission now.

"You seem intrigued by the wings, Thea." My voice dips again in her presence. She steps closer to me, looking up with a beautiful smile. "Let me know if you have questions. I'll show them to you any time you want."

Thea nods with a mischievous look. "I'd love to see them. I have so many questions now that I'm not in shock mode."

"Done," I breathe out as her sisters join us.

I don't miss the way Wren's eyes drop to my hand on Thea's waist. I want to declare my formal intentions in front of them all, but this isn't the time or place. Instead, I smile at Morgan, who's got her cell in her hand.

I point toward the ward, its translucent surface visible twenty yards in front of us. "Ward magic is kind of finicky.

Because of the map, we knew you were coming, so the town's glamour was up when you arrived. That's why you didn't see the ward. The glamour also meant time worked normally within Ever while the glamour was up. Now that the glamour's down, there's an odd time vacuum right by the ward."

I gesture for the girls to follow me, and they do like a little trail of ducklings. I point at the visible, smooth surface.

"Twenty feet on either side of the ward is a weird time-space where your cell will work, but you're still on Ever time. You could go outside the ward a little way and still be on Ever time. Any farther than that and you're back on human time. But right here by the ward itself, you can call or text and it'll work."

"What a mindfuck," Wren mutters, looking at the ward's surface.

"We could just leave right now, right?" Morgan asks.

I glance over, trying not to let my irritation show.

"You could," I say slowly. "But you'd miss the adventure of a lifetime. Would you not regret that? Are you in such a hurry to go back to your normal lives?"

Before she can answer, the Keeper emerges from the shadows, his bag of pixie dust still clutched in one hand. Morgan's eyes narrow as he skirts our group with only a curt nod. He doesn't look back as he swings one long leg over his motorcycle and revs off toward town.

"What an adventure!" Morgan snarks in an irritated tone.

I'd love to tell her she's wrong, that the Keeper is the person I most respect in this entire town. But the words die on my tongue after my earlier conversation with him.

"He's complicated," I offer, not sure what else I feel comfortable sharing.

Morgan's unhappy look softens when Wren and Thea both smile at her. She sighs. "It's not a big deal. We came for a girls' weekend. We can still do that, I just want to make sure I don't cross the Keeper's path. He seems happy to steer clear of me, and that's fine."

Her mention of their weekend reminds me that I can't hog all of Thea's time, even though I want to steal every single one of her moments.

I point to the ward. "I'm going to check in on some paperwork in my office inside the gas station. Find me if you need anything, okay?"

My mind is a whirl of emotion as I give Thea a quick smile and then leave the girls so they can have a bit of privacy.

Once inside the gas station, I go into my office and stand at the window so I can keep an eye on them. I'm not worried about thralls in the daytime, but given their behavior has been especially erratic in the last month, I've got to remain vigilant.

I'll protect Thea with everything I have. I've just got to hope her sisters aren't the ones who pull her away from me.

THEA

I try not to stare at Shepherd as he stalks to the gas station and disappears inside. But damn, that ass. I could bounce a coin right off it; it's so muscular and round. Goddamn.

Wren clears her throat helpfully.

I whip around to my sisters, who both give me snarky looks. "Shit, did I say any of that out loud?"

"Pretty much all of it," Wren laughs. "Why do I get the sense our girls' weekend might involve a little more dude action than we expected it to."

"No, definitely not," I remind my sisters. "You two are my priority. Sandersons all the way, right?"

Morgan snorts. "Yeah, but if there were the off chance you could get laid, we would never stand in the way of that. It's been a minute for you, girl. Plus, we can still have fun, too." She seems to feel the topic is settled because she takes out her phone and stares at the screen.

I'm about to comment on her bringing up the fact it's been a while since I dated, but she gasps.

"Jesus," she says, her tone full of awe. "We arrived at Annabelle at two a.m. on Thursday, and it's just after three a.m.

now. On fucking Thursday. How is that . . ." She looks around in confusion.

I grab her cell and verify what she's just said. "We should check in with Aunt Lou. Just verify nothing is weird timeline-wise."

"At three in the morning?" Wren is the voice of reason, like always. "If we call Lou at three a.m. she will lose her shit. She'll think something's wrong."

"How about a text?" I say. "Just to let her know we arrived."

Morgan seems in agreement and types a message on her phone. She presses send and gives us both a look, then slips her phone into her pocket. I don't think any of us expect an answer from Lou at this time—assuming the time is accurate—but we might as well wait a few minutes to see. I'm still having trouble believing the time difference, but when I look down at my watch, it jives with what I saw on Morgan's screen. I thought it had just stopped. I stroke the worn leather band, remembering the day my father gave it to me. It was a police academy graduation present. Even if it's useless for telling Ever time, it's never coming off my wrist.

Behind my sisters, the ward shines a faint green. It looks like a flimsy film, but before I can say anything, Morgan reaches out and touches the surface.

Wren and I shout at the same time, but the film shimmers and shakes and appears to expand outward slightly under her touch.

"It's beautiful," she says with reverence.

"The Keeper just dusted it, so it's extra strong right now." Shepherd's deep voice is practically a stroke along my skin as he rejoins us, striding out of the gas station's rickety door.

My cheeks heat at the visceral reaction my body has to him, but I've got too many emotions about it to even process. He's not human. He lives sheltered away from my reality in a town full of other monsters. Time passes slowly here. I'm still a little overwhelmed about it, but trying to be cool. Because the beef-cake who pauses next to me and gives me a sexy little smile? I'd like to do dirty things to him, no matter what I've learned.

I want to slap myself.

And I'm only here for a weekend. Except that, based on the available evidence, I could stay here for quite a while, and it would only be a weekend outside Ever's wards. This is totally insane.

His smile broadens, and I wonder if he can read minds or if any of the monsters can. Because the look on Shepherd's face is the look I imagine he'd have if he knew I was thinking about that wingspan and what it means for other . . . things.

Morgan's right—it's been a long time since I dated anyone. My mind is firmly in the gutter, monster man or not.

"Earth to Thea," Wren laughs as she slaps my shoulder. "Get your head out of the clouds, Sarah!"

I snort at my Sanderson sister nickname but give him an apologetic look. Has he ever seen a movie? They've got a movie theater on Main, but how does that even work?

"Oh, I get the reference," he chuckles. "Even though time moves differently here, the Keeper has it rigged so we still get movies from the modern world. Don't ask me how he does it, but I've seen *Hocus Pocus*, and it's not a stretch looking at you three to guess that's the reference."

I grin like the Cheshire cat. Could he be more perfect? Right now, I don't think so.

I realize I'm staring at Shepherd and his ridiculously hand-some face when Wren not-so-subtly steps on my foot.

"Get it together," she hisses under her breath, giving Shep-herd a neutral look.

I blink several times. I'm not usually shy around men, shit I work with a predominantly male police force. I love dudes, and I'm very comfy with my sexuality—but this man has my usual ease a little off-kilter.

I'm sure it's the fact that he's a goddamn gargoyle, so I decide to cut myself a break. Nobody could be cool under these circumstances.

Moving on.

I look up at Shepherd. "Well, we've verified it's only been a little while out there . . ." I gesture at the ward's shiny surface.

"Okay," Shepherd says agreeably. "This is your girls' weekend, right? Can I make a few suggestions for how to enjoy Ever?"

Bold of him to assume we're sticking around. I think I like it, though. A twinge of disappointment settles somewhere in my chest when I think about not seeing him tonight, but I shove it aside. I didn't come here for a man, no matter how much this one entices me. I don't know him, not that I need to know him to wanna climb him. But still.

"Might as well!" Wren says.

Next to Wren, Morgan frowns. "Actually, I'd like to ask a very pointed question before we engage in fun times."

Shepherd inclines his head. "Sure, Morgan."

My triplet looks up at him. For the first time, I realize how worried she looks. I try to think about this from her perspective. If the Keeper is to be believed, he called us here with the map because she's his mate, even though he doesn't seem to want anything to do with her. Everything about that is weird and off-putting. We have lives outside of Ever. She's a well-respected doctor with a thriving pediatrics practice in the city.

My suspicions are confirmed when she crosses her arms. "Tell me about the map and the Keeper. He said I was his mate, but he's unfriendly, to say the least. I'll be blunt. You seem into Thea, but we're only here for the weekend."

"Morgan!" I hiss.

She throws both hands up. "I'm just saying. We arrived in a hidden monster town, and all of a sudden, there's a lot of damn interest in us, including an entire resident orientation." She barrels on while Wren and I stand and stare. "And then there's the whole Keeper's mate comment, which freaked me the fuck out. I just don't want to end up stuck here. That's not what this was supposed to be about." She looks up at Shepherd. "I don't know why, but I trust you to tell us the truth. What's the endgame in all this?"

Shepherd's been listening silently, his big arms crossed over his chest.

When she's done, he looks directly at her, holding her fierce gaze.

"Monsters . . . connect differently than humans. Most monster species believe in the concept of fated mates or love at first sight. For many of us, once we identify who we want, relationships progress quickly. That's a *nearly* universal monster rule. Trolls and orcs are the only exceptions to that."

My cheeks are on fire from Morgan specifically calling out his interest in me, but his explanation has the wheels of my mind spinning like tires on slick pavement.

"So, your interest in Thea is what?" Morgan presses on. "You think she's your fated mate? Even though we don't live here and don't plan to stay?"

I want to stomp on her foot so hard. This whole interaction brings me back to the time my dad cleaned his gun while grilling my first boyfriend about his intentions. It was such a weird thing to experience the cliché firsthand like that.

It scared my boyfriend shitless, though.

On the other hand, Shepherd looks anything but scared. There's a confident smile on his face as he answers Morgan's pointed question.

"Nobody in Ever would ever force you into something you don't want, but having a new resident isn't all that common for us. You'll all be the objects of a lot of interest. That's natural, but any monster in this town would respect it if you were simply not interested in something romantic."

Morgan frowns. "And what about the Keeper calling me his mate?"

Shepherd shrugs, his big shoulder muscles flexing under a shirt that can barely contain him. "It surprised me when he admitted to that. You'll have to ask him about his intention in calling you. He's . . ." He seems to search around for the right word. "The Keeper is blunt and unfriendly, but he's the best Keeper I've ever worked with. He's highly respected in the Keeping community. We're safe because of the many, many sacrifices he makes."

"Like what?" Morgan presses. "What does he sacrifice?"

Shepherd looks at me, but the smile on his face is sad when he turns back to Morgan. "He's been alone a long time. Being a Keeper means he keeps odd hours. He's always working, always obsessed with our safety. He's both the heart of our community and its only self-imposed outcast. It's an honor to be a haven's Keeper, but it's a horrible role to fill."

Morgan's frown disappears, but she turns to Wren and me. "Okay, I don't feel bad for him, but I suppose it's nice to understand where he's coming from. It doesn't matter because we're not here forever, right?"

"Right," Wren says, but her voice is distant and thoughtful.

I can't even agree because the words turn to ash in my mouth when Shepherd looks at me.

We've been here for such a short time, but I know one thing for certain—I want to know more about this town and its inhabitants, in particular the big male standing in front of us with a hopeful expression on his face.

~

"Alright." Shepherd claps his big hands together.

I marvel at the way his three fingers look in comparison to my five.

"So, you're in a monster town. We're nice though, so it'll be fun to get to know us. I'd suggest visiting Main Street. The general store, aptly named the General Store, has a unique mix of items, and Ohken's an even better storyteller than Catherine. If you want an early dinner, Herschel's is perfect for something a little fancier than the Green Bean. After that, go to Miriam's Sweets and meet her. Her desserts are magical."

The happy look on his face is almost infectious.

"Wait," Wren laughs. "Just so we're clear. They're magically delicious, or they're actually full of magic?"

"Both," Shepherd laughs. "Plus, she's got the hardcore hots for Alo, so it would be fun for you to meet her. Then I'll have someone besides Catherine to talk to about how Alo should ask her out."

"You're the town matchmaker then?" Morgan's laugh seems to come easy.

I'm glad to see her relaxing a bit.

"Not hardly," Shepherd snorts. "But Miriam is perfect for Alo if he would get it through his thick skull. If you want, swing by his place and grab Iggy for the dessert bit. He adores Miriam, and he loves her shop. No pressure, but Iggy's a little comedian."

"Done," I say without looking at my sisters.

Something about the teeny gargoyle toddler calls to me. I was shocked as shit to see him that first time, but he's kinda cute.

Morgan looks at Wren and me. "Okay, so Main Street and early dinner? I'm good with that."

Wren nods, and I risk a glance up at Shepherd. The corner of his plump, dark lips is turned up, a deep dimple visible on one side. He watches my sisters carefully but turns to me as if he feels me looking.

Finally, he grins. "I'll ride back with you three."

"Will you fit?" Morgan laughs and gestures at his much larger frame. "You've got to weigh like three hundred pounds and Thea's car is a POS."

"Hey now," I protest, giving her a haughty look as I twirl my keys.

The big gargoyle looks over at me, dark eyes hooded as fangs descend from his upper lip, curving to touch the bottom one. I should be frightened because it makes him look more predatory. But somehow, the devious smile on his face just makes me hot.

"I'm not at all worried about fit," he murmurs, his voice husky and low.

My nipples turn to rocks in my shirt as my sisters fade away toward the car, leaving me with Shepherd, who reaches out and grabs one of my belt loops, tugging me close to him. His eyes don't leave mine until he leans down and brushes my hair away from one ear. When he leans down, his lips brush against the curve of my ear.

"I want you to have a blast with your sisters, but I want time with you later, Thea. Are you okay with that? To be clear, I mean a date." His breath is warm against my ear, heat waves radiating down my front.

I stammer out an affirmation of some sort as he straightens up and smiles, threading his fingers through mine and leading me to the car.

When he attempts to shove himself into the backseat with me, he does not fit. He looks sad about it, but he flares his wings wide and flies in front of us as we head toward town.

Wren looks at me with an amused grin. "I'm pretty sure we're all just staring at that peach of an ass, but Thea, please tell me you're gonna tap that at some point and tell us every single thing. Good god, look at it. I'm thirsty as fuck."

"He asked me on a date," I mumble as I prop my chin in my hand.

We all stare at the monster flying in front of our car.

"Get it, girl," Wren confirms, letting out a sigh of appreciation at Shepherd's big, muscular figure.

"He's got a fucking *tail*," Morgan mutters. "There's a damn shovel attached to the end of it. He could kill somebody with that thing."

Kill my cooch is more like it, if I'm honest. I've read monster romance. He is every single gargoyle, minotaur, harpy, shifter fantasy I've ever had come to life. His tail whips out behind him as he flies, the spade-shaped end fluttering in the wind like a flag.

I'm entranced by the way his leathery wings catch the air as he leads us back to town. By the time we arrive, my panties are soaked and my sisters mercilessly poke fun at me. I agreed to go on a date with a gargoyle. A gargoyle!

We park at the Annabelle, and my sisters go inside—I assume to check in with Catherine or maybe change. I hover like an idiot, waiting for Shepherd to land, but Iggy shows up first, fluttering out from a bush to land on top of my car.

"Thea! Thea! Did you go see the wards? Did you check the time? Are you staying?" He peppers me as Shepherd gracefully descends out of the sky, landing quietly on the sidewalk and tucking his wings behind him like a superhero cape.

I'm suddenly curious how he can have wings but still be wearing a shirt. I'm so curious how it all works. Now probably isn't the time to ask questions, though.

"Iggy," Shepherd greets his nephew, coming up next to me until my side is pressed against his front.

I look back at the adorable toddler. "To answer your question, yeah, we're staying for a bit. We're going to go see the shops on Main for a bit, but want to come to Miriam's with us later?"

Iggy fists both hands and punches upward victoriously. "Yessss! I'm not even asking Dad, just come get me 'kay?"

"I'll tell your dad," Shepherd corrects before looking at me. "Have a good time, Thea. Catch you later?"

"Yeah." Is my voice breathless? It sure as hell sounds that way to me. Everything he says has a double meaning. Catch me later? Yes, please.

CHAPTER ELEVEN
SHEPHERD

I don't actually have to work this afternoon, but I didn't want to intrude on the girls' time together. So, I hang out with Alo and Iggy for a few hours until the triplets show up to take Iggy to Miriam's. It's hard not to trail after them and watch Thea obsessively. But I remind myself that it's good for Alo to have time away from Iggy, and I'm getting time with Thea later. I have to because it's harder and harder not to snatch her up and carry her to my nest.

I'm beginning to understand my parents' obsession with each other a little bit better.

Alo and I share a half barrel of troll mead from Ohken's private stores. Godsdamn, he makes the best mead. I shudder a little when I think of what sorts of ingredients might be in it. I stopped asking, and he stopped telling me a long time ago.

"Earth to Shepherd. You're so distracted!" Alo slaps my wing, something I'd only allow him to do.

It would be rude for anyone else but a family member or partner to touch me like that.

"Thea's mine." I turn in my chair to face him. "It's such an odd sensation for your body to recognize someone as yours but to still need to get to know them."

Alo looks skeptical. "Just be careful, brother. The girls said they weren't staying. You don't want to love and lose, believe me."

He falls quiet, taking a sip of his mead as his eyes drift off to the thin strip of trees behind his cottage home. Catherine's garden spills over into his backyard a little more every year.

I give my older brother an aggressively pointed look. "Why don't you ask Miriam out? She's wanted you to for ages, and you've been single for years at this point."

"Iggy keeps me busy," he hedges.

"You're scared, and it's understandable," I say. "But Miriam isn't she-who-must-not-be-named, so you've got to leave that behind you."

Alo lets out a warning growl, his horns flexing when he turns to me. "When you finally claim your mate and your heart starts beating, it's fucking glorious, Shep. To feel it stop? I don't want to go through that again. I'm an empty shell all the time, brother. It aches, deep inside, and nothing I do now is gonna change that."

I don't believe it, but Alo's hung up on the pain of losing his mate, shitty as she was. I never liked her for him, and I'm glad she's gone. She was a terrible mother and a terrible mate, and they're both better off without her.

Still, I can't imagine connecting like that only to have it ripped away. I hope I don't ever find out, but his comment reminds me that I know who my mate is. And there's a solid chance she won't stay here and I'll be in the same boat as Alo. I don't want that for myself, and I'm resolved to do everything I can to win Thea over and get to know her as fast as possible.

Eventually, Alo and I run out of things to talk about. Iggy shows back up, high on sugar, and with a box of sweets from

Miriam for Alo. He takes them, and when he opens them, a note falls into his hands. Oh boy.

Alo opens the folded paper and scans it. A red blush colors his dark cheeks, and he clears his throat, studiously avoiding my gaze. I'd give my right horn to know what's in that note, but it's obvious he doesn't plan to share. I look at my nephew as he zooms around the back porch like a wild animal.

"Come on, Iggy, let's get ready for bed." I grab his tail and drag him toward the stairs.

Iggy yawns but launches into a story about the triplets. I pull him upstairs to his room and help him get into his pajamas. Eventually, Alo joins us, but he's flushed, his horns pressed tight against his head. I resist the urge to ask him what about Miriam's note has his horns in a knot, but I suspect I know.

An hour later, we've read Iggy a hundred books, and he's asleep in the crook of my arm.

I don't know if Thea's still out with her sisters or if they're back at the Annabelle, but it's time for me to find her. Anticipation coils like a snake low in my belly.

"Get outta here," Alo says gently, sensing my change in focus. "Good luck, brother."

I smile, plant a kiss on Iggy's forehead, and leave them to head next door to the Annabelle. That's the first place I'll look.

Flapping my wings, I ascend to the room Thea took—the gargoyle room. Thank you, Catherine, for comm'ing me that helpful tidbit—and peek inside. The sight inside shocks me so hard that I forget to hover and fall ten feet before I regain my composure. She was in her room, shirtless, unclipping a bra. Gods, I didn't think this through.

I fly back down to the ground and find a few small stones, tossing them against the window to let her know I'm here.

Moments later, she shows up in the window, sliding the ancient wooden frame up to stick her head out.

"You were right about Miriam," she laughs. "She's got the hots for Alo."

Laughing, I press hard off the ground and fly to the second story, hovering just in front of her. "Do tell."

She chuckles again and hops into the open window frame. "Morgan made a point to mention Alo and every time she did, Miriam got all blushy and flustered. So cute. She's amazing, by the way. And Iggy freaking loves her, it seems like."

She's confirming what the entire town knows. Miriam is perfect for Alo if he'd just get his shit in gear.

I want to ask more about her night, but I don't want to hover outside her window like a teenage asshole sneaking around. Holding my hand out, I give her what I hope is a charming look. "Come to my place for a drink? I want to hear about your afternoon."

Thea's cheeks turn a bright pink, and her blue eyes drop to my outstretched hand and then to the ground two stories below us.

"I would never let you go," I growl. "You're safe with me, Thea."

She nods once, placing her tiny hand in mine. I marvel at the color of our skin next to each other's. Mine's a smoky charcoal gray, and hers is so beautifully pale. Even the back of her hand has tiny brown freckles on it. I never could have foreseen that my mate would be human. Honestly, it never crossed my mind. But now that I know she is, I'm fascinated by our differences.

I pull her to the edge of the window sash and give her a rakish look. "You're gonna have to trust me for a sec, okay?"

When she smiles, I wrap a hand around her waist and pull her into my arms, her back to my front. Quickly, I thread her legs through mine, pinning her against my body with one hand splayed over her chest. It's a sensual, intimate embrace. I'll never carry anyone else like this; it's a position reserved only for my mate. If I do a good enough job wooing her, I might get to fuck her like this one day. We're not there yet, though.

It's just like I told her and her sisters earlier—monsters move quickly once we identify the one we want. I know humans don't work the same way, but based on the way Thea's body molds to mine, I'm hopeful.

"I've got you. You okay?" My voice is rough in her ear as she squirms.

"Don't you dare let me go." She laughs a little, but her tone is shaky with obvious nerves as I flap my wings and bullet straight up.

Thea screams, but the scream morphs into a joyous laugh as she spreads her arms wide. I fly above the thin strip of forest between the Annabelle and the part of Ever where I live.

"Every home here is a little different, I'm excited for you to meet mine," I share as we fly.

My lips are right by her ear. I'm rock-hard against her back, and I suspect she can feel it. I want her to. I want her to know exactly what she does to me.

I grab one of her arms, wrapping my fingers through hers and using my grip to point below us. "That series of cottages is the street many of the orcs live on. The rolling hills behind them are the centaurs' farm. Some of them live in the forest too, like Taylor, who you already met. I'll give you a full tour of Ever outside of downtown tomorrow if you want."

"Okay!" Thea's voice is pure excitement as she points to a house just below us. It's all curved walls with a mushroom-shaped thatched room. "What's that one, it's adorable! Look at that garden!"

"That one's mine," I whisper. "I can't wait to show it to you."

THEA

I'm flying! I'm freaking flying! I'm flying with a rock-hard dick smashed up against my ass! Because let's be real, Shepherd is hard as hell behind me. I can fully admit to thinking about him for the majority of girls' night, even though we had a fantastic time and it felt *almost* normal. Aside from all the monsters walking around and behaving like humans.

Shepherd swoops low to a curvy, concrete path leading up to the cutest hobbit cottage I've ever seen. Except this cottage is incredibly tall. I wonder if he can fly around inside. The beautiful plants lining his walkway sway in the air with a gentle breeze when we land on the path. Shepherd carefully disentangles us and sets me down.

"The house is excited to meet you," he laughs. "She never sends a breeze around for new people."

I whip around. "The house sent the breeze? Do they all control the weather?"

"Nah," Shepherd says. "Mine's connected to my garden. My home is very lowkey, you'll see that, but she usually loves people. She's just never expressed that much excitement to meet someone. Then again, I don't bring women to my home, so she knows it's a big deal."

He says it with a serious look on his face. It's another statement hinting that he's got romance in his sights. Somehow, despite the absolute rollercoaster of a day I've had, it doesn't scare me like it maybe should. If anything, I'm curious to know more.

I smile brightly up at him. "Tell me more about the house connecting to their owners bit," I ask. "I don't get that, other than the Annabelle seems to react to Catherine and us."

"That's pretty much the gist of it," Shepherd chuckles. "Houses pick their owners. If you decide you want one, one will simply pop up for you and you'll know it's there. You'll feel called to it."

I don't know how much more information I can absorb today.

"This is all in the welcome packet, you know," Shepherd jokes. Dark eyes fall to my lips. "Read it later. Right now, come inside with me and tell me everything about your afternoon." His dark eyes crinkle at the corners as he drags his gaze back up to meet mine.

I think I recognize the myriad of emotions in the way he looks at me. There's heat and desire and joy.

Shepherd steps closer, and his bright, clean scent wraps around me. He's intoxicating, looking at me like he wants to eat me alive.

I move toward him until my chest touches his body. Dark eyes flash as he reaches out to tuck my hair over one ear.

"I'm having a hard time not putting my hands all over you, angel." His voice is a pure, possessive rumble, his fangs poking at his lower lip.

Angel? I could get used to that.

I open my mouth to say something, anything, but nothing comes out. No saucy retort, no sexy statement. I'm just . . . overwhelmed by the tension between us.

He seems to get it, though, because he gives me a heated smirk and turns, tugging me toward the front door. He swings it open, steps inside, and cuts the lights on.

I follow him in and gasp. A tiny wood-paneled hallway with a coat stand opens quickly into a cozy living room, where a fire crackles in a stone fireplace that soars to the arched ceiling. Criss-crossed beams above us form a star that holds up the roof.

Directly in front of us, the entire wall is taken up by an enormous round window looking out onto a babbling brook. I can't even see any other houses, but I cross the room to be sure.

Shepherd trails me as I round a carved wooden coffee table and two plush-looking sofas. I move to the gigantic window and press myself against it.

"This view is straight out of a storybook," I murmur, admiring a lovely stream of water that runs just behind Shepherd's house.

Dense pine trees should be dark and ominous, but tiny lights zip in and out, illuminating the scene with an otherworldly, pale glow.

"Pixies." Shepherd stops beside me, leaning against the glass as he slides both big hands into his pockets. "They harvest one of the ingredients for their dust from the pine trees. Although, they might just be being nosy too."

A hot blush spreads across my cheeks as I look up at him. "Nosy? Because of me?"

Shepherd removes one hand from his pocket and reaches out, placing it on my lower back and pulling me close. His dark eyes glitter in the pixies' light.

"It's a small town. Bringing you here is big news." His black eyes fall to my lips. He reaches up to brush his thumb over them.

My lips part, the rough pad of his thumb stroking along my top lip. He grits his teeth, a muscle in his jaw working. He looks at me with a possessive intensity, like he could eat me alive. Should it terrify me? Perhaps?

This has been a day for the record books.

"Just to be clear," I joke. "Monsters don't eat humans, right?"

Shepherd's low, rumbly laughter sends a jolt of heat to my clit. He leans one big arm on the glass and bends down to hover his lips above mine.

"Why, Thea? Are you afraid to get eaten?"

Those damn dimples tease me. His pink tongue slips out to run along his lower lip.

Lust strikes hot between my thighs as wetness seeps through my panties. I clench my legs together.

Shepherd lets out a soft, low rumble. It's almost a growl, but there's no warning in it. If anything, it stokes the flame burning inside me as I resist the urge to climb him. He is an absolute master of the double entendre, and I think it's my favorite thing about this whole town so far.

"You look so thirsty," he murmurs, his voice husky.

His thumb stops and presses against my lips, almost daring me to nip at it.

Instead, I do what any sane woman would do after discovering a gargoyle has the hots for her—I open my mouth and lick up the pad of his finger, never breaking eye contact with him.

The effect is instantaneous—Shepherd's nostrils flare. His horns move from their relaxed position to flatten along his scalp. It's fucking fascinating.

Just as quickly, he removes his thumb from my mouth and steps back. I almost reel from the loss of that touch. Did I misunderstand this heat? I don't think so.

He rolls both shoulders as if working out a kink, and then a smile splits his handsome face. "Come. Tell me about your day, and I'll make you a drink." He reaches for my hand, his grin infectious.

I place my hand in his, watching as his fingers curl around mine. I'm fascinated by those fingers and how strong they look, tipped in dark claws a few shades more purple-gray than his skin. God, they look sharp. Would they cut me if he touched me? Or maybe they retract . . .

I'm still focused on that while Shepherd leads me around the fireplace. We head down a short hall that opens into a dark kitchen, where he flicks the light on and turns with a smile.

"I'll give you the full tour any time you want, but my place isn't huge. There are two nests upstairs. But—"

"Nest? Like a bird's nest?" I hope my question isn't rude, but I'm picturing him curling up on a bed of sticks and it just doesn't seem right somehow.

Shepherd laughs and pats the countertop. "Up here, angel."

I follow his direction and hop onto the long, thin island, noticing how much closer it puts me to his face. He could easily lean in and press those beautiful, dark lips to mine.

His nostrils flare again, black eyes dropping to my mouth.

I'd bet my right tit he's thinking the same thing I am.

I bite my damn lip like a horny teenager.

"You thirsty, angel?" His voice is husky, his eyes focused on my mouth.

"God, yes," I admit.

All this double entendre has me ready to rip my clothes off. What would it be like for Shepherd to say the dirty shit he's thinking outright? I want to know right now.

He steps between my thighs and places a hand on either side of me. I'm caged in close to his chest. He leans down and brings his lips close to mine.

I whine when he cocks his head to the side and drags the tip of his nose up my neck, huffing softly against my skin. Warm lips trail a teasing path up to my ear, and this time I'm certain he growls. It's a low rumble that sends a zing between my thighs.

"I'm going to pursue you, Thea. Consider this my formal statement of my intention." His voice is pure gravel, and it shocks me when he nips hard at the skin beneath my ear.

I yip and jerk in his arms, but he's not done.

"I need to get to know you, sweetheart. I need time with you. You feel it like I do, right? This connection. Tell me you wanna know where it could go . . ."

My mouth drops open as I gasp for air. His lips are still tickling my neck. Just kiss me already, is what I want to shout. I don't, though.

Shepherd lets out a throaty chuckle and steps away, turning to the fridge.

I stare at his muscular back and wings. They're tucked closely together, but from this angle, it's easy to see major bones and leathery material are between those bigger sections. Just looking at them has my cheeks flushed and my clit throbbing in time with my heartbeat.

"I hope you're coming back for more," I demand, finally finding my voice.

I used to be such a good tease, but I'm off my game here.

"Oh, I'll come back for more," he laughs.

He grabs a giant glass jar of something dark that bubbles like beer. He sets it on the countertop next to me and then retrieves two glasses from a cupboard behind him. It's all so normal and human that I pause for a second to recenter myself.

Monsters live in a town just like I do. They have fucking refrigerators. They declare their intentions to pursue.

"What did you mean?" I ask. "That you intend to pursue me? And don't think I forgot about the nest question you haven't answered."

I give him a cheeky grin as he pours the dark liquid and then hands me one.

"I'm gonna show you my nest in a minute. It needs to be experienced because it's magical."

"Literally?"

"Everything in my house is magical, that's how a monster house works."

On cue, a bowl slides across the countertop of its own accord.

It's filled with oranges, and Shepherd laughs, pointing to the bowl. "She thinks you'd like an orange in your mead. Want to try one?"

I look up and around at the house, at the beautiful, exposed wooden rafters and the wall of plated windows behind me.

The house just moved a damn bowl. By itself. Across the counter.

"Thank you," I whisper, unsure of precisely how to interact with a cottage.

There's a groan and a shudder, and Shepherd laughs again. "She says you're welcome."

"Do you speak in some sort of language, or do you just understand the creaks and groans?"

Shepherd slices the orange and drops a slice in my glass before handing it to me. "Tell me if you hate that, and I'll make something else while I answer your questions."

I take a quick sip, and a myriad of flavors burst across my tongue—oranges, strawberries maybe, but there's a hoppy feel to it, sort of like beer. It's got a bitter aftertaste that I love.

"God, it's good," I admit. "You said it's mead?"

Shepherd nods. "This one is from Ohken's stores. He does the best mead, just don't ever ask him what's in it. The ingredients are always weird."

Oh god. "Like what? Eyeball of newt or zombie's tongue?" My voice is barely a whisper as I eye the glass like it's a spider.

"Well," he laughs. "Last time I thought I tasted strawberries, it was earthworms."

I clap my hand over my mouth and set the mead down. "I'll come back to that in a minute," I mumble.

Shepherd's deep laugh warms me as the house shudders around us playfully. I think she's laughing with him. God, this is so weird.

"Okay, let's see about your questions," he muses. "I'll go in reverse order so we can end on the sexy pursuing stuff. That's my favorite part."

He gives me a playful wink and takes a sip of his mead, then sets the glass down. Swear to god, I hope he's not drinking earthworms. But even that couldn't make him any less sexy.

He leans against the bar with one hip and gestures around the kitchen.

"Our houses don't speak, but they make their wishes known. That shuddering noise is the way she laughs, but when she's pissed at me, the floors creak loudly. You'll learn those noises in time if you stay," he adds at the last moment, and some of the smile fades from his eyes.

It comes back after another sip of mead. "There are two nests upstairs, the guest nest and my nest. Nests are oval-shaped, so I suppose they're like a bird nest. And it's built up high on the second story, but that's pretty much where the comparison ends. I'm gonna show you in a minute because of your third question." His cheeks flush a little darker and shiny, white fangs slide down from his upper jaw to poke at his lower lip. "Intention to pursue simply means I'm telling you that I'm interested in you, that I want you, angel."

There's that nickname again. I take a quick sip of the troll mead. I hope it's not made out of earthworms, but I need to do something with my mouth before I blurt out some ridiculous response. My brain, the helpful bitch that she is, supplies an image of fun things I could be doing with my mouth, and I choke on the mead.

Shepherd remains quietly watchful, black eyes focused on

me while he waits for me to recover and respond. After a heated moment, he takes my glass from my hand and sets it down. Big hands come to my ass, and he pulls me to the edge of the island, flush with his broad, muscular chest.

"I won't apologize for coming on strong, Thea. But if I'm ever too much, you can tell me, alright? I'll attempt to tone it down."

I shake my head. I hate that idea. I don't want Shepherd to tone himself down.

"I don't want that," I state. "But maybe explain things along the way because I don't know what's normal for monsters or what your traditions are. But I want to know."

Shepherd tips my chin up with one finger. "Good, Thea. Because I want to play with you in my nest. I'd like to show it to you, if that's alright?" Dark eyes are focused intently on mine, a dark red blush covering the tops of his angular cheeks.

Oh god. He's just told me that the nest is his bed, and he wants to take me there.

Am I about to go see it? Hell yes, I most definitely am.

CHAPTER THIRTEEN
SHEPHERD

I can barely believe it. Thea's here, my mate's *here*, in my cottage, after so many years of hoping and waiting and wishing for her. I'm pressed between her pretty thighs, her heartbeat a steady drum I'm quickly becoming fascinated with. What would it be like to claim her and feel my own heart come alive?

I reach out to trace a vein in her neck. Her heartbeat throbs there, too.

"Gargoyle's hearts don't beat until we claim a mate," I muse, watching the blood rush through her veins. "The sound of yours fascinates me."

When I look up, her blue eyes flash with something that looks like need. Her woodsy, caramel scent fills my nostrils. All gargoyles have strong senses—it's necessary to be good protectors. I got a hit of her natural scent while flying, but it soaks the air in the small space of my kitchen.

She worries at her plump lower lip. "I don't know what it means to be someone's mate, Shepherd. It sounds a lot more intense than a date on a girls' weekend."

Her voice is soft, maybe even a little nervous. She's gently reminding me that she's not here for long.

Something pinches in my chest at that, but I bend down and press my lips softly to hers once, then pull away. Her girls' "weekend" will be nearly three months in Ever time.

"I'd be a liar if I didn't admit that I hope you like me enough to stick around, Thea. But let's take it one date at a time. If it goes nowhere and you leave, I'll understand."

I won't understand, but I'll try to. And no matter what, I won't chase her if she chooses not to stay. Neither of us deserves that drama. I might have recognized her soul as part of mine, but we still have to end up in love, and being fated doesn't guarantee that will happen. Alo is the perfect example.

Thea nods, but she seems lost in thought, glancing away.

When she says nothing else, I grab our drinks and help her off the island. I jerk my head toward the living room. "We can drink these upstairs, I'll give you the tour."

She follows me silently, which seems out of the norm for her based on our interactions so far. She's the goofy, funny triplet, and I want to hear everything she's thinking out loud. I don't sense she's afraid at all, but I suspect she's overwhelmed from the day she's had. Still, every sense I have tells me to just get her to the nest, that she'll be comfortable there.

"A gargoyle's nest is our refuge," I explain as I walk around the opposite side of the stone fireplace, down a second short hall, and up a set of curved stairs. I walk backward while Thea trails me. "Gargoyles feel most at home in their nests. It's a place of rest and rejuvenation. It's where we connect with our partners. It's a place where our young play. It's the center of a gargoyle home."

Thea chuckles. "Sounds like a human living room."

"I suppose so," I admit. "But there's no tech in the nest aside from a comm watch. A nest is a paradise away from everything else."

I don't know how to explain a gargoyle nest in any other way, but when I open the door to mine and step aside, ushering Thea in, all I feel is pride. It swells in my chest until it's almost hard to breathe. My tail lashes from side to side in excitement, but I wrap it around my thigh to keep from looking like an angry cat.

Thea looks around with a little gasp. "Holy shit, this is . . ." She paces around the edge and examines every detail with excited focus.

I try to see it from her perspective. Every inch of the three walls is carved with stories from my family. Alo and Iggy are there, along with my mother, father, and grandparents. The only wall that's not carved is the one at the head of my actual nest. I'll carve that wall when she and I start to make memories together. That wall is ours.

The actual nest in the middle is large and oval with plush sides that curve up. I suppose it's like a bird's nest, but it's soft and firm like the perfect pillow. The raised edge is not only comfortable, but it serves a dual purpose as support for . . . activities. This is the place I'll claim Thea if she stays long enough for that. All I need to do is court her and show her why we should both want this.

I watch her for a moment, her elegant fingers trailing the art on the wall. She points to a tiny gargoyle. "Iggy?" A smile splits her freckled cheeks.

I nod. "I carved all of these stories." Pointing up at the ceiling, I explain the basic functions of the nest. "That angled, long window opens to let in a breeze, or to fly out, or to enjoy the weather and the stars." Grinning, I point at the actual nest. "The squishy bed part is for relaxing, and other things."

Thea blushes, but stands and points to a long metal bar that's visible outside the window. It sticks out into the air like a flagpole on a house. "What's that for?"

I frown because I already dread sharing this tidbit. "Once a month, gargoyles sleep for twenty-four hours. It's called stone sleep, and it's vital to maintaining and growing our power. Once a month I perch out there and turn into stone. I'm unreachable during that time."

Her eyelashes flutter softly. "Does it hurt?"

I shake my head. "Not at all, it's a reprieve. We dream deeply in stone sleep."

"Wait, what does Alo do when he's stone sleeping? Does Iggy sleep? God, I have so many questions."

I set our drinks down on a small table next to my oval-shaped nest. "Iggy won't stone sleep until he comes of age at fifteen. For now, he comes here and stays with me when Alo sleeps." I give her a sneaky look. "I feed him a shitload of candy and we watch movies like crazy. Or we come up here and cuddle. He loves that."

"So, basically, you're the coolest uncle ever?" Thea's tone is playful as she reaches out and runs her hand along the edge of my bed to stroke the soft fabric. "God, this is amazing. It feels like chinchilla, although I hope it's not an animal skin." She looks up at me with a hopeful grimace.

"Not chinchilla. It's a fabric woven by gargoyle seamstresses specifically for nests." I reach out and pull Thea to me, clutching her to my chest as I fall into the nest and flip us onto our sides. Relaxation floods my system at having her in my arms. "My nest is home in every sense of the word." I stroke her pale hair up over her shoulder. "Having you in it feels perfect."

Thea smiles, her cheek propped up in her palm. I shove one of my legs through hers. All I want is to be closer to her. Like this, she's almost riding my thigh. I want her riding my cock, falling apart on me.

Earlier today I did some quick research on humans at the historical society. Apparently, humans do things like *dating*. Gargoyles don't do that for an extended time. When we find a partner, we take them almost immediately to our nest and fuck for days. I want to do that with her, and there's an obvious attraction between us, but I'll try to take things at human speed.

"What are you thinking about? You look lost in thought, maybe a little concerned." Her voice is playful as she reaches out to lay one tiny hand on my chest. Suddenly there are far too many clothes between us. Grabbing her hand, I shove it up my shirt so we're skin-to-skin. A soft, satisfied groan leaves me, my horns flexing hard against my scalp.

"That's better," I murmur, shifting closer to her so she's forced onto her back with me hovering just above. Her lips part, her thighs clamping around mine. We're dancing on the edge of something here, and I don't think I can hold back. Not with her body wrapped around mine. Not with her in my godsdamned nest. I thought I could take things slowly, but the smell of her arousal assaults me. I want to rise to the occasion in every possible way.

My tail lashes anxiously against the bed, and Thea shifts up onto her elbows to look at it. "Are you a cat, Shepherd?"

I growl out a playful warning and slap her thigh with the spade-shaped end. "Not hardly, little human."

She reaches out and strokes the end of my tail thoughtfully. The move sends intense heat streaking along my tailbones and up my thighs. It coils deep in my balls, filling them to the point of pain. God, she doesn't know how intimate tail touching is for me, clearly, or I suspect she wouldn't be stroking me like that. I can't wait for her to learn every inch of me. And I can't wait to learn every inch of her.

"I'm not human though, right?" Her tone is wistful.

She grabs my tail just behind the tip and pulls it to her chest, clinging to it as if it comforts her. I hold in a groan as my cock leaps in my pants.

"True," I admit.

I lean over her to bury my nose in the hollow at the base of her throat. She arches back, giving me better access. I know she doesn't know what exposing her neck like this means to me, how it's an invitation for my teeth, but some part of me hopes she senses it. At the very least, she trusts me enough to show all that soft, vulnerable skin.

"What are you?" I murmur as I brush my lips across her collarbone. "Besides mine . . ." I add on that last bit to see how she'll respond, but where I expect some resistance, her scent blooms stronger. It calls to me, practically a plea for her to be sated.

"I wish you had some mystical way to know what I am if the Keeper's to be believed." Thea's voice is small as I scent my way back along her collarbone, following the touch with a brush of my lips.

When my tongue runs softly into the base of her throat, she gasps. I groan. All this fucking clothing is so uncomfortable. Snarling, I roll on top of her and pull her to me. I roll until she's straddling me and I'm seated upright against the back wall of my nest.

"Better," I snarl as I wrap my fingers through her long, pale hair. It's so incredibly soft and silky. "I wish I could answer that question for you, but we can approach the Keeper together if you like."

Thea's eyes flash, her nostrils flaring. A vein throbs in her neck, her heartbeat galloping as her woodsy, caramel scent spills stronger into the air. My nest will be saturated with this scent after she leaves. I can't fucking wait to smell her here all the time.

My other hand comes to her lips, and I stroke my fingers across them. "These need kissed, angel. I'm trying to be a gentleman and woo you like a human would. What would a man do next?"

"But you're not human," she counters. "And apparently, neither am I. So what would a gargoyle do in a situation like this?"

"Oh, that's an easy one." My voice is hard gravel as I drag her head carefully back and bite my way up her neck to her ear, which gets the same rough treatment from my fangs. "A gargoyle would break you apart on his thick cock until you never want to leave his nest." I rock my hips once, reveling in the way it feels when hers roll to meet mine.

Thea lets out a soft, needy whine, and I can't hold back any longer. Everything in my core aches with a need to claim her. My mouth waters at the idea of getting between her thighs and licking. I can't keep teasing like this.

She wants me. She needs me. And it's time I did something about that.

CHAPTER FOURTEEN

THEA

My clit is on fire, literally on fire. I notch my hips against Shepherd's thigh, desperate for enough friction to get off. His mouth is warm under my ear, his fangs pricking just enough to remind me that I'm in bed with a damn gargoyle. How is it possible that forty-eight hours ago, I didn't even know Shepherd existed? Or that a whole town full of monstrous beings was hidden from my world . . .

The truth is, I couldn't care less that he's a monster. If anything, I'm fascinated. My damn curiosity might not get me killed, but it might get me fucked by a monster. I'm not even confused about my stance on this topic anymore. I want it. I want *him*.

"Shepherd," I moan. "Please . . ."

What am I even begging for? I think for this slow torture to end.

"Tell me what you want, angel." His voice is gruff and commanding as his hips roll to meet mine. An obvious erection presses against the front of his pants, rubbing against me with every movement of his big hips.

"Too many clothes," I gasp out.

I need to see him in all his glory. A voice of reason in the back of my head says I should take it slow—we've never even been on an actual date. But somehow, I feel as if I know Shepherd's soul. He's strong, good, and kind, and I want to unravel his layers as fast as I can.

Including what he looks like completely naked and underneath me.

One of Shepherd's big hands circles my neck, his thumb pressed into the hollow at the base of my throat. "My tee unbuttons at the shoulder and along one side. Remove it for me."

The gravelly command in his voice has me out of my mind with desire. Fingers trembling, I find the buttons along his shoulders and undo them, peeling the shirt down to reveal a stacked chest peppered with soft black hair.

His chest rises and falls with quick, shallow breaths. My hands move to his left side, where I find more buttons running along the seam of his tee. I rip them open and then pull the whole shirt away from his body, tossing it beside us in the nest.

I'm in a fucking gargoyle nest.

Gargoyles have nests.

And it's the best, most comfy dog bed on a platform.

"Are you even real?" The words come out before I can stop them, my eyes drawn to Shepherd's.

His eyes glitter shiny black in the low light. He moves his hand from my throat but then grabs my wrists and brings them to his pecs. He's not as warm as a human would be. That's the first thing I notice. The second is that the planes of his body are rock-hard. There's not an ounce of fat on this man, which makes sense, because he's not a man at all. His skin is soft and velvety, slightly more textured than mine.

"Feel real enough to you, sweet girl?" Shepherd's voice dips low as I explore his chest, running my hands over one dark gray nipple and then down the side of his thick-cut abs.

He lets out a soft growl, full of pleasure, and it makes me wonder just how loud I might be able to make him. Something tells me Shepherd wouldn't hold back in the bedroom, that he'd let me know exactly how much he enjoys me.

"I keep expecting to blink my eyes and wake up back in the city," I admit as I stroke his stomach absentmindedly.

Shepherd gives me a neutral look, but it's easy to see there's something he's not saying.

"Don't hold back from me," I demand, halting the progress of my hands. "Never hold back, please? I always want to know what you're thinking."

Shepherd grabs one of my hands in his. I marvel again at the three fingers that wrap around my wrist and bring it to his mouth. He kisses the inside of my arm as he pulls me gently forward, my upper body pressed flat to his. My breathing grows shallow and rocky. I could kiss him like this. We're close enough.

He nips at the heel of my palm, never taking his eyes from mine.

"I was thinking about how I don't want you to leave Ever. About how I want to please you so well that you'll never want to go. I want to keep you, Thea."

His eyes sparkle as two of my fingertips disappear between his dark lips. The gentle suction feels like it's pulling at my clit too. His soft tongue swirls over my fingers, a tease of how he might apply that tongue to other parts of my body.

Shepherd's eyes dip to my chest. "The color of your skin makes it so easy to see how you feel about what I'm doing. I'm gonna learn you fast, angel. Starting now."

My heartbeat gallops in my ears when his tongue trails along both fingers, swirling around the ends. He groans, deep and low and then moves so fast I can barely track it. He shifts and flips us. One enormous wing curls around me at the same time. Then I'm cocooned with a wing underneath me and the other surrounding us both, shielding us from view.

Not that there's anybody to view us. It's dark inside the shelter of his wings, but they're almost warm underneath me, soft and pliant. I reach out to stroke the thick membrane between his bones. There's an audible growl, but it's so dark in here, I can barely see Shepherd's face.

Big hands come to my pants and pull them off my hips. His voice is low as his lips trail the pants down one of my thighs.

"Wings, tail, and horns are erogenous zones for gargoyles. Then all the usual spots you might expect." He lets out a soft chuckle as I reach down and touch the tip of one of his horns.

They move in my palm. I gasp.

"They flatten along my skull when I'm aroused." Shepherd shifts forward and grabs my hand, guiding it to one long, curved horn and helping me touch it. "Fuck, Thea. Your hands on me are pure bliss."

There's a low growl, and I arch my hips when his lips come to my lower stomach. God, he's headed straight for the candy shop, and I honestly haven't shaved in who knows how long.

All those troublesome thoughts fly away when his warm tongue licks straight up my slit, over my panties. I gasp at the sensation. And then he does it again, and again, before dragging the tip of his nose through my folds. I flood my panties as Shepherd's fingers come to the fabric and shift it aside. A ripping sound fills the air before they're yanked from my body. Tattered, if that noise was anything to go by.

Shepherd growls again. "Tell me what feels good to you, little human." His hands come to my thighs, and he presses them wide.

Can he see in the dark? Is he staring at my pussy right now? I can't tell, and all I can hear is his steady breathing. And all I can feel is his warm breath on my soaked cunt.

Shepherd closes his lips over my clit and sucks. Bliss rockets through me as I cry out, the sound muffled in the cocoon of his wings. He sucks again. My hips buck. I'm going to fucking come already. My hips gyrate as I grapple for something to hang on to. But there aren't sheets and pillows below me; it's just his wing. So I grab the only thing I can reach, one of his wing claws, and I hold on for dear life.

Shepherd buries his face between my legs and growls as he licks his way up both sides of my pussy, then along my clit. He alternates licking and sucking, and moments later, a wave of pleasure hits me like a hurricane. I scream his name over and over as I grip his claw tight. It's never been like this with anyone else, never so all-encompassing, never so fucking good. And he never stops, licking me through the longest orgasm of my life.

When the pleasure finally recedes, he lets out a soft whine. "That was far too fast, Thea. I need to learn to tease you better, to make this last for hours."

"God, are you grumbling about how good you are at that? Jesus," I sob. "Hours?" I let go of his claw. "I don't think I'd survive hours."

Shepherd chuckles and shifts forward until his big body covers mine, his lips brushing my mouth. They're soaked with my release, and the fact he doesn't seem to care makes me want to devour him.

"I'll work you up to it, sweetheart, because you're gonna need that stamina. Gargoyles fuck very thoroughly. Hours are always the goal, my sweet. We're . . . different from humans."

"I can see that," I groan. "That fucking tongue."

He laughs again, and then a sudden whoosh of chilly air hits me as he unwraps us and hops nimbly out of the bed, giving me a knowing look.

"You need sustenance, and then I need to take you back to the Annabelle. If you stay here in my nest, I'm fucking you, Thea. You've had a helluva day though."

I don't even know what to say to any of that. I want what

he's referencing, but it *was* a long day. So I roll onto one side as I watch him. He tucks both wings elegantly behind his back, but my eyes are drawn to the long, hard length pressed to the front of his pants.

"You sure we shouldn't do something about that first?" I tease, pointing at the obvious erection pressed to the front of his pants. "Because I really, really want to."

Shepherd leans forward, both hands on the edge of the bed as his lips hover above mine.

"Sweetheart, if you touch my cock, I'll lose the last shred of self-control I possess. I'm exercising it at this moment to keep from fucking you for days, but I'm only so strong. Don't tempt me unless you're ready to be locked up here for a solid twenty-four hours."

I feel saucy after that fan-fucking-tastic orgasm, so I nip at his lower lip, pulling it between my teeth.

Shepherd groans, but he doesn't pull away.

"I taste myself on you," I whisper when I release the bite.

"Thea . . ." This time his voice is a soft whine, like he can barely take it anymore and he's a dam about to burst.

God, I want him to, all over me, all inside me. I'm not ready to go home.

But he straightens and takes a step back. "Snacks," he mutters, running both gray hands through his hair. "Snacks and the inn."

Without another word, he trots out of the room.

I roll back to the middle of the nest and stare at the carvings on the walls around me. This room is so beautiful, so perfect. I don't ever want to leave it. I think I can understand how a nest is a refuge, because right now? It feels like home.

Shepherd returns a few minutes later, carrying a spoon and a small dish. I push myself back against the bare headboard wall. He slides into bed and straddles both my legs, showing me the dish, which turns out to be crème brûlée.

"I made this for you. There's plenty for your sisters too, if they want to come by. Or I can bring some to the inn." He smiles and dips the spoon into the burnt sugar topping, breaking it.

"God, that looks good. You cook?" I don't know why I'm surprised. He's fucking perfect.

"I love to cook, it's my hobby," Shepherd laughs. "I don't know if human men feed their women, but it's definitely a gargoyle trait." He spoons a bite of the creamy dessert and brushes it against my lower lip. "Open, Thea."

My core clenches at his command, but I'm a good-fucking-girl and I obey, my lips closing over the spoon he inserts between them.

"Fucking, god . . . lord," I mumble as my eyes roll back into my head. I manage to swallow. "This is incredible, Shepherd."

He preens, his horns flattening to his skull. I laugh as I open for another bite.

"So I guess the horns are for you what my blushing is for me?"

He nods and bends over, planting a tender, soft kiss on my shoulder. Suddenly, having a shirt on feels like too much since I'm wearing no pants, but I don't want to stop eating the delicious dessert long enough to fully undress.

Shepherd solves that problem. He grips my tee at the neck and cuts a line straight down the front with his claws. He shoves it down over my shoulders with an appreciative hum.

"That's better." A devious smile follows. "I don't wanna take you home, angel. I want to devour you all night and feed you snacks, in no particular order."

"Sounds good to me," I laugh.

This is so easy with him, this playful banter. I've never been this comfortable with a man in such a short time. Maybe it's because he's so open, so clear about what he wants, and I don't have to worry about where I stand.

"Is there anything not perfect about you that I need to know now?" I'm half joking, but there's a serious undercurrent to my question. When he sits up and gives me a look, I expand on my thought. "I don't even know what I don't know about Ever and you. And *me*, for that matter. The Keeper says we're not human, but..."

He sets the crème brûlée aside. "If you had to guess, what do you think you are, Thea?"

"A witch," I laugh. "A long lost Sanderson sister."

He gives me a wicked smile and wraps his strong fingers through my hair to fist it. It's not a gentle touch, and it sends a wave of heat through me.

"I'll help you figure that out as soon as you want to," he growls. "We need the Keeper though, he's got the right connections to test for monster blood."

I look up at the big gargoyle. His eyes are hooded lustfully, his gaze hot as he nips his lower lip.

Trailing my tongue along a groove between his muscles, I nip one ab playfully. "And what would you guess I am, Shepherd?"

He groans and grips my hair tighter. "Something very fucking compatible with gargoyles. Gods, Thea. Stop licking me, please. I don't think I can make you stop, and your tongue is so godsdamned soft."

Heat builds in my core as I place a series of hard bites down his stomach to his hip. I don't want to stop. If anything, I want to throw myself into his arms and eat him alive. But he asked nicely, and I have to assume he wasn't kidding when he said he could barely hold back.

With a soft whine, I shove myself back into the plush pillows, watching the monster in front of me. But instead of noticing the wings and the horns and the tail that lashes from side to side behind him, I notice the heat in his eyes and the clench of his jaw, all telling me how much he wants me.

Join the club, buddy. I want everything he's not offering right now. He's probably right that I should head back to the Annabelle.

The thing is, I don't want to go.

CHAPTER FIFTEEN
THEA

When I yawn for the third time, Shepherd insists on returning me to the inn to get some rest, so I leave his nest reluctantly. I fall asleep in his big arms on the way back. Flying is so damn relaxing. Or maybe it's just that being nestled against his broad chest feels perfect. Either way, I barely remember him swooping through my open bedroom window or depositing me on the bed.

I do remember him tucking the sheets around me and stroking my hair away from my forehead. And I most definitely remember his whispered promise to find me in the morning and bring more snacks.

The following morning, aggressive banging on my door wakes me up. When I blink my eyes open, the sun is already higher in the sky than it usually is when I wake up. I must have slept in. Rolling over, I let out a muffled noise, and my sisters pry the door open and fly in, throwing themselves across me.

Morgan gets in my face immediately, examining me like I'm a scientific specimen.

"Wren saw Shepherd fly away with you last night. Spit it out, tell us everything."

Wren gives me a no-fucks-given shrug and sips a to-go coffee in her hand with green whipped cream on top of it. What in the hell?

"Aww, you two already went to the Green Bean?"

Morgan snorts. "Higher Grounds, the coffee place. And the Green Bean? Been here long enough to shorten the name, have you?"

I shrug. I don't know if I'm ready to explain how Ever feels homey to me and I'm not anxious to leave. Especially after what happened last night.

I shift upright to sit against the pillows and make eye contact with my sisters. "Shepherd showed me his house last night, and it was so pretty, you guys."

"What else did he show you?" Wren's normally sarcastic voice is even dryer than usual as one chocolate brow travels upward. A gleeful smile spreads across her face as if she's trying not to break out into laughter.

"He showed me less than I wanted to see," I counter. "But he did get partially naked, and we did a few things, and let me tell you, I don't know if I could go back to a human man after that."

Morgan gapes. "You're being obtuse! What exactly did you do?!"

A knock at the door has all three of us leaping upright. It reminds me of the time we found an old porn magazine in my aunt Lou's room and we were skimming through it when she caught us.

My neck flushes as Catherine peeks her head in. "Shepherd is downstairs with a gift for you, Thea. Shall I let him in?"

My sisters' heads swivel around to me as I struggle to swallow. God, he did say he planned to formally pursue me last night. I didn't think much of it at the time, enamored as I was with his mouth.

Catherine gives me an understanding look. "I don't mean to

interrupt, but may I come in? I feel I can provide a little clarity here, and I've known Shepherd most of his adult life."

When I nod, she lets herself in but leans against the wall and crosses her arms. She looks every bit the beautiful school mistress as she smiles at us.

"Monster dating rituals vary, but the biggest difference from humans is the speed itself."

My sisters are silent as Catherine continues. "Gargoyles will typically make a formal intention to pursue, and then the gifts begin. They'll gift items not just for the object of their affection but for your family as well. Being a protector species, it's highly important to a gargoyle male that he be seen as a capable provider. Hence Shepherd, downstairs with three boxes of cookies." She shrugs as if this is all normal.

Wren pats my leg as she looks at our hostess.

"I say let him up because three boxes of cookies sound perfect. Who knows what new secret we're gonna learn today, so I'll need to get my sugar on to handle it."

"That seems perfectly reasonable," Catherine laughs, looking at me for agreement. When I nod, she taps on her comm watch. "Please tell Shepherd to come in."

I fly out of bed and run to the mirror to pull my fingers through the bird's nest on top of my head. God, there's no saving it, and I can already hear his quiet footsteps on the creaky, wooden stairs.

I grab a tee thrown over a nearby chair and toss it over my bra. The door opens softly, and Shepherd steps in with a big smile.

His jeans hug his enormous thighs, and his white collared shirt is rolled up to his elbows. It's unbuttoned at the top just enough for that dusting of chest hair to poke out. Because I took his shirt off last night, I notice small buttons along the seams of this one too.

"Good morning," he rumbles.

I swear that voice is so deep it sounds like rocks breaking.

His eyes are on me, and despite my disheveled state, he looks thrilled at what he sees. He steps further into the room, three small boxes in one hand.

He gives Catherine a soft smile and then crosses to me, handing me the topmost box. "I made these for you, Thea. I wasn't sure what you liked, so it's a random mix. But tell me your favorites and I'll make more."

I take the box and open it, and goddamn, it's heavier than it looks. Inside are rows of assorted cookies. Their sugary scent hits me, and I take one and try it as he turns to my sisters and hands them each a box.

"These look amazing, Shepherd, thanks." Wren sets her coffee down and grabs a cookie, taking a bite and groaning. "Holy shit. So good."

He laughs and shrugs. "Snack up, shack up—the gargoyle male's motto. We've gotta feed ya to keep ya."

Wren chokes on her cookie. Morgan and I burst into hysterics, and Shepherd just grins.

"Oh my God." Morgan cackles. "That should be a sticker. I'd slap that on my e-reader so fast. Shit, Shepherd, find me a gargoyle man because that motto is pretty much perfect."

Shepherd leans against one of the bed posts with a pleased grin on his face. "You don't need a gargoyle male because you've got me for snack duty." He glances at Wren, who's still pounding herself on the chest. "It sounds like you had a fun time last night. I'd love to take all three of you out tonight if you're up for it. And I've asked Ohken to give you a behind-the-scenes tour of town today, as long as you don't have other plans."

Wren shoots off the bed fast as lightning. "Errr, what time is that, Shepherd?"

He laughs. "No pressure, just if you want him to, I can cancel if you have plans."

"Oh no." She waves his comment away with a chuckle. "Dinner and behind-the-scenes sound great. I'll get ready." She lifts the box of cookies and nods. "These are amazing, thanks again!" Without another word, she darts out the door, her footsteps echoing behind her.

Shepherd winks at Morgan. She rolls her eyes. "I don't suppose I can expect a box of chocolates from the Keeper anytime soon, huh?"

Catherine chuckles as she comes over and wraps one arm around Morgan's shoulder. "That is not his style, my friend. To be honest, I'm not sure what style I'd expect from him when it comes to courting. I suppose I think he'd be very blunt."

"That part has already proven to be true," Morgan grumbles. "There's just no courting."

"Do you *want* him to court you?" Shepherd asks the question I've been mulling over since we saw the Keeper at the gas station.

His announcement about Morgan was weird and shocking, but I have to wonder if there might be a cinnamon roll somewhere under his gruff exterior.

"I don't," Morgan asserts. "I really don't. If you're gonna show up with presents for all three of us, then that's enough for me."

Shepherd takes a step closer, grabs Morgan's hand, and rubs the back of it with his thumb. "I'll always be here if you need something, okay? If nothing else, you can count on *me*." His voice is a low promise, and I swear I see the hint of tears in Morgan's eyes.

His dark eyes drift over to me, and despite how serious the moment feels, I'm thankful for him. If I'm honest, we've all been adrift since our parents died. Lou has always had our back, but it's still unmooring to be without the people who raised you. Having Catherine here as our hostess and Shepherd taking care of us feels good. It almost feels like family.

I rub the watch around my wrist. I don't want to miss out on a single minute of this.

CHAPTER SIXTEEN

SHEPHERD

I confirm dinner details with Thea and Morgan, but eventually, I have to head to work with the Keeper. My day passes at the speed of molasses, but I'm thankful when he demands I dust the wards and then go to his castle for a review of the ward monitoring system there. It's a chore we do every few months, but we always do it after a new resident arrives. We've only ever had one security breach in Ever, and it came from within.

Never again. Not on my watch and not on the Keeper's. Our processes have changed in the last few decades. Despite the serious work, I find my mind wandering to Thea and our upcoming date.

If the Keeper finds me distracted, he doesn't comment on it. Then again, that's not his way anymore. Eventually, it's time for me to get ready. That part, at least, flies past, and before I know it, I'm letting myself into the Annabelle to pick up the triplets.

Catherine's smile is the first thing I see. She rounds the check-in desk and claps her hands together. "You look wonderful, Shepherd. The girls have been getting ready for . . . ooh, quite some time now. They're very excited."

The inn chuckles around us, pipes groaning somewhere in the distance.

I lean against the worn wooden desk and smile. "I don't think Thea expected me to ask all three of them out tonight. Am I screwing this up?"

Catherine shakes her head. "We want the Hectors to stay in Ever. You're an excellent ambassador, my friend. You'll know when it's time to be alone with your mate."

Your mate.

The words send a thrill through me as I stand upright, my horns flattening to my skull.

Catherine glances up at them and purses her lips but holds back a smile.

The inn shimmies a little bit. She's laughing at me.

But then time stops because there's a flash of white, and Thea's warm caramel scent fills the entryway. I look up to see her descend the stairs in a body-hugging white floral sundress. It cuts off at the knee, and then she's wearing white combat boots with black soles. It's effortlessly cool, and I can't resist pulling her into my arms the moment she's close enough.

I lean down and bring my mouth to her ear.

"You look incredible, Thea. I could eat you alive like this."

I keep my voice low enough that Catherine won't hear. Thea giggles and places one hand on my stomach, giving me a teasing grin.

"You said monsters don't eat people, remember?"

I open my mouth to tell her exactly what I want to eat, but her sisters bound down the stairs to stop a few steps above her.

Pulling Thea to my side, I smile at her family. Wren's dressed in head-to-toe black. She looks like a badass goth princess. Morgan wears skinny jeans and a tee that says "Bite Me."

"Trying to send the Keeper a message?" I snort, pointing at her shirt.

She shakes her head with a playful laugh. "Not necessarily,

but hey, if he takes it that way, that's fine." She crosses her fingers in the shape of an X as if to ward him away from her.

I grin. "The Keeper is a vampire, Morgan. So if anything, your shirt will seem like an invitation."

Morgan's face pales. Catherine claps a hand over her mouth. Wren and Thea both double over in laughter.

"I—that's not what I want," she stammers. Her face turns beet red.

"You might wanna change," Thea snarks and slaps her sister on the stomach. "Imagine if we see him and he looks at your shirt and he just comes up and bites you. Shit, it might be possible, Morgan! Who knows!"

A pink flush steals across Morgan's cheeks. I can't help but wonder if she's thinking about the Keeper biting her and not finding it as repulsive as she'd have us believe. If he's right, and she's his mate, there's a solid chance my read on her is accurate. Only time will tell. If anything is clear, though, it's that neither one of them seems ready for that.

Morgan darts upstairs as Thea turns to me, her hand resting on my arm. "Thanks for the heads up. Although I've got to admit, I would have liked to see that play out."

"Watch out for this girl, Shepherd," Wren warns. "Thea might look like the sweet and innocent one, but it is so far from the truth."

Thea beams up at me.

"Can't wait to find out," I muse, smiling back down at her.

I don't want sweet and innocent. I want her to be as dirty and depraved as all the things I want to do to her. I want her to welcome my corruption because I'm a gentleman, but I fuck like a monster.

～

Two hours later, we finish a lovely dinner at Herschel's. Herschel himself came out from the kitchen to say hello to the triplets. After I pay the bill, he gives me a wink. I get the sense he's trying to help me make a good impression, but I hope I don't need the help.

Dinner with the triplets was easy and fun. They fit in here, despite their initial surprise at learning what Ever is.

After we box our leftovers, we walk to Scoops for ice cream.

We're not there two minutes before Iggy flits through the front door and perches on my shoulder. "Uncle Shepherd, Dad said not to bother you while you're with your mate, but you always let me get chocolate sauce on my sundae and he doesn't. Can I just hang out with you for a minute?"

I risk a glance at Thea, but she doesn't look concerned that Iggy called her my mate.

Instead, she pats her shoulder and gives him a sly look. "What if we do chocolate sauce and caramel too, and we won't tell Alo a single word."

I give Iggy a faux surprised look, and he pushes off my shoulder, landing carefully on Thea's. She looks slightly uncomfortable when he wraps his long tail around her neck, laying the spade carefully against her chest.

"This is common for younglings," I offer, hoping she doesn't find it too unusual.

Still, it warms my heart to see her be so friendly with my nephew. I wonder what a half-human, half-gargoyle child might be like. Gargoyle genetics tend to dominate others. Every half-breed I've ever met still looked like a gargoyle. But maybe our babies would have her beautiful blue eyes.

I try to stop my mind from going there. This is our first actual date, and both her sisters are here. But seeing her with Iggy does things deep inside my chest.

She reaches for my hand, and by the time we order, I'm

ready to leave. Her palm is warm in mine, her skin warmer too. All gargoyles run cold. I want to feel that warm body naked under mine. I need to pleasure every inch of her.

I've done my duty and courted her family. We had a wonderful dinner. But I'm anxious to be alone with her.

We grab a spot at the picnic tables outside, people watching on Main as everyone enjoys their cones. The next half hour passes in a blur as Iggy regales us with tales of his adventures today at school. But all I can focus on is Thea's pink tongue every time she licks the rocky road she picked out. Her tongue looks so soft, and I try desperately not to let my horns flatten to my head. Iggy will notice and ask about it.

I shift on the bench seat, trying to adjust my aching cock.

Thea looks up at me, licking the ice cream, and then I realize she's teasing me. She gives me a sultry look.

Little minx. She teased me last night too, and I nearly exploded all over her.

There's a polite cough, and we both look over at Morgan. She pats her shoulder and gives Iggy a huge, friendly smile. "Hey, kiddo, your uncle and Thea have plans, and we're heading back to the Annabelle. Let's get you back to your dad, okay?"

Morgan's an angel for reading the room the way she is. I mouth a quick thank you. Her grin broadens.

Iggy hops across the picnic table, his tail lashing side to side. "Okay," he hedges. "You won't tell him about the chocolate and caramel though, right? It's our secret?"

"Scout's honor," Morgan laughs and holds her hand up.

I don't know that saying, and Iggy doesn't either, but he seems to take it as a promise. He slaps her upheld hand in a high five and leaps onto her shoulder, wrapping his tail around her neck.

I almost laugh when she gives me the same disconcerted look Thea did earlier. But this is gargoyle life. It'll be years before Iggy grows out of this habit.

I point at his tail. "The tail thing teaches about connection and balance. When he comes of age, he'll use his tail to cement himself to a spot to stone sleep, a deep, restorative sleep we do once a month."

Morgan glances over at Iggy, and he leans in to rub his horns playfully against the side of her head.

Wren reaches out and pats the back of my hand. "Shepherd, thank you so much for a lovely evening. We had a wonderful time." Her voice is warm and kind, and without really meaning to, I grab her fingers and squeeze them lightly.

The protective side of my nature has me bristling with pride. I'm courting Thea, and her family is pleased. I don't want to hope it's enough to convince them to stay in Ever, but we're off to a good start, at least.

Wren, Morgan, and Iggy leave, and Thea turns to me on the picnic table's bench, swinging one leg over the long seat so our knees touch.

"Now what?" she asks, her voice breathless.

I reach out and tuck her pale hair behind one delicate, round ear, marveling at how different it is compared to mine.

"I want to take you for a walk in the garden, and then I'll take you to my nest." My voice is practically a growl, but I've been on edge since our tease in the early hours of the morning.

Thea's nipples are prominent against the thin fabric of her dress. Goosebumps cover her arms, and I don't think it's just the chill now that the sun has gone down.

Still, I pull her sweater off the back of her chair and hold it for her to slip her arms in.

"There are other ways to get warm, you know," she teases, looking up at me with a devilish grin.

Fuck me, she's a tease. And I want that. I want to protect her, to care for her—and then take her home and go wild in my nest.

Our nest.

Godsdamn, I'm falling for her so fast. This could be a problem, a huge problem, if the triplets decide not to stay in Ever. It nearly killed Alo when his mate left. I don't want that, but it could be a moot point. Despite having spent a short amount of time with Thea, I'm lost in her.

"You look all wistful and dreamy. What are you thinking about?" Her question breaks through my thoughts as I stand, offering her my hand.

I lift her off the bench and steer her toward the garden, thinking about how best to answer that question. Ultimately, I decide the truth makes sense. She's absorbed every new piece of information about our town with shocking resilience.

"It's killing me not to have you underneath me in my nest already," I growl.

Thea slides her arm through my elbow and grabs my bicep. I flex it a little, wanting her to feel my strength, my power. I want her to know I can protect her and her family. I want to shoulder their burdens and be a part of all their highs and lows.

"Are you trying to mate me, Shepherd? Aside from what I assume is a physical act, what all does such a thing entail?" Her question takes me by surprise because that's exactly what I'm trying to do.

I've danced around the topic and told her we'd take it slow, but damn. We get along really fucking well.

I look up into the sky, trying to summon the right response. The reality is that all gargoyles have an alpha male personality, but I've tried to tone it down a little with her because she's new to the monster world. She hasn't grown up watching people find their mates and claim them the same day.

"Mating you is my intention," is the best answer I can summon. But I stop us on the sidewalk and turn to her, tilting her chin up so she can see the truth on my face. "I want you, Thea. I won't deny that." I lean down and bring my lips to her delicate ear, relishing the way she shudders and presses closer to me. "I want my mark on your neck, angel. And I'd do it right this moment if you asked for it. But I'm aware you didn't grow up with that version of normal, so we'll take it as slowly as you need to." My voice is a rasp as I nip gently at the shell of her ear.

Her hand slides inside my shirt and comes to rest over my heart. It doesn't beat now; I've never heard the sweet sound of its steady thump. But I will when I claim her. If I get a chance to do that.

Her voice is steady and confident. "Be patient with me?"

I pull back and smile, even though her words crush me. They're understandable, but there's a small part of me that hoped our obvious connection would be enough to get her to throw caution to the wind.

"Always," I murmur, turning us to walk again.

Thea squeezes my arm. "So tell me why you want to walk through the garden."

I smile as we round the corner from Main Street and the community garden comes into view. It's lit up in brilliant swaths of neon color, pixies zipping all over as they work. It's hard to see any specific individual when they're small sized like they are now, but the light trails that follow their movements trace patterns in the dark sky.

"God, that's so beautiful." Thea's voice is wondrous as we head for the entrance.

I point toward the closest light trail. "Right now they're in their small form, but they have a full-sized form too, like when you met Miriam at her sweet shop. They switch easily between the two, but all pixies live here in the garden."

"So Miriam lives here?" Thea looks around as if she might recognize someone, but then gives me a frustrated look.

We reach the garden's outer barrier of shrubs. They're so large they form a wall almost as tall as Thea. Stepping through, I point to our right, where a long row of gourds hang from an A-frame trellis.

"There are rows of homes throughout the garden, but Miriam lives in this row. Third gourd on the left."

Thea looks up. "Can I take a closer peek or would that be considered rude?"

Nodding, I tug her inside the A-frame and thrum gently on the third gourd. There's a small hole in the front, and a light appears there. Miriam's small form smiles at us, and Thea gasps.

"Miriam, hi! I'm so sorry if we bothered you, Shepherd was just showing me the garden, and your . . . gourd is lovely."

Miriam zooms out and then poofs into her full form with a big smile. Her brilliant green hair waves slowly behind her ears, almost like she's underwater. Matching veined wings flap softly against her back before she folds them. She pulls Thea to her for a quick hug.

"Come visit me whenever! If I'm not at the shop, I'm probably here. Some time, if you want, I can dust you, and you can come inside for tea. Would you like that?"

It's a perfectly pleasant offer, but I don't know that Thea knows—

"Dust me? Pixie dust, you mean?"

Miriam laughs joyously. "Yes, girl! I'll dust you and shrink you and make you tea. It's so cute inside our gourds. Plus, it's kind of fun to experience the world in another way. I'll show you anytime. I can even fly you around in small form, although, I suppose . . ." She gestures up at me.

Thea looks confused. "I thought the pixie dust was for the wards. I'm still not clear on that, to be honest."

A light flashes off to our left, and Miriam sighs. "Shepherd, I know you can explain that, and Ezazel is calling. It's my night to stir the dust, and I wish I had the excuse of the shop, but Caroway is working tonight's shift. Ugh, give me any other job than stirring dust!" She moans again, then snaps her fingers to switch to her small form.

She darts off into the darkness, a trail of green light following her.

"Holy shit," Thea breathes. "I'm in absolute awe. Am I ever going to feel like I know everything about this place?"

I tuck her hand back through my arm protectively. "Well, let's start with the pixies and the garden. Every date I take you on, we'll explore something. How does that sound?"

Thea looks up at me with a big smile. "I'm curious to learn more about gargoyle nests too, if we're making lists of things to explore."

Heat floods my system as my cock throbs in my jeans. "You don't know what you're doing to me," I whisper. "You're an excellent tease, angel."

"Well," she quips, tossing her hair over her shoulder, "it would be best to know what I'm in for, right? I mean, god forbid we lack sexual chemistry."

She drops that bomb, and I stop us again, turning her to face me. There's such a bratty, devious expression on her face as she bites her lip and tries not to laugh.

Victorious joy fills my chest. She might not feel the urgency I do, but she's playful and comfortable around me.

I fucking love it.

"Something tells me you'll be an absolute brat in the nest, Thea," I whisper. "Tell me I'm right . . ."

"I'm *such* a brat," she confirms. "Do you like to chase, Shepherd? Because that's something I enjoy, if we're sharing."

I hold back a groan because I don't want to be rude to the pixies and start fucking Thea right here.

"Chase, hold down, bite, spank, collar. I could go on." I keep my voice low so it's just between us. "I'll break you, Thea, and then put you back together. What do you think?"

"As long as you don't call me a good girl," she whispers. "I feel like that's so overplayed. It seems like every dude in the world got the memo that women love that. I'm over it, to be frank."

I don't know whether to laugh hysterically or toss her over my shoulder and head home. Maybe both.

Blue eyes blaze with intensity as she looks up at me, the smile gone from her face. Her cheeks are flushed and rosy, color spreading across her chest.

"I think we should make this tour short," she suggests. "Informative but quick. Can we do it?"

"Fuck yes," I agree. "Let's get to the good part, shall we?"

CHAPTER SEVENTEEN
THEA

I'm naturally a joker. Any kind of joke is good. A sexy joke, a dad joke, I love them all. But I'm not usually comfortable enough with new people to be myself right away. It takes me a minute or two to warm up, and I blame that on being a triplet. Wren and Morgan are my girl gang.

Sisters before . . . everybody else.

God knows what's come over me with Shepherd. Well, I suppose I do know.

I'm comfortable around him in a way I've never been around someone new. And that might mean something. Could I be somebody's mate? And is it even fair to him to pursue this if we don't intend to stay in Ever?

A pang aches deep in my chest when I think about leaving him behind and going back to my job. It hasn't been the same since Dad died, and I don't know if I'll ever be able to work in that office with his ghost.

My mood goes somber, and I pick at the watch around my wrist.

Shepherd's long fingers wrap through mine and bring me

back to the present. When I look up, his eyes dip to the watch and back to mine. "Where'd you go, Thea? Wanna talk about it?"

I squeeze his fingers but raise the watch so he can see it better. Its scratched, worn surface is a comfort to me.

"My dad gave me this watch when I made detective. It was given to him when he made detective a million years before. It's almost a comfort blanket to me at this point, like a little piece of him is still with me even though he and Mom are gone."

Shepherd pulls my hand to his chest and strokes the back of it. "You've mentioned him a few times. It sounds like you were very close."

"I am a total daddy's girl," I admit. "I loved my mother fiercely, but she and Wren were two peas in a pod. Neither of my parents would ever admit to having favorites, but Morgan got the shit end of the stick if I'm honest."

"That explains a lot, actually," Shepherd murmurs, looking toward the Annabelle, which is across the street from the garden. "Morgan seems to wear her emotions and confidence almost like a set of armor to protect herself. Maybe she finds it easier that way."

It hurts my heart a little that he can tell that from just a few days around us, but he's not wrong. My parents loved all of us, and I know Morgan felt loved, but she's always joked about not being anyone's favorite. Except I don't think it was much of a joke. At least, not a funny one.

"Maybe she'll find her place here," Shepherd says. "Maybe all along, she was just waiting to get here to fit in perfectly."

"With the Keeper?" I snort. "And her 'Bite Me' shirt?"

"Oh, I give him a couple of months before he's losing his mind," Shepherd says. "Nobody's meant to be alone, Keepers least of all. He's the only unmated Keeper I know of in any of the havens."

I laugh at that. "Morgan isn't the type to be a politician's wife. It's almost laughable."

Shepherd's grin grows bigger. He nods at the garden behind me.

"Let me give you the rundown on the garden. Ohken and the pixies work together to keep it growing. It acts as an engine for all of Ever, keeping our weather like this year-round. The sole purpose of the garden is to generate pixie dust."

I look up, confused. "Does pixie dust come from a plant, or what's it a byproduct of? You mentioned some ingredients come from the pine trees."

"Moonflowers are the primary ingredient." Shepherd smiles, pointing to the nearest wall-sized shrubbery. "Although the pixies use a few other ingredients as well. Moonflower vines grow all along the garden's outer edge, sometimes trailing into the edge of it. Pixies tend the garden because the natural ebb and flow of plants in a garden feed the moonflowers. They, in turn, grow moonflowers, and those, along with the other four or five ingredients, are harvested into pixie dust."

God, that sounds complicated. What happens if something screws up the weather or a raccoon eats the plants?

Shepherd seems to sense my confusion. "It's a full-time job to care for the garden, but it's the unique responsibility of pixies in every haven that protects itself with wards."

"Some don't?" I haven't thought too much about the other towns like Ever, but now my mind spins.

"Most do," Shepherd confirms, walking me down a sandy path with rows of vegetables on either side. "Some havens are built within castles or compounds or natural landscapes like the interior of a mountain."

My mind is blown. I swear I'm gonna have dreams about secret monsters in underground tunnels now.

Shepherd jerks his head over his shoulder. "The forest behind downtown is where the centaurs and wolves have their homes. They guard the northern and western borders, and I focus on the south and the east since they're closest to downtown."

"What does that mean?" My voice goes small because talking about how it's Shepherd's entire job to protect the town makes my heart clench.

It's not lost on me that he's a protector, just like my dad and me.

"The Hearth assigned me to Ever the day I came of age, but—"

He stops in place, and his long, pointed ears twitch. A low growl leaves his throat as he glances around, sniffing at the air. I watch with growing horror when sharp spikes emerge along the tops of both his horns. Matching, stony-looking spines burst through his shirt in a line along his shoulders and down his arms.

Dark eyes morph pitch black, his voice deep as gravel. "Go to the Annabelle now. Wait there. Don't come outside."

He opens his mouth, and an ungodly roar echoes out of it. The pixies dart around us, the garden abuzz with noise. I struggle to understand what's happening, but everybody is freaking the fuck out here in the garden. Something's wrong, but I don't get it.

"Now!" he commands me, giving me a gentle shove toward the garden's entrance.

A roar that matches his echoes from across the street. I blanch but sprint toward the garden's edge. I know Shepherd wouldn't tell me to hide if it wasn't important.

A crunching sound comes from behind me, and when I turn, Shepherd is crouched down in the middle of the garden. He seems bigger and brawnier. Long, sharp-looking spines emerge down his thighs and legs and the entire length of his tail. He braces and then pushes off the ground with a flap of his wings that knocks me back and into the bushes.

He disappears into the night sky as a winking light appears

in front of my face. Miriam. She shouts at me, but she's so small I can't hear her.

I grimace, but she darts out of the garden's entrance and across the street toward the Annabelle. I run after her, lifting my comm watch.

"Call Morgan or Wren!" I shout into it.

Morgan's name pops up immediately, her voice worried.

"We're with Catherine at the inn, where are you?"

Thank fuck. Oh, god. "I'm on my way," I shout as I sprint up the front steps.

I yank the door open and leap inside, slamming it behind me. The Annabelle feels stone-cold like a grave. I press my hand to the wall.

"Are you okay? What's going on?" I whisper.

Am I talking to the fucking house? Will she understand me? Is Shepherd okay?

The wood slightly shudders under my palms, but it feels like a reassurance, and then the house stills again.

The pound of footsteps echoes through the house, and my sisters appear at the top of the stairs with Catherine.

"Oh, thank god you're here," Morgan shrieks, leaping down the stairs. "We knew you were with Shepherd but still."

"Shepherd told me to come here and then took off." I glance up the stairs at Catherine. "What is this? It's the bad monsters, isn't it? Shepherd turned into . . . shit, I don't even know. It was like he went into fucking battle mode."

Catherine clutches one hand to her chest, her pale cheeks flushed. "I hate that you girls are here to see this. Thralls have only ever gotten into this town once in my entire life, and someone let them in that time. It could only be that, but Annabelle will protect us."

An eerie howl splits the air, just like that night at the gas station. Without thinking, I turn and sprint to the front door. My sisters both whisper-scream, but there's no other sound.

Something draws me to look out the glass-paned front door, that fucking curiosity Morgan is always chiding me for. But what I see stops me in my tracks.

A shadowy figure moves up the street. It's shaped like a panther with a long thin body, walking on all fours with a bushy black tail that sweeps the street behind it. It almost looks made out of lava, but when I see its face, that's where everything goes from bad to worse. Because its body is an animal's, but its face is uniquely human, its features contorted in a painful-looking grimace. Flame-filled eyes dart from side to side as it pauses and sniffs the air.

I hold my breath as Morgan and Wren join me. Wren claps a hand over her mouth, her eyes wide. Catherine joins us as we peer out from either side of the front door's clear panes. Even the inn seems to be holding her breath.

This must be a thrall—I can't imagine what else it might be. We've only been in Ever for a few days, but every last person has been kind and inviting. The beast in the middle of the street gives off a malevolent, violent aura.

It looks around again, sniffing the air, and then it swings its head to the right, toward the garden. With a quick leap, it darts through the open entrance and disappears from view.

"No!" Catherine shouts, bringing her wrist up. She speaks directly into the comm watch. "Message Shepherd, Alo, Ohken, the Keeper. Thrall in the garden." She turns from us and sprints back up the stairs without another word.

"What the fuck?" Morgan hisses. "Was that the thing they told us about? It's got to be!"

I can't concentrate because there's movement in the bushes that form a wall around the pixie garden. They heft and sway like something's pulling at them, and then a long strip of vine falls into view in the garden's arched opening.

It's a moonflower vine. I just know it is. And the thrall is ripping it down. From what Shepherd shared earlier, the vine is critical to the safety of this place. That's the moment I realize I'm falling for this little town. I like it here, and I don't want something bad to happen to it.

Wrenching the door open, I tear outside. My sisters shout, but the noise fades into the background. I vaguely hear footsteps behind me, but I sprint across the street, pausing only when I reach the garden's opening.

Hands wrap around me almost immediately, but I throw one hand up to silence my sisters. When I peek around the corner, I see the thrall. I was right—it's tearing at the moonflower vines with reckless abandon. Nearly one full hedge is down. When I look to the right, I can see the pixies in their homes, their glow illuminating the gourds from within. I'm confused why they aren't coming out in their full size to fight, but maybe that's not how this works.

I turn to my sisters. "We have to distract it until Shepherd or the others get here."

Their eyes widen.

"Are you fucking nuts?" Wren says. "Did you see that thing? How are you going to distract it, Thea?"

"I'm gonna get it to chase me. We just need it out of the garden, the garden powers the wards. So if it rips the flower vines down . . ."

"The wards come down, and more of those things could get in." Wren finishes my sentence and gives Morgan a resolute look.

Morgan crosses her arms and shakes her head, but I can see she's quickly coming around to the idea. She looks up, her dark eyes blazing with intensity. "This plan sucks."

"I've got a better one," a voice hisses from behind us.

We whirl to see Catherine stride across the street with three shotguns. She keeps one and holds the other two out for us. Wren and I take them.

Morgan shakes her head. "I'm the fastest. Let me do the running portion of this shit-ass plan."

"Head directly for the Annabelle," Catherine says. "She'll protect you."

This is a terrible plan, but the gargoyles aren't here, and all I can do is pray they'll respond quickly to Catherine's message.

Morgan gives us a quick smile and sprints into the middle of the garden, whistling with two fingers in her mouth. God alive, she's loud as fuck. The thrall spins around and narrows its blazing eyes. A shudder runs through me. Morgan picks a tomato off a nearby plant and throws it at the creature, pegging it square in the ear.

It lets out a godawful roar and shakes its head. She hits it again and again, and then the beast makes a quick leap for her.

Time seems to slow and speed concurrently. Morgan flees the garden with the thrall in pursuit. It sprints past us without even looking, focused as it is on her. I pull the shotgun to my shoulder and focus on the thrall. Letting out a breath, I aim the barrel. I pull the trigger once, hitting the creature in the back left flank just as it follows Morgan up the Annabelle's front steps.

Morgan manages to slam the door shut in its face, and it whips around as Wren and Catherine get shots off.

We pause just long enough to reload, and in that time, the thrall throws itself through the glass front door and into the foyer, knocking the Annabelle's door off its hinges.

"Morgan!" Wren and I scream at the same time.

I fly across the street as fast as my legs will take me, but the Annabelle goes into attack mode before I reach the porch. Her wooden floors ripple, carrying Morgan deeper into the house and the thrall back out the destroyed front door. The porch ripples too, tossing the monster into the street in front of us.

It clambers back to its feet and lets out an earsplitting shriek.

I drop to a knee and get off another shot, hitting the thrall right in the neck. It snarls and roars, whipping around to face us with its tail lashing angrily side to side. Its human face is frozen in an angry sneer, and long fangs peek out from thin, bloodied lips.

Suddenly, another bellow rends the night, and a blast of wind knocks me backward onto the concrete. The shotgun clatters from my hands.

Two dark figures descend like freight trains out of the night sky, landing in the street between the thrall and us. Alo and Shepherd.

The thrall roars, but the street is silent as a grave.

And then the gargoyles move as one.

CHAPTER EIGHTEEN
SHEPHERD

We've already killed one thrall. A second is right in front of me and far too fucking close to Thea and the others. My desire to spill blood rides me as the thrall's tail whips back and forth. Thea stands frozen behind me, and just the fact that it's close enough to endanger her is enough to drive my blood lust sky-high.

Alo and I move in concert. He darts left, and I go right. The thrall jumps straight up and twists, but Alo slides underneath it as I pounce from above, stabbing at it with my wing tips.

We split it through the stomach, and its severed halves drop to the street with a squishy thud.

My chest heaves with the exertion of killing two thralls tonight—both headed for different parts of town, which is odd. Usually, they beeline for the closest unsuspecting monsters. Coming to the garden is new behavior.

Alo shoots me a sharp look.

There's a sharp intake of breath. I look up to see Thea's eyes widen. Her lips part, and she says something, but I'm so focused on the bloodshed that I don't even hear her. And then she starts running to me.

Without thinking, I smooth out my battle spines and open my arms. She throws herself into them, pressing her face to mine, both hands coming to my cheeks.

"Are you okay? Are you hurt?" Her voice is worried as I press my lips carefully to hers.

I tremble with the need to cement us together. I'm furious that the thralls were able to get through our wards. Now of all fucking times. It's been forty years since we had a thrall in Ever, and that was an inside job.

My comm watch chimes. When I glance down, I see it's the Keeper. His voice follows. "Ohken's got the other body, we're headed to Doc Slade's. Meet us there." He signs off without another word.

Thea strokes a steady path down my cheeks and my neck and along my shoulder where moments ago I bristled with spines. My body relaxes with her safe in my arms.

Iggy zooms out of hiding and across the street, wrapping around Alo's head and neck as they reunite. Morgan comes out of the inn to join Wren next to Catherine. They look fucking horrified.

Alo joins me and gives me a resigned look. "Let's get this thrall to Doc Slade. We need to understand how the fuck they got through the wards. It shouldn't even be possible."

Thea slides out of my arms, her expression neutral. This is the worst fucking timing. We were connecting so beautifully, and despite my role here in Ever, all I can think about right now is how she'll probably leave after this bullshit. How I'll never get a chance to woo her long enough to keep her.

I grip her chin and tilt her gaze to meet mine. "Come with me to Doc Slade's?"

Blue eyes bore into mine, and she nods her agreement. Behind her, her sisters seem to be in shock.

Alo jogs around the back of his cottage to grab a wheelbarrow. We dump the two halves of the thrall into it. Catherine speaks softly with Morgan and Wren. I hope to gods she's saying something that'll convince the girls this isn't an everyday occurrence. I'm heartsick that this happened when Thea's only just arrived.

This is the reality of our world, though, and it wouldn't be fair to pretend otherwise.

Our group is silent as Catherine and the triplets trail us to Main Street. I try not to focus too hard on Thea, but she walks with her sisters, their arms linked together.

We hook a left at Main and head to the far end, where Doc Slade has his office in a refurbished bungalow. I notice the cottage has sprouted front window boxes since I last had a visit. He must have taken up gardening. The dark elf himself opens the front door and gives me a look, his black horns shining in the low light from his front door.

"Take it through the back, Shepherd. I've already got the other one there." His gaze goes over my shoulder, his mouth curving into a friendly smile. "Ah, the Hector triplets. It's awful to meet you like this, but come on through, please." He opens the door wide, and Thea goes through first, giving me a gentle squeeze on the arm as she passes.

Gods, I'll be fucking destroyed if she doesn't stay.

I grit my teeth and wheel the thrall around the back of the cottage and through double doors on Slade's back porch. Ohken and the Keeper are there already, standing in a miniature autopsy theater. The other thrall lies in pieces on one of two autopsy tables. Black blood drips onto the floor as I wheel the second in and dump its remains on the second table. In front of the autopsy tables, two rows of seats form a half circle around Doc Slade's workspace.

Thea and her sisters come through the theater door from inside the cottage. Slade follows them. He glances at Thea, then shoots me a sorrowful look. I can almost see what he's thinking, how fucking unfortunate it is for this to happen now, of all times. He gestures for Catherine and the girls to seat themselves in the first observation row.

I resist the urge to grab Thea in my arms and disappear to our nest. I need to comfort her, and I need the comfort of her touch. I'll never regret killing to protect my family, but most gargoyles are highly lustful after an expulsion of that sort of energy. Connecting with those we put our lives on the line for is important. I ache to touch her, but her gaze is locked firmly on the blood dripping from each thrall into a drain below their respective tables.

Slade looks around the small, quiet room. "I'll forgo a long introduction. I'm Doc Slade, Ever's primary physician, and I'll be conducting an autopsy on the thralls."

"How do you know more aren't coming through the wards as we speak?" Morgan asks the question.

The Keeper turns to her with a neutral look, his lips pulling into a sneer. A long, bloody wound runs down the side of his head from our fight with the first thrall. Blood is dripping onto his lower lip. He looks feral.

"Aside from my monitoring system, which detected them when they came through, gargoyles can sense thralls. Alo, Shepherd, and Iggy would know if more were within our borders. The castle is scanning the wards again now, so it'll pick up how they got in in the first place."

Shit, that was a lot to unload on her. They haven't been to the Keeper's place. They don't know how tied into Ever's defenses his castle is.

Thea looks at her sisters and then back at Doc Slade. "We'll hold our questions for now because this autopsy seems important. But please know we'll have a million questions when you're done." There's a grim look on her face. Her whole body looks tense.

"Fair," Slade agrees, and then he rounds the autopsy table with a scalpel. He's tall and lanky enough that he can stand in one spot and examine the thrall from head to toe. The room is silent while he looks at the first one. "This one was a wolf shifter, based on the head shape," he murmurs, showing the girls the thrall's head.

"It's the only element of their former self that thralls retain." He points to the second one. "You can see that one was something humanoid, not that it matters. Once a monster is enthralled, there's nothing left of who they were, and as far as we know, there's no reversal."

There's a sharp intake of breath from one of the triplets. Ohken rounds the Doc and stands in the doorway to the main part of the house. It's a protective move, and I notice him look up at Wren when he does it. Even standing in the doorway, he's tall enough that his head is the same height as hers. She glances over and gives him a soft smile, but she looks terrified.

Slade bends over the thrall and lifts one long hind leg. He sighs and gestures for the Keeper, who crosses to join him. They peer closely at a section of mottled, burnt skin on the animal's thigh.

The Keeper looks up at Catherine. "I don't recognize this sigil, it's not Wesley's."

Catherine's hand flies to her mouth, her eyes closing in what looks like relief.

"Who's Wesley?" Morgan asks.

The Keeper answers curtly. "Wesley was a previous Everton. He was a powerful warlock, but he did not share our beliefs. He tried to take over this haven about forty years ago. We fought him and won, but he escaped. We haven't heard from him since."

Catherine shakes her head, then stands and excuses herself, brushing past Ohken to head for the front of the cottage.

We watch her go, but when I turn, Thea's eyes are on me, burning a hole in my chest.

Fuck. Claim. Protect. Cherish.

Those are the thoughts that run through my head as I gaze

back at her, willing her to understand that this isn't our normal life.

I swear to you, I promise wordlessly. *I swear I will always come for you when you need me.*

The Keeper's comm pings and his address pops up. The castle is calling. He lifts his wrist, and an automated voice echoes throughout the theater.

"There is a three-meter-by-three-meter hole in the southeast corner of the ward. No other foreign entries. The wards are knitting together as we speak."

"Three meters?" Alo hisses. "Something's not right."

The Keeper looks up at the triplets in their stadium seats. "No," he murmurs. "It's not."

Morgan stands, bristling at the insinuation in his tone. "You can't think we had anything to do with this. You called us here in the first damn place!"

The Keeper looks over at me and then back up at Morgan. "It's my current hypothesis that your arrival affected the wards somehow, Miss Hector. I intended to allow you to find out about your monster heritage at your own pace, but we can't risk it. We need to figure out what you are. Otherwise, I can't protect the town."

Morgan slumps in the seat and exchanges a skeptical glance with her sisters.

"It won't take long," I assure them. "And it'll be better for you to know anyway."

"What if we want to just go back home," Morgan snaps, her green eyes narrowed on the Keeper.

"You can't leave," he states. "Not until we figure this out. What if you leave and you're somehow the key to fixing what's wrong with the wards? I can't allow it."

"And here we are," Morgan says. "Prisoners, despite what you said that first day."

The Keeper sighs. "If I determine you're not a threat, you can go as far away from this place as you like. Until then, don't venture out of downtown. Am I clear?"

"Crystal," Morgan snaps.

Thea glances over at me, and ire that matches Morgan's, burns in those crystal blue eyes.

Fuck.

~

Half an hour later, we've taken two cars to the Keeper's castle in the northwest corner of Ever. His home is buried deep in the woods, down a long, twisty dirt road. He loves being remote like this, and the castle itself suits him. I tried making a few Dracula jokes when it first appeared, but the Keeper had already lost his sense of humor by then.

The triplets are quiet as we pull up a black cobblestone drive and park out front. I hop out and open the door for Thea. She brushes my hand with hers as she steps out and looks up at the Gothic structure. She seems less rigid and furious than she did when we left Doc Slade's.

"Alo wouldn't look out of place perched on one of these escarpments," she murmurs, leaning in as if telling me a secret.

I bump her hip with mine and thread my fingers through hers, relieved she can find some humor on an otherwise awful day. Wren comes to my other side and loops her hand through my arm. It warms my heart because it means the girls see me as a safe and comfortable space, and I want to be that for them.

I look at Morgan and give her a teasing wink. "Want a piggy-back ride?"

She rolls her eyes but purses her lips to keep back the smile that threatens to take over her face. Of the sisters, she's the tough nut. It makes a lot of sense after Thea shared about their parents and Morgan not being anyone's favorite.

The Keeper strides around us and right up the gangplank to the front door. The castle opens for him, creaking softly when we step onto the gangplank together.

Morgan looks up at the armored doors. "God, this place is beautiful, isn't it?"

The castle shudders slightly, but the doors press open a little wider. It's not lost on me that if the Keeper is right, and she's his mate, then this is her home. I wonder if she's thinking about that right now.

Unfortunately, there's no time to ponder it because the Keeper drags us quickly through the house without explaining anything about it. The girls brim with questions, that's easy to see, but they follow quietly until the Keeper opens a wooden door and steps into a small, dark room. One entire wall is filled with screens and cameras and all the tech that powers the monitoring system. It looks like a damn command center.

He stalks across the room and opens a hole in the wall, pulling out a flat disk about the size of a dinner plate. He tosses it into the center of the room without explanation.

"Call Moira."

I sigh. "These disks are how we call monsters in other havens," I offer as the triplets stare at the disk in shock. "Every home has one."

Thea opens her mouth to say something, but a figure pops up from the disk and surprises her.

I try to see Moira as Thea might. Moira's a harpy, and well, she's far less humanoid than the Keeper or me. She ruffles her feathers, cocking her head to the side in a birdlike move. Thea pushes against me until I wrap one arm around her waist.

Moira croons, her eyes crinkling at the corners as the longer feathers on top of her head perk up in interest. It's the harpy version of a smile. "Keeper. How good it is to see you."

He clears his throat, gesturing to the rest of us, and Moira turns. She inclines her head as she examines each of us in turn, giving me a simple nod.

"Who are you?" Wren's question is soft and polite, more curious than anything.

Moira smiles and spreads her wings wide before they settle against her back, her head twitching from side to side in the way most bird folk do.

"Oh, that's easy, I'm the Keeper's betrothed."

CHAPTER NINETEEN
THEA

You could hear a pin drop after what this . . . person, bird, whatever-she-is just said. Morgan and Wren are stiff as boards next to me. I don't know if Morgan is relieved, pissed, or shocked into a stupor. But she crosses her arms and glares daggers at the Keeper. We can see through the bird-person to him. She must be a hologram of some sort. On the other side of her, the Keeper looks at Morgan with a neutral, almost bored expression.

I'm starting to get mad. Real mad. He's been less than pleasant since the moment we met. He declared Morgan was his mate, and now he's betrothed? Oh, hell no. Not just hell no, *fuck* no.

"Listen here," I start, pointing my finger right at the Keeper.

"Oh!" The bird lady jumps in surprise, then soothes her feathers with two dark chocolate-colored wings.

She has wings instead of arms. She has fucking feathers instead of fingers! Holy shit.

"I think I see what's happening," she continues as she gives me a disconcerted look.

"Yeah?" My voice is a little ruder than I'd like, but the Keeper is now looking at this woman like . . . well, with an almost affectionate expression.

Fucker.

The woman ruffles her feathers, not unlike a parrot. She lays them flat down and coos softly like a pigeon. "I'm Moira, as I imagine you heard when the Keeper called me. I work for the Hearth, although based on Ab—"

"Moira." The Keeper's voice is stern. When she turns to look, he shakes his head as a warning.

"Okay then," she says with a little eye roll. Suddenly, I'm liking her a little better. "Based on how the Keeper called me, I'm guessing this is off the record?" She glances over at him with a raise of chocolate-brown, delicately feathered brows.

He nods, this time in agreement. "They arrived a few days ago, but somehow the wards are suddenly full of holes. I need to know what their ancestry is."

"Full of holes?" Wren and I shout it at the same time.

"Not hardly," I continue. "Just one hole, and you're not gonna pin that shit on us, or so help me god, we'll leave, no matter what you said."

I don't look at Shepherd because I don't want to see the look on his face at the mention of me going. I know it would hurt him. Shit, it would hurt me to go, but I won't stand for any more of the Keeper's bullshit.

"Let's take this a step back," Moira warbles. "You're unaware of any monster ancestry, but the Keeper thinks it could be important. Let's sort it out, shall we?"

"Off the record," the Keeper presses. "Once I know more, and if they decide to stay, we'll register them with the Hearth."

"The Hearth will not like it if you delay, Keeper," Moira counters. "It would be better to register your new residents quickly."

"Off the record, Moira," he commands. "I'm serious." His dark eyes are focused on the bird-woman, and like this, I'd almost find him handsome if he weren't so fucking off-putting personality-wise.

"As you wish," Moira says. She turns to my sisters and me with a gentle expression. "I'm a peacekeeper for the Hearth, which is a fancy term for the person who figures out what monsters are when they don't know. Well, that's part of my role, anyhow. If you'll reach out and touch my feathers through the hologram, I'll be able to learn what sort of monster blood you have."

Wren and Morgan both shift next to me. Wren looks over at me, and then Morgan kicks my foot.

"Go on, Thea," Morgan chirps. "By all means, let's see what we are so we can be of service to his royal keepness."

Next to me, Shepherd clears his throat, but I'd swear he's just holding back a laugh. I don't dare look up at him though, because, through Moira, I can see the Keeper glowering at Morgan.

My hands go clammy. Oh, god. I've tried not to think about what sort of monster I'll be, but it seems we have to find out whether we want to or not. I turn to Shepherd, a sudden worry rocketing to the forefront of my mind.

"You're still gonna like me, right? Even if I turn out to be some kind of weird iguana lady. Or an abominable snow-woman. Or—"

"None of that would faze me," he agrees with a seductive smile. "Sounds like fun."

I blow out a breath and look back at Moira, who seems amused. She lifts her wing and shimmies it at me, encouraging me to touch it. When I reach out and place my hand on the tip of her feathers, a zing travels up my arm. It feels like one of those pens with a battery inside that shocks you. And then it's done. She rolls her eyes skyward in thought, scrunching her beak up before smiling at me.

"White witch. A protective designation, meaning you'd typically work with your haven's gargoyles and Keepers. The Keeper can find you a tutor unless you'd like one assigned by—"

"No, thank you," the Keeper states. "I'll handle it internally. Catherine will be glad to help, I'm sure."

Moira purses her lips but looks over at Wren and Morgan. Wren steps up next, and a flush crawls across her cheeks. She doesn't look so discombobulated now that she knows I'm a witch.

A witch! I want to talk to Shepherd about it, but it's Wren's turn. He must sense my urgency though, because the arm around my middle tightens, his fingers playing at the hem of my shirt.

Wren touches Moira just like I did and is declared a green witch, something to do with supporting the garden. Morgan steps up, and the Keeper shifts a little closer, his gaze utterly focused on her hand when it touches his girlfriend's. Morgan grits her jaw when the zing hits her, but Moira gives her a big, genuine smile.

"Black witch. That's lovely, nobody has received a black witch in ages."

Morgan smiles a little, despite her earlier ire, but takes her hand back. "What does that mean?"

Moira preens, her feathers popping upright and then settling flat again. "Well, black witches are healers, but they're incredibly rare." She turns to the Keeper. "Are you certain you don't want to involve the Hearth? We've got some incredible teachers these days."

The Keeper shakes his head, but Morgan puts both hands on her hips.

"What if I want that? What if I'd like to have a teacher to learn about *my* power? Why do you seem to think you speak for all of us?"

Moira casts an inquisitive look between them. Maybe it's uncommon for someone to disagree with their town's Keeper like this. For whatever reason, he doesn't seem to want the Hearth involved, and Shepherd trusts him.

I tap my sister on the elbow. "Let's talk about it later, Mor. This day has been wild. We could all do with processing time."

If Moira's offended that we don't seem to want her employer's help, she says nothing. After a long, awkward silence, she gives the Keeper a soft smile. "Ring me later if you want to chat this through, alright?"

He nods, but his eyes are squarely on Morgan in a clear visual standoff.

Morgan opens her mouth to speak, then zips it back shut.

When she says nothing, the Keeper gives Shepherd a terse look. "Alo is patrolling the wards with me tonight. Get some rest. You're on in the morning."

It's a clear dismissal as he turns to the wall of monitors and begins fiddling around. I give my sisters a look.

It's time to get outta here.

CHAPTER TWENTY
SHEPHERD

The girls are silent as we leave the Keeper's command center and pace back through the dark halls. Normally I'd offer them a tour of his impressive keep, but I sense there wouldn't be much interest in that right now.

Witches. It's not wholly surprising because they look so completely human. Still, it could have gone in a few different directions.

By the time we get to the car, I can see Morgan practically boiling over. She opens her door, gets in, and slams it shut. I hunch into the driver's seat of the car and glance over at her.

Wren and Thea are quiet in the back seat.

"Let's talk about it," I encourage. "I can probably—"

"Betrothed?" Morgan hisses, crossing her arms as she glares out the windshield, her upper lip curled into a sneer. "Fucking betrothed. He's more and more of a catch by the minute."

I wait to see if she's done. Thea pops her head up between the seats.

"Did you know?" Her voice is soft.

I want no miscommunication here, though.

"I didn't know," I say. "The Keeper is secretive about his

private life. Although, I can't say I'm surprised, given how hard the Hearth is on him."

"What does that even mean," Morgan questions as she turns in her seat to face me. "You guys talk about the Hearth like it's some evil organization, but I don't understand. Why doesn't he want the Hearth's help to teach us?"

I sigh because there's so much to unpack there.

"The Hearth is our governmental organization, but I can't say that most havens have a positive relationship with them. Their rules are strict until a rule doesn't benefit them, and then the rules change. Still, without the Hearth's intervention all those centuries ago, the haven system wouldn't exist."

"The Cerinvalla Accord of 482, right?" Wren questions from the back seat.

When I agree, she smiles. "I read the welcome packet. There's quite a bit of info in there about the Hearth and how it got started." Her smile falls. "But they don't say a lot about why Ever seems at odds with the Hearth."

I don't know how much to share with them, but I decide they deserve a little more of the Keeper's story, especially since he seems disinclined to share.

"All haven residents go through an official process to be assigned designations for haven leadership if they possess the right qualities. Alo and I got assigned to Ever after requesting it. Protectors aren't that uncommon, so many protector-type species end up in that role, and most havens have a team of protectors. Keepers are exceedingly rare, and they seldom end up in the havens they came from.

"The Keeper never underwent the designation process because he lived outside of havens for a long time. Eventually, duty called him back, and he agreed to go through with it. I think he was more surprised than anyone when the test showed him to be a Keeper."

"He lived outside a haven? In the human world?" Morgan seems surprised to hear this.

"Yeah," I chuckle. "He wanted to know what it was like, and he didn't want the pressure his family put on him to live up to their expectations. Still, he eventually returned, and then when he was determined to be capable of becoming a Keeper, he had no choice."

"Please don't tell me this shit to make me try to like him," Morgan grouses. "Every time I turn around, I learn some fresh new bullshit about him."

I put the car in drive and head back toward town. It's late at this point, and I know the girls must be exhausted.

When I park in front of the inn, they file up the front steps in a line like ducklings. Thea dallies at the back, waiting for me.

She slides her hands into her back pockets, a sorrowful look on her face.

I resist the urge to pull her into my arms. If I know anything, it's that she's mine. Being close to me would comfort her. But her body language isn't giving me an invitation.

"Today was a shitshow," I offer. "I'm sorry you and your sisters had to see that. It's never happened as long as I've lived here."

One of her pale brows lifts upward. "You mean except for the time the guy who lived here let the thralls in?"

"Right," I admit. "That was . . . different. And forty years ago. Ever has always been a safe place, and I'm so frustrated this happened when you've only just arrived."

Thea shrugs, pulling her hands out of her pockets to cross her arms over her chest. My mouth goes dry at the way it pushes her breasts up higher. I ache to sink my teeth into her, to please her. But this isn't the time, no matter what typical gargoyle-courting behavior dictates.

"Do you think the Keeper's right, and it's our fault what happened to the wards?"

I fucking hate that question. Because the logical one that follows it is, if we leave, would everybody be safe?

I shake my head. "I can't say for sure, but he'll figure it out. He always does. And in the meantime, we can learn more about your power, if you like."

She looks behind me at the garden. Even now I hear the buzz of the pixies working fast to get it back into shape. Thea gestures to the Annabelle's door, already restored by Ohken and the pixies. "Walk me in? Wren and Morgan might have more questions for you."

I nod and follow her in, wrapping my tail around my leg to avoid wrapping it around her and pulling her into my arms. When we get inside, Wren and Morgan are talking with Catherine. The mood is somber.

Catherine's eyes are rimmed with red, but she rubs Morgan on the shoulder. "It's been a shocking day. Why don't you girls get some sleep, and we'll wake up early to talk about what it means to be a witch? If you want to learn, I'd love to teach you. But I won't be at my best this evening."

"We understand," Morgan says in a gentle tone. "Do you want to talk about the Wesley thing? It seemed to upset you."

I unwind my tail, lashing it from side to side as anger rises in my chest. Wesley did his level best to rip Ever apart forty years ago. Not finding his sigil on the thralls tonight doesn't mean he's not somehow involved, though. It just means he didn't direct the two who attacked us. Someone did, though. Someone directed one of the two to head for our damn garden. That's no accident.

Catherine shakes her head. "You three deserve answers, so I'll tell you what I can in the morning. I just . . . I could use some rest myself."

Morgan looks over at me. "Tonight was scary as fuck, but thank you for protecting us. I'll thank Alo tomorrow, but it's clear to me now why your role is so important."

"The world isn't completely safe anywhere," I remind her. I'm really speaking to Thea though, hoping she'll take my words to heart. "The human world is dangerous in many ways too."

Morgan nods slowly, but it's clear she doesn't fully agree with my words. She gives Catherine a quick hug, grabs Wren's hand, and pulls her sister to the stairs. Thea turns to me when Catherine disappears down the hall toward the kitchen.

"You were amazing today," she murmurs, both hands going back into her pockets.

It won't do. It won't do at all.

Whipping my tail out, I wrap it around her waist and drag her close. I stroke my fingers through her pale hair before gripping the back of her neck.

"I will always protect you and yours. You know that, right?"

Thea bites her plump lower lip and nods.

"You want to be with your sisters tonight?" My voice is gruff. I want her to be with me, but I sense the triplets might get more comfort from one another at the moment. There's probably a lot they want to discuss.

Thea sighs, then looks around me up the stairs. "I think so. I'm all out of sorts, and—"

"I can make it better," I growl, running one hand up the back of her shirt to flatten it between her shoulder blades. "I can help you forget, angel."

Pale lashes flutter as she gifts me a soft smile. "Rain check, but I'll take you up on that tomorrow if you're free?"

"Sure," I say.

A long, tense beat drags out between us before she turns and heads for the stairs. I follow her to her room, but all I can think is that I want to toss her into the bed and shower her with affection. I want her to feel good, to forget about the bullshit that happened tonight. Because the thralls? That's not Ever, that's not our normal. I'm worried she and her sisters won't be able to look past that.

~

Ten minutes later I'm back home, trudging upstairs to my nest with a hard-on pressed to my thigh. I've been in a state of permanent frustration since I met Thea. I don't blame her, she's human. Well human*ish*. She grew up with human customs. All I want to do right now is fuck her senseless, show her my power, and make her feel safe after a horrible day.

I press my palm against my cock as I fling open the door to my nest. The strength of my need for her grows by the moment. I can't have her right now, but I can take the edge off. Ripping my jeans open, I fall into my nest and close my wings around myself. I work my dripping length, soaking it with my seed as I remember what Thea smells like. My imagination works overtime as I roll onto my back and rock my hips, shoving my cock through my slick but rough fingers.

"Thea," I growl. I'm going to come fast, too fast like this.

My balls tense up tight against my body as my dick jerks in my hands, spurting more precum.

My comm watch pings. Is it—

Aloitius Rygold.

Bah.

I let go of my dick and hop out of the nest, zipping my pants back up. I don't immediately answer, but head for the kitchen where I wash my hands and grab a drink. I can't talk to my brother with a cock in my hand.

I give myself a moment for my dick to go down, and then I comm him back.

"Sorry I missed you. What's up?"

Alo's voice is tense and curt. Just like me, he feels responsible for what happened. I know the weight of keeping everyone safe rides him just as badly as it does me.

"I need to patrol with the Keeper. Can I send Iggy to you for the night? I wouldn't ask, but—"

"Of course," I growl. "Any time, Alo, you know that."

Normally, he fights me on this topic. He doesn't want to be a burden. But Iggy is never a burden to me.

"I'll fly him over now," my brother says before clicking off.

Sighing, I grab a bottle of water for Iggy and head back up to the nest where they'll meet me.

When I get there, I set the water down and fly up to the window, propping it open for my nephew and brother. A few minutes later, they arrive. Iggy snakes up under the window and rests on the ledge, looking up at me with big, worried eyes.

Alo hovers just outside, his face a neutral mask. I know he's seething like I am, though. I can sense it in the family bond we share.

I give my brother a quick smile. "I'll bring Iggy home tomorrow sometime. Get some rest after you patrol, brother."

Alo nods and ducks under the open window pane to give Iggy a quick hug. My heart squeezes as I watch them. When he leaves us, Iggy watches him go with a solemn look, his tail fluttering morosely behind him.

"Dad said I couldn't help tonight. And I tried to follow him, but he yelled at me to come to your house 'cause of what happened today."

There's a lot to unpack there. I swoop gently back down to my nest. Iggy follows and lies down on one of my pillows, looking at me expectantly.

Lying down next to him, I curl my left wing around us so we're cocooned in the darkness. "Your dad wants to keep you safe."

"But it's my *job* to keep everybody safe, just like you and Dad," Iggy mutters, his tiny voice full of frustration.

I pull at the end of his tail, wrapping it around my forearm to hold him close to me.

"You *will* protect everyone. But not until you're full-grown, remember? Your only job right now is to listen to your dad and practice your stone sleep."

"Sleeping sucks," Iggy grumbles. "It's so boring, and—" A yawn cuts his words off, his dark eyes fluttering closed.

The warmth from my wings is soothing to him, and within a few minutes, he's fast asleep, snoring with his chin tucked on the underside of his arm. His tail stays wrapped around my right arm protectively.

My comm watch chimes, and Thea's name pops up. Unfurling my left wing, I lay it against the edge of the nest and answer.

"Thea. Is everything okay?"

Her voice is soft through the watch. "Everything's alright. My sisters are asleep. I just . . . I felt bad we didn't get a chance to talk earlier. Wren and Morgan are taking all of this better than I thought they would, but we're all freaked out."

I want to tell her to come over, but I obviously can't kick Iggy out. He's fast asleep, his snores punctuating the otherwise silent room. And I wouldn't want her walking here alone at night. It's not far, but after what happened today . . .

"I'd invite you over, but Iggy's crushing my wing at the moment, snoring like a banshee."

There's a soft laugh on the other end. "Do banshees exist? Or is that just a saying?"

I join her in laughter. "No banshees. How are you feeling about earlier?"

Thea's quiet for a moment. "It didn't scare me like I thought it would, seeing the thralls. Before you got there, I ran into the street and Catherine and my sisters helped me distract it. It was tearing the moonflower vines off the wall. I just . . . I was terrified of what might happen if they were successful."

This is new godsdamned information. "You ran into the garden?" My voice is a hiss. I'm furious, terrified, and trying not to wake Iggy up. "You could have been killed, Thea. You could have—"

"I was fine!" she insists. "I wasn't even really afraid." She pauses. I try to collect my fucking thoughts. "Do you think it's because white witches are a defensive thing?"

I flop back down on the pillows. With everything that happened tonight, her witch designation has been the last thing on my mind. But maybe it shouldn't be.

"I don't know," I admit. "I'd like to join you when you and Catherine speak about it if you're alright with that. I know the Keeper will probably want to as well, but at least me."

"Yeah, of course," she says. "Anything if it'll help Ever."

And there it is. The type of statement I've been dying to hear from her since we met.

"You like it here?" I don't mean to ask the question aloud, but I want to know.

I just hope I'm not going to hate the answer.

CHAPTER TWENTY-ONE

THEA

I know exactly why Shepherd's asking this question. It's something I've thought about pretty much since the moment we met. *I* encouraged my sisters to stay once we found out the truth about this place. *I* ran out into the garden tonight, hopeful that I could help protect Ever.

"Yeah," I agree. "I like it here, and I want to spend some time with you alone, Shepherd. Can you clear your schedule for me tomorrow?"

There's a rustling noise, and then the soft sound of snoring reaches me. It must be Iggy. The idea of them snuggled up in bed makes me want to run to his house and join, but given what happened today, it doesn't seem like a great idea to run around in the dark.

"I'm always available to you," Shepherd murmurs, his voice deep but low. There are soft footsteps and then the closing of a door. "What are you doing right now, Thea?"

Oh lord. There's a seductive lilt to his voice that makes me wonder if we're about to do what I think we're about to do.

I hoist myself deeper into the pillows and prop my arm up so

I can listen to Shepherd without holding my wrist up to my face.

"I'm lying in bed," I admit. "Wishing I was in that nest with you. We've been teasing around the idea of doing dirty things in there, haven't we?"

"Fuck, angel," he growls. "I'd like nothing better than to bring you to this nest right now. But there are . . . complications."

I laugh. "He's never a complication, but that's why you need to pencil me in tomorrow. I don't know what'll happen in the future, but I want to learn more about you, Shepherd. Shit, I want to learn more about me, too."

There's a low, huffy groan and the sound of something hitting the floor.

"Was that your pants?" I tease.

"Yeah."

"So you're naked?"

"I am."

I bite my lip, slipping my hand between my thighs. I've had the hots for Shepherd since minute one. This has been a long time coming, figuratively.

"Tell me more," I whisper. "Tell me everything."

Shepherd's breathing goes heavy, and all other sound fades. I can just imagine his wings cocooning him up against a wall, one hand splayed on the wood so he can speak right into the comm watch.

"I'm hard for you, angel. I've tried to be such a fucking gentleman, but it doesn't come naturally to me. I suspect you know that though, don't you?"

"Yes," I admit. "You strike me as a particularly filthy man. Male. Fuck," I grumble. "I don't know the right terminology."

There's a deep laugh. "Nothing about me is like a human man, Thea. If you were here, I'd show you."

Fuck me, the seductive growl he lets out is nearly enough to make me combust.

"I'm dripping for you," he growls. "So ready to fill you and make you scream, Thea. Do me a favor, angel."

"Anything," I gasp, desperate to catch my breath as my cheeks and chest heat.

A sensation builds between my legs and throbs in time with my heartbeat.

"Slip one hand between your legs and tell me how wet you are for me, only for me."

I cry out softly at the command in his voice, but I do what he asks, sliding two fingers down into my panties. They're soaked, and my fingers come away soaked too.

"What did you find, Thea?"

"So wet," I groan, keeping my voice soft. "If you were here, you'd—"

"Slide right in," he breathes. "Put you up against the wall, pin you with one wing, and spank you with the other while I fuck you senseless. I'd be satisfied when you black out from the pleasure, my little witch."

"Oh fuck," I moan.

"My little witch" has a nice ring to it. I've barely wrapped my mind around that news, but there's a near future where I suspect it'll excite me to lean into it.

Shepherd groans softly. "Godsdamn, Thea, I'm ready to explode. I need to hear you come. Lick your fingers and roll them over your clit. Imagine it's my big, strong hands instead."

I don't need to be told twice. Sucking my fingers loudly in my mouth, I revel at the taste of myself on them.

"Tastes good," I tease.

"Thea," he warns, his voice laced with gravel.

He sounds ready to fly to pieces, and I want to hear it.

I reach down and rub my clit in gentle circles, my back

arching at the heat that swirls through my body, building and igniting deep in my core.

"I want you here," I cry out, past the point of caring if anyone hears me masturbating into my damn comm watch.

God, I hope this thing isn't connected to some town-wide system. I grit my teeth and groan as pleasure floods through me. A rhythmic slapping sound echoes through the watch. I imagine Shepherd's dark fingers moving fast along his cock.

"I want to be there, angel," he growls. "Tomorrow you're mine, Thea."

"Yours."

"Mine to fuck. Mine to spank. Mine to please."

"Yes," I cry, right on the edge of the abyss.

I move my fingers faster, flying over my swollen clit as I bite my lip to keep from screaming his name.

"Come for me, little witch," he growls.

And I detonate. Starbursts crash behind my eyelids as I open my mouth in a silent roar. Waves of bliss radiate from my center, my channel pulsing around emptiness as my orgasm batters me. Rolling onto my side, I moan Shepherd's name desperately into the watch.

A stream of expletives echoes through it, and then a choked roar sends a searing new wave of heat through me.

"Thea . . ." he groans, his voice broken and desperate.

The slapping sound slows, but I can just imagine it now. Did he paint the wall with cum? Is he trying to catch his breath and still hot from what we did?

"How hard did you come, Shepherd?" My voice is husky as I stare at the opposite wall, basking in the afterglow of the best orgasm I've ever had.

"As hard as I knew I would the first time I offered to come for you," he growls, bringing me back to the night we met.

Call me, and I'll come for you. That's what he said to me.

I grin into the comm watch. "Good night, Shepherd. I can't wait to see you tomorrow."

He sighs softly. "I'm counting the minutes, Thea. I miss you."

I toss and turn all night despite the incredible orgasm. I blame it on wishing I was wrapped up in Shepherd's muscular arms. When I wake in the morning, I manage a warm shower. Someone knocks on the bathroom door just as I get out and wrap a towel around myself.

Wren enters the bathroom without waiting for a response. Ah, the joys of sisters. She hands me the spray-in conditioner with a haughty look.

I scoff. "This is mine, bitch! I knew you took it. I've been looking for that shit for two weeks. The snarls have been indescribably horrific, Wrennie."

Her chuckle tells me she doesn't believe my ire. I'm not the triplet with the temper. Cough cough, Morgan.

"Being sisters results in a what's yours is mine is ours effect. I thought we agreed on that," she mutters.

I hear stompy footsteps before Morgan shoves her way into the bathroom as well. "Catherine suggested the Galloping Green Bean for breakfast to talk about the whole witch revelation."

Wren gives Morgan a curious look. "I still find it odd that none of us seem particularly fazed about the whole witch revelation. We're witches, bitches!" She does jazz hands out to both sides as I snort.

Morgan shrugs. "I'm half in disbelief over the last few days and half unsurprised because we've fashioned ourselves after the Sanderson sisters our whole lives. It fits, ya know? I'll probably turn out to be the hated one like Winifred though."

She's joking, but there's tenderness under her tone.

Holding my towel carefully, I throw myself into my slightly-older sister's arms. "Just because the Keeper isn't acting gaga over you doesn't mean you're our Winifred The Despised. He's a dummy."

She nods, but it's easy to see she's lost in thought.

"He's betrothed," she huffs. "How lucky for him to have a betrothed and a mate. I wonder if he's nicer to her than he is to me."

"Nice doesn't seem like his modus operandi," Wren says. "Although now that I'm not in shock, I wish he'd explained that whole betrothed comment for your benefit, Mor."

Morgan scowls, something she's done nonstop since we came here.

"If he's betrothed, and he thinks I'm his mate but wants nothing to do with me, why the hell did he even bother to announce that at all? Why not just leave me be?"

We all fall silent because the only person who has the answer to that question isn't here.

Half an hour later, we're all dressed and walking with Catherine to the Galloping Green Bean. We cross Main and head behind the first row of buildings, the diner's shiny metal 24 Hour sign blinking at us. The sign seems almost friendly, and I wonder if the diner gives off that vibe to welcome us like the inn does—it feels homey to me. I think the Green Bean is one of my favorite things about Ever.

When we arrive, Alba greets us at the door. Seeing her in centaur form again is a wild experience. The day I met her, she was just the buxom, saucy waitress who gave Shepherd a hard time. Now everything below her ample waist is horse-shaped and covered in silver horsehair. She still wears the same sarcastic expression, though, as she shoves purple horn-rimmed glasses to the tip of her nose. She grabs four menus and turns to lead us to a table, glancing over her shoulder.

"How are you ladies today? Not upset about the attack, I

hope?" Alba's voice is surprisingly relaxed considering the insanity of yesterday.

"Oh, we're good," Wren deadpans. "We attacked a thrall, we're all witches, and the Keeper won't let us leave. So yeah, we're fine."

Alba whips around, her ass-end knocking into the table next to us. Everyone at the table gives her an irritated look, but she crosses her arms.

"Witches? I knew it. I told Catherine the day after we met, didn't I Cath?" She barrels on without waiting for Catherine to get a word in. "Well, if you're monsters, then you certainly belong here, so there's no reason to leave."

"We do have jobs, you know. And an aunt who adores us and would very much miss us if we just moved to Ever," Morgan mentions.

"Are the jobs something you really wanna go back to?" Alba counters as she motions to the diner around us. "When you could be living this life all the time? Filled with magic and mystery and love? Just bring the aunt here too."

"That's enough, Alba," Catherine says in a gentle tone. "It's been a rough twenty-four hours, let's cut the girls a break."

Alba rolls her eyes and lets out a noise that's half whinny and half snort. "Listen. There's a craft fair today. We opted not to cancel it despite what happened yesterday. Hang out on Main and see a little more of what makes Ever so charming. There's danger everywhere, girls. I've heard terrible things about the human world—sex trafficking, kidn—"

"Alba," Catherine insists a little more sharply.

Jesus, she's intense for this early in the morning.

She's not wrong though, whispers the devil on my shoulder. And we're from New York, so we're plenty used to the dangers of the human world.

The centaur rolls her eyes and directs us to a red and turquoise pleather booth with a great view of Sycamore Street. She takes our drink order, then clip-clops toward the long bar that runs down the back wall of the restaurant. She heckles a couple of other monsters who sit at the bar. It makes me smile. I suspect being up in everybody's business is her standard operating procedure.

Then time slows as a giant figure swoops out of the sky, landing gracefully just outside the diner's retro door. He runs both hands through his wavy, dark hair, tucking his wings neatly behind his back. Today, Shepherd wears a black tee and jeans that hug every inch of his thick, muscular thighs.

Did those thighs quiver last night when he came with me? I wanna know. I'll be asking about that later.

A few moments later, Shepherd joins us, sliding into the booth on the same side as me. One big hand comes to my thigh and squeezes possessively. I resist the urge to purr at how good his touch feels.

My concentration is broken when Alba returns with our drinks. She gives me a knowing look, and it takes everything I have not to snark back.

"Good morning, friend." Catherine sounds tired, and I have to wonder if we're pushing too hard for answers.

I don't know if she slept a wink last night. I barely did for a myriad of reasons.

"I patrolled with the Keeper early this morning," Shepherd says. "The wards look good. The hole knit back together overnight, and we reinforced it with extra dust." He looks at me. "Maybe you can help me with that sometime." A hint of a smile plays on his lips.

"Because of the whole white witch protective thing?" Wren asks.

Catherine and Shepherd both nod, but it's Catherine who speaks up first. "Witch blood isn't all that uncommon, but having enough of it to sense a designation is. That would mean someone in your very close family tree is a full-blooded witch."

I shift back in my seat, surprised. "Are witches always women?"

"Yes," Catherine smiles. "The men are called warlocks, but their powers are the same."

"Lou," I mutter. "It's gotta be her."

My sisters nod, but Catherine gives me an inquisitive look. "Who is Lou to you?"

"Our mother's sister," Wren offers, gesturing around for help. "How do I explain Lou?"

Morgan laughs. "Sharp, intuitive, good at everything she sets her mind to. Perfect, amazing. Shall I go on? Our aunt Lou has always been our favorite person outside of our folks. She's closer in age to us than she was to our mom, but she's the easiest person in the world to be around. She's a national treasure, and we adore her."

"Do you think she'd want to come here?" Shepherd asks the question.

I don't think my mind has even fully wrapped around *us* staying here, much less asking Lou to come.

To my surprise, Wren nods. "Lou is all about the natural world and believes there's far more out there than humans know about. I bet you could bring her here and she wouldn't blink an eye at all this." She gestures around the diner.

It's busy this morning with all sorts of monsters. A few I recognize, but most I don't.

Shepherd gives me a look. "She's the one you texted from the gas station, right?"

Catherine looks up at Morgan. "Not your parents?"

My heart clenches at that. We haven't shared anything about our parents with her.

"Our folks are dead," Morgan says simply. "They died in an accident about six months ago. Lou's been our lifeline. I would want to invite her here since we can do a weekend over the course of three months. Maybe she and I can be crazy cat ladies in a little house near downtown."

I snort at that. There's not a single cat-loving bone in Morgan's body. That's more Wren's and my style.

I slide a hand under Shepherd's arm and lay it on the inside of his thigh. He stiffens, but the corners of his mouth turn slightly up. He steps his feet out wider, which gives me plenty of access to touch whatever I want.

Wren glances at Catherine. "I think we can worry about Lou later. We don't even know what the three of us plan to do yet. I want to know why Thea wasn't terrified by that thrall and how we can all learn more about our power."

Catherine smiles. "Taking to your witchiness quickly, I see. I'm thrilled. The Historical Society up on Main can help us with witch history, and I can guide you at a high level. There aren't any other witches in Ever at the moment, but you could travel to Kenmore in Scotland for training at a school there." She looks around at each of us, her smile growing. "To be honest, girls, most witches learn how to access their power, and then their control grows naturally. Take Wren, for instance."

Wren takes a contemplative sip of her coffee.

Catherine continues. "Wren's a green witch. I can teach her a few basics, but then it makes sense for her to work with Ohken in the garden. That's where her power will grow best. He's an excellent instructor, very hands-on."

Wren chokes on the coffee, spitting it all over Morgan and the table as she coughs and sputters.

I swear the town itself has a sense of humor because moments later, a giant figure in the booth behind her turns with a wicked smile.

Ohken. Bridge troll, Ever Question Master, and all-around hottie.

Based on the satisfied look on his face, I'd guess he heard our entire conversation. I resist the urge to laugh at how comical it is, but Wren is still coughing her head off.

Ohken shifts so he can look over the booth's leather top. "What's this I hear about a witch needing instruction?"

Wren whips around, her eyes bleary as she pounds herself on the chest.

I pipe up, always helpful. "Wren's a green witch. Wren doesn't know shit *about* being a green witch."

Ohken's russet eyes flash. "Hmm. A green. Very handy indeed. I'll be in the garden all day, Wren. Come find me, if you would. Assuming you want to be taught, I suppose." His voice trails off.

She nods but still can't seem to catch her breath. Shepherd's body quakes, and when I look up, he's stifling a laugh behind his big hand.

Morgan sops coffee off the table until Wren gets control of herself. I know she's dying to say something about this turn of events, but with Ohken seated right behind her, she won't. It's a sort of delicious devilry to watch her cheeks go pink. I see what's happening, she thinks he's hot.

He is, in an enormous, I-can-break-you-in-half-with-my-pinkie sort of way. He's hot. Ohken looks like the Daddy Dom version of the jolly green giant, complete with a sexy auburn man bun. Oh lord, I can't wait to grill her about this later. Usually, she's the cool cucumber of us three. She's off her game, though, because she isn't usually discombobulated around men. But something about Ohken has her sputtering and gaping like a fish.

"Later, then," Ohken murmurs.

He gives Wren a long, assessing look. The rest of us stare at them. Finally, he flips back around and returns his attention to a newspaper on the table in front of him.

Catherine looks at me. "You and I can cover some basics about being a white witch, but the majority of your learning should come from the Keeper, Shepherd, and Alo since they protect the town. Gargoyles and haven keepers always work with a white witch, when possible."

Heat flames across my cheeks. Teaching could potentially lead to sexy teaching, and I'm nothing if not a model student.

"How convenient for you," Morgan deadpans. "Do tell my lovely mate I miss him dearly and I'm wringing my hands waiting for him to show up and carry me off on a white horse."

Catherine chuckles, Shepherd laughs aloud, and then the whole table dissolves into hysterical cackles. I don't think any of us can imagine the Keeper making that sort of effort, not based on his behavior so far.

When the dust settles, Catherine wipes tears from her eyes. "He'll probably call a quick town meeting at the gazebo in a bit. There hasn't been an attack here in forty years. He'll want to address it."

"Since Wesley, you mean?" The question is out of my mouth before I can stop it.

I feel immediately bad for asking, but I think we have a right to some information about the danger we're in.

"Yes," Catherine nods, wrapping both hands around her mug. "Wesley was an incredibly powerful warlock." She looks up, gray eyes shining with unshed tears. "He was my mate."

CHAPTER TWENTY-TWO
SHEPHERD

The table is silent as Catherine shares. I squeeze Thea's leg a little tighter, imprinting the feel of her under my palm.

"I never saw his darkness," Catherine admits. Her pale eyes move from me to each of the triplets. "Nobody did. Everybody loved him, even the Keeper. Wesley was so charismatic and friendly." She pauses to take a sip of her coffee, then looks out the window like she can't bear to face us while she recounts the story.

"We were mated for about a year when I started to notice odd occurrences around the Annabelle. She didn't like him. And she'd do mean things, like trip him going up the stairs or burn his coffee. I thought it was because it had always been her and me, and he upset that balance. But I should have paid attention."

The girls look entranced when she continues.

"One night, he slipped out of bed. He'd started to do that. He always dealt with insomnia, so it didn't surprise me. But it turned out he was punching holes in the wards that night. The thralls outside were his, waiting to come in and attack."

"And what happened? Was anybody hurt?" Thea's voice is impossibly small when she asks the question.

"No," I confirm, wanting to be clear on this topic. "Alo, Ohken, the Keeper, and I were able to fight the thralls, along with help from some townsfolk who no longer live here. It was close, but no one was hurt."

Catherine rubs at the side of her coffee cup and looks back at Thea. "To be honest, I've always been worried he'd return. I think I've always known he *would*, someday. I don't believe for a moment that the attack this week was someone else. It's Wesley, it has to be."

"What's his endgame?" Thea questions.

She's shared her job with me, and I love that in the outside world, she's also a protector. I can see that in the way she goes into investigative mode.

"Ever is a large, thriving haven," Catherine shares. "Many powerful beings live here, even royalty from a variety of species. To spell and enthrall monsters with that level of power would make it easier for Wesley to take over this entire haven. And taking over one haven puts all the rest at risk because of how we're interconnected."

I pick up where Catherine left off, glancing at Thea but ensuring I connect with her sisters too. "Each haven has a direct connection to one other. We connect to Hel through the motel. I mentioned that the night we met."

Thea groans, Wren slaps her forehead, and Morgan shoots me a deadpan look.

"Dammit. You literally told us the motel was a gateway to hell. This is what you meant, isn't it?"

"Exactly," I chuckle. "It's just Hel with one *l*, though. Not hell like the Christian belief. But from Hel, there's a traveling station to any other haven. Each haven is connected, and you can access the rest from their assigned station. That web is part of how the havens are tied together and secure. But you can imagine how taking over just one haven would start to break that down."

Thea looks over at Catherine. "And that's Wesley's goal? To break down all the havens so he can enthrall people and what, take over the world?"

Catherine's lips are pursed tightly, her eyes full of sorrow as she nods her agreement. "It turned out Wes didn't believe monsters should hide from humans at all. He believes we are inherently more powerful for a reason, and he wants the monster universe to live in plain sight, ruling the human world."

"Jesus," Wren says, taking a sip of her coffee.

I feel a pressing need to continue the story. "Even so, we were able to stop Wesley's attack, despite how well-coordinated he was. And then the Hearth stepped in for a while with extra support. We haven't seen Wesley in almost forty years. His attack was the only time in monster history that an attack came from within a haven, versus the outside."

I expect the girls to have questions, but they fall silent. I hate that it seems I have to dump a shitload of news on the Hector triplets every day. It's been surprise after surprise for them since they arrived.

Catherine gives me a worried look. She's convinced Wesley is to blame for the thralls, even though the evidence doesn't support that.

Our food comes, delivered by Alba's nephew Taylor, but the table is mostly silent. The triplets look lost in thought.

I'm driven to remind the girls that Ever is still an incredible place and that violence and bullshit aren't an everyday occurrence. So, I suggest a little bit of fun.

"There's a gorgeous lagoon in the forest I'd love to take you three to later. You can meet the mermaid school. They've been asking about you, according to the Keeper."

Thea drops her fork and gazes up at me in awe. "Mermaids? Honest to god, mermaids?"

She looks so excited I burst out laughing.

"Of all the things you've seen here, mermaids are what jazzes you, huh?"

She blushes and eyes the wing spikes behind my shoulders. "I mean, it's *all* super cool, I'm just a huge Ariel fan . . ."

"Alba mentioned a craft fair of some sort, too," Wren says. "Can we go to that also?"

I smile. "Of course. The craft fair goes on until about three, so let's check that out first. I'll take you to the lake after for a swim, and then I've got a date tonight."

I swear Thea preens next to me, but her sisters share a look and smile. They must have talked about me, and that makes me happy as fuck. I've given Thea space. This was originally a girls' weekend, and I haven't forgotten that. But their "weekend" takes up nearly three months here. I can steal time with her.

The rest of breakfast passes in a blur. Catherine talks the triplets through a learning plan to see how much witch power, if any, they can access. Afterward, we head to Main Street for the craft fair.

Wren and Morgan link arms, but Thea makes a point to hold my hand. I keep her close to me, keeping my eyes open for anything amiss. I always rely on my gargoyle ability to sense thralls, but I'm doubly on edge because of what happened yesterday.

Still, when Catherine and the girls stop at Miriam's stall to sample pastries, I relax a little.

I hear Iggy before I see him, his tiny wings beating the air as he zooms up the street. To my surprise, he lands on Thea's shoulder and wraps his tail protectively around her neck, the end dipping down into her shirt. She steels herself under his weight but reaches up. One hand goes carefully to his side.

If my heart wasn't full of this woman before, it is now. Watching her accept my nephew with such ease is the best thing I've ever experienced. Better than the chemistry, better than her smiles. What's happening right here is all about family. Which is precisely what I want with her. I want to build that together.

That's the moment I know I won't be able to let her go. Not now. Not ever. I don't care what I have to do to convince her to stay, but it's happening.

Alo joins me, slapping my tail with his as he leans close to my ear. "Think your thoughts could be any more obvious, brother?"

I slap him back, making sure to dig the pointed end of my spade into his side. "Maybe you should make yours a little *more* obvious, Alo."

His eyes flick over to Miriam, rubbing lime-scented candy lotion on the back of Iggy's arm as he laughs joyously.

I turn so the girls can't hear me and get in my brother's space. "You're gonna lose what's right in front of you. Grab happiness where you can."

Alo growls at me, but his eyes never leave Miriam. I swear to the gods, I don't know what push he needs to get him to make a move. She's made her interest obvious, but she's not going to wait around forever if he doesn't return it.

An hour later, we've visited every stall. Iggy's eaten three ice creams and now zooms in tiny circles around our group, high on sugar. Eventually, Alo grabs him by the tail and drags him on top of his shoulder.

"Ignatius Zion, chill out." Alo's voice is sharp, but Iggy slaps his father on the head with his tail as he settles himself on Alo's shoulder.

It's a youngling's equivalent of pfft. I make sure not to laugh out loud and encourage him. Gods help Alo when Iggy comes of age and they're the same size.

Thea catches my eye, opening her mouth to say something when a gong echoes.

She waits for the long, resonant noise to stop. "Lemme guess, we aren't saved by the bell?"

I don't get that reference, and I'm about to ask when Ohken joins us.

"The Keeper called a meeting about yesterday's attack. We'll get his thoughts on it and his plan to ensure it doesn't happen again." His striking eyes flick to Morgan and Catherine and finally land on Wren. "We'll keep you safe, don't worry." His voice is a low rumble.

Thea and I swivel to look at Wren, but her gaze is firmly planted on Ohken, a blush staining her cheeks pink.

"Earth to Wren!" Thea shouts.

Wren jolts upright, green eyes fluttering before flicking over to her sister. The gong rings again, and we head toward Town Hall.

I'm feeling a little devious, maybe even a little matchmakey. I glance over at Ohken.

"I'm taking the girls to the lagoon after our meeting. I'd like to remind them what a fun place Ever is. Wanna join us?"

If I didn't think the blush on Wren's round cheeks could get worse, I was wrong. She's practically purple at this point. The look she levels at me would kill a lesser male.

I grin back at her.

Ohken keeps his steps slow as he walks next to her. He looks down at Wren with a mischievous grin. "I suspect Shepherd hasn't been forthcoming about all the details surrounding a trip to the lagoon. Has he explained how the lagoon is a nude experience?"

"Fucking no, he hasn't," Wren glares at me.

"Don't pop a vein, Wren," I snort. "I'd call it more clothing optional. You can leave it on, if you want."

Ohken laughs, smirking before he focuses on her once more.

"Much as I'd love to join, I'm patrolling the wards with the Keeper tonight. Rain check on naked swimming, though. It's always fun."

Next to me, Thea practically vibrates with humor. Even

Morgan beams as she watches her sister attempt to respond to Ohken but fail to come up with any words.

Thea taps me on the side. "I don't have a bathing suit, anyway."

I'm nearly breathless at the thought of her naked in the water. I don't know if swimming nude is common for humans, but in Ever, that's how we always do it.

I lead our group toward Town Hall. The gazebo's wooden timbers groan as it stretches to fit the whole town. It takes ten minutes before the stragglers join us, the Keeper standing at the front as always, dressed in head-to-toe black.

He doesn't bother with pleasantries, launching right into the details we discussed sharing.

"Many of you are aware two thralls broke through the wards yesterday."

Concerned murmuring fills the gazebo, but he continues. "Alo and Shepherd immediately neutralized the threat, but we discovered a sizable hole in the ward that the thralls came through. It's patched now, with help from Ohken and the pixies. We are working overtime to keep you safe, and nobody was injured."

"Why now?" someone shouts from the back of the crowd.

Grunts and whistles of agreement follow the question. I shuffle my wings behind my back. I hate this. Ever has always been safe. It's been four *decades* since we had an issue.

I try to remind myself my townspeople are scared precisely *because* they've always felt safe here.

"I can't be certain," the Keeper continues, his voice neutral and emotionless. "But I think the arrival of the Hector triplets played a part."

Oh fuck. I don't know if he realizes what he just said, but like a damn horror movie, every being in the gazebo turns and looks at the girls. Morgan and Wren squish close to Thea, who steps back into my arms.

Morgan lifts her chin, ever the defiant one. "If we affected the wards, we don't know how. It wasn't purposeful, but if we can keep it from happening again, we will."

"How on earth could you help?" someone else shouts.

"They're witches," the Keeper continues. "White, green, and black. A blessing, if they've got significant power. We just don't know yet."

"Wow," Wren mutters, giving me a disbelieving look.

It's easy to see that the sisters feel singled out.

Shit, even I feel like he's singling them out.

His typically harsh expression softens a little. "We've never had witch residents in Ever. I know we'll all support the Hectors in learning about their power. They could be important allies for us if this attack is part of something larger."

Silence descends for a long, heavy moment before the Keeper glances around. "The ward monitoring system that Ohken helped me develop worked like a charm yesterday, and our protector team went into immediate action. We were ready, as evidenced by the fact that nobody was injured."

"What about the garden?" someone shouts.

He crosses his arms and runs one hand through his gelled-back hair. The Keeper's face pulls into a displeased sneer. It's a stress tell from him. I hate that he carries such a heavy weight by being responsible for our town.

His answer is brusque. "A quarter of the moonflower vines were pulled down, but the pixies are working hard to get them back up."

Ohken clears his throat, and the focus moves from the Keeper to him. He's always been such a commanding, confident presence. I'm a little surprised he didn't present as a Keeper when he came of age and got tested, but I'm glad for his partnership every day.

"The pixies and I have already managed to thread about half the vines onto temporary supports. It'll take some time to get them back on the hedge, but we'll be fine. This is why we always keep more dust on hand than we need. This doesn't set us back."

Murmurs buzz through the air, some more understanding than others. When there aren't any other questions, the Keeper folds both long arms behind his back, glancing around to work the room.

"That's all for today. As always, comm me, Ohken, Alo, or Shepherd with questions." He pauses there, and the crowd begins to dissipate.

I'm surprised by the number of Evertons who stop by and offer to help the girls with their power. By the time everyone's gone, the triplets don't seem so stiff.

Once everyone has gone, the Keeper strides toward us, his footsteps heavy on the wooden floor. He peers at Morgan.

"I'll need to help you with your power, Morgan. Healers are rare, and there's a chance we'll need your particular set of skills. Let's set aside time to—"

"No thanks," she snaps. "Now that you threw us all under the bus in front of the entire goddamn town, I'm not feeling particularly friendly. I'll work with Catherine and Shepherd."

The Keeper sighs as if he doesn't know how to navigate emotion. I suppose that's true, in a way. Keeper training involves shutting off a lot of what makes beings emotional so they can see the logic in every situation.

"I'm the most natural person to assist you, Morgan." His tone is curt and insistent.

She crosses her arms. "And yet I don't get the sense you'll be a particularly kind teacher. I need that. I don't know shit about being a witch, and I don't need your negativity while I'm trying to learn. If I even stick around. Because frankly, this bullshit with thralls and pixie dust and blaming us when we got here a few days ago is a dick move."

He blanches, and for a moment, I think I see remorse in his eyes.

The Keeper straightens, nodding briskly. "I'll allow that for now. As soon as Catherine tells me you've got the basics down, I'll have to take over. The security of this town is at risk, and somehow, the three of you are connected to what happened."

"I don't know why you'd think that," Thea states, irritation plain in her voice.

The Keeper turns to her with an eye roll. "It's probably specific to *you*, Thea. White witches work with gargoyles and Keepers to protect their havens. It's entirely possible that your being here is causing your latent power to build and rise. And somehow, without even being aware, you probably put that hole in the ward. We need you to learn to control your power so it doesn't happen again."

I don't think he could have shocked Thea any worse if he'd slapped her. Her muscles quiver.

I growl at my lifelong friend. "That's enough, Keeper."

He stares at me, dark eyes narrowed to slits before he turns and strides purposefully out of the gazebo toward Main Street. I watch him go, alone like he always is, and all I feel is sadness for the person he used to be before he was responsible for our safety.

"Goddamn, he's a charmer," Morgan chirps, but she sounds devastated.

Alo sighs next to me and pats Iggy, still perched on his shoulder. "Well, I need a drink. I'm gonna swing by my place, but I'll meet you four at the lake. We could use a swim."

Iggy leaps off his dad's shoulder in excitement, but Alo grabs his son's tail and places him back where he was.

"You come with me, kiddo, I need your help."

Iggy nods. Despite her tiff with the Keeper just now, Morgan lifts her palm for a high five. Iggy slaps it with his tail spade and a little snort of laughter. Kids move on from things so easily. I love that despite how frustrating today must be for them, the triplets still make an effort to be sweet to him.

CHAPTER TWENTY-THREE
THEA

E very morning I wake up, I think to myself how the prior day was wild, and nothing else is gonna surprise me. But the reality is the Keeper just tossed us in front of a moving bus, and it was very uncool.

It's not lost on me that some folks offered to help us after, while others steered clear. He just built a huge divide between us and the rest of town. I would have thought he wanted us to stay here, but maybe not. I decide I'm going to ask him the next time I see him. If it's true that I'm a witch and I have protective power, then he and I might work together soon. But I refuse to work with an asshole, especially given the grief he continues to direct at Morgan.

I turn to Shepherd. "Listen, I want to skip the lake. If it's true that we affected the wards, and we have no reason to believe it's not, then I want to learn about my power fast. I don't want anyone in danger because of me."

Shepherd's eyes soften, and I expect him to disagree, but he nods. It's like a knife to my heart realizing he thinks that's best too. Does he agree with the Keeper that I'm at fault? Even if I have no idea how I could be? I force my lower lip not to tremble, even though he's looking at me with a soft, tender expression.

Catherine's kind voice breaks through the spiral of my thoughts. "It's probably for the best, Thea. Morgan, Wren, how do you feel about your first magic lesson?"

"Let's do it," Morgan agrees. "No more of this let's-blame-the-Hectors bullshit."

"Definitely not," Wren agrees. "Plus, if I can help fix the garden, I want to do that."

Ohken watches the exchange silently but taps Wren on the shoulder when she mentions the garden. "I'd love your help with the garden. Catherine can get you started, but I may be able to help with your power too. Comm me when you've got time to speak about it?"

"Absolutely." She gives him a determined look, and pride soars through me.

My sisters are absolute wonders. Despite what Ever has thrown at us in the last four days, they're taking it in stride way better than I could ever hope for.

Morgan grabs Wren's hand but bumps me with her hip. "We'll head back to the Annabelle and get started. See you two in a minute, okay?" She gestures toward Shepherd, despite the fact he's standing right the fuck next to me.

I see what she's doing, and I thank her for it with a playful wink.

Catherine and my sisters leave the gazebo and head toward Main. I turn to Shepherd with a cheeky grin, both hands pressed to his broad, muscular chest.

"Do you think the hole in the wards is my fault?"

Shepherd's long, flexible tail snakes around my core and drags me close. One big hand cups the back of my head. His eyes search mine, drinking me in.

"Witch power can be unpredictable when untrained," he hedges. "But what I know with certainty is that you would never hurt the wards purposefully. I'm committed to helping you figure it out. That's what good partners do, right?"

Jesus. I think that's about as good of an answer as I could expect. I don't know if it's my fault either, but I want to find out fast so it doesn't happen again.

When I smile up at him, he matches my expression. His nostrils flare, and the playful smile morphs into more of a deviant smirk.

I let out a soft, irritated huff. "I'm really sad not to see you naked in the lagoon, but we're still on for tonight, right?"

He blows out a breath that seems to match mine in frustration. "It's a shame about the lagoon. Gargoyles are excellent swimmers. I was looking forward to you staring at my dick underwater. The lagoon holds infinite teasing possibilities."

"Oh, you know I would," I laugh. "Although, I think the girls would too, if it was flopping around in front of them."

Shepherd snorts but leans down and presses his forehead to mine. He brushes his nose against my own. "I love it when *you* look at me, Thea. I love that you look at me like you can't wait to sink those blunt little teeth into my skin."

"You're into that?" I say. "Biting?"

"Oh yeah." His voice is a deep, sensual rumble. "Gargoyles are aggressive lovers. I can't wait to bring the same out in you."

"I could be a pillow princess," I counter. "Just lie there lazily and let you do all the work."

Shepherd growls. "Oh, we'll do that, too, but sometimes I'm gonna make you work for it, angel."

My clit throbs in time with his hand stroking at the nape of my neck. "Good," I breathe out. "I need that later. I'm probably gonna be frustrated as hell when I learn I have no power or it'll take years to build. And meanwhile, I'll blow enough holes in the ward to turn it into a cheese grater."

Shepherd pulls my hair over one shoulder and returns his grip to the back of my neck. His eyes are soft, his lips parted. I swear to god, if he kisses me right now, I will not pass go or collect two hundred dollars, it'll be straight to his nest. I'm already on fire from last night's tease, and being around him makes that so much worse. Especially knowing he doesn't blame me. He's in my corner, and it feels really good. I've always had my sisters and Lou, but since my folks died, my corner has felt a lot more empty.

"I'm here to help, Thea. The Keeper too, despite that bullshit earlier. None of us will pressure you to protect Ever, but I adore that you want to."

I stroke one hand down his pec and over his nipple. It's hard and raised, and he sucks in a breath when my fingers brush over it.

"You're playing with fire, little witch." Shepherd's voice is a low, focused growl, his pupil and iris indistinguishable from one another. "Keep going, and the only thing you'll be learning is how to take my dick in your pussy and my tail in your ass."

I snicker, even though my cheeks are on fire and I can't seem to fill my lungs with enough air. "I hope I *do* learn that tonight, but I'll stop teasing you for now. Though you should know, in general, I'm a huge tease. I can't stop myself."

Shepherd's grip on my neck tightens to the point of pain. I'm caught, unable to move or tear my gaze from his. Thick fingers tangle in my hair, and then he yanks my head back so all I can see is the gazebo's angular, paneled ceiling.

I'm so exposed like this, and when a huff of breath brushes against my skin, I clench up tight.

Shepherd releases a satisfied, possessive growl, and the sharp prick of teeth pulls a gasp from my lips. Soft, wet warmth tickles its way along my skin. His tongue. Fuck me, it's warm and smooth. He bites and nuzzles his way down to my collarbone, and then he bites that as goose bumps sprint along my arms.

"I'm a tease too, angel," he breathes into my ear.

He slips his free hand under my shirt and bra, his fingers playing with my nipple. It raises and hardens under his expert touch. Fuck, we're in public. Anybody could walk by and see him teasing the hell out of me right here in front of Town Hall.

He pinches hard enough to make me squeak, then bites my neck at the same time. Warring sensations fill me—pain, lust, need.

He growls against my skin. "I'll go help Ohken and the Keeper while you're with Catherine. Find me the moment you're done. I'll cook for us tonight, and we'll do something about this heat, Thea."

"Okay," I agree, breathless with need. "It's gonna be a long day."

"An even longer night," he promises.

He brushes my cheek with his lips and then pulls me in the direction everyone else went. I resist the urge to tackle him and do something about all this aching right *now*, but responsibility lies in front of us.

Offhand, I wonder if this is how the Keeper feels all the time. This weighty sense of being responsible for the town and wanting to help. It sounds like it consumes him. For the first time, I feel a little bad for him.

We walk past the Galloping Green Bean and cross Main, heading for the Annabelle. We arrive in time to see my sisters cross from the inn to the garden. Miriam appears in the garden's open archway and waves at us as we approach. Green and pink wings flutter rapidly at her back.

"We've never had witches in Ever, so cool." She sounds thrilled to death that we're witches.

I'm still not sure how I feel about it myself. A little stunned, kinda overwhelmed, and totally disbelieving. Quite possibly guilty of opening a damn gate in the ward to let hideous monsters in.

Wren laughs. "Well, if I can magically fix what the thralls did to the garden with a snap of my fingers, I'll get excited."

Miriam laughs again. "You three are going to be amazing. Catherine is an excellent teacher. Come work in the garden. It's got a great vibe for lessons."

Catherine rubs my back, her touch motherly and sweet. It reminds me of the way my mother would always stroke my hair when I was sick. "I'm happy with the garden if you three are okay with it. I forgot something in the Annabelle. I'll be right back."

On cue, the house's front steps clatter like piano keys. I don't know what it means, but Catherine laughs.

My sisters follow Miriam into the garden.

Shepherd plants a tender kiss on my lips. "I'm going to find the Keeper. Comm me when you're coming over. I'll be ready."

"I can't wait," I admit. "Maybe I'll take to this whole witch thing hella fast and spell something for you when I get there."

"No doubt," he laughs. "As long as it's a sexy spell, I'm down."

With a quick wink, he pushes off the asphalt and rockets up into the sky.

I watch until he's nothing but a tiny dot, and then I join my sisters and Miriam. On the far side of the garden, there's a round picnic-style table. Everyone's seated and seemingly waiting for Catherine.

I slide in next to Wren and press my shoulder to hers. So much about our lives has been uprooted in the last few days. She and Morgan have handled everything with amazing grace and perseverance, but I'm glad we're going through it together. Despite it all, I'm still somewhere halfway between frazzled and fascinated. Is frazzlenated a word? Because that's what I am.

Wren bumps her shoulder back against mine. Catherine joins us a moment later, carrying a small package in her hand. Whatever she's got is wrapped in a dark red tattered cloth. She sets it down in the middle of the table and smiles.

"When I was younger, I trained with the Hearth as a teacher, and although that's not my role in Ever, I can get you started with your magic. The reality is a lot of magic is innate, but what's not can be learned. Some spells must be learned from other witches, though, so there's a point where you'll likely travel if you decide to pursue your powers to that extent."

"What are the other havens like?" Morgan asks.

Catherine laughs. "They're all wildly different, to be honest. Hel is the most similar to Ever, but it's in Romania. So picture an adorable small town but set deep in the snowy mountains."

Morgan slaps her forehead. "I still can't get over the whole gateway to Hel comment from Shepherd when we met. I just thought he meant the motel was gross."

Miriam titters joyously. "Yeah. The motel is almost its own little world. It's only ever busy when we have sporting events because otherwise people stay at the An—"

"Hold the phone," shouts Morgan. "Sporting events? Oh my god, tell me you play Quidditch. I'll stay forever if you play Quidditch."

We all burst into laughter at the same time. Of the three of us triplets, Morgan is the sporty one.

Miriam continues. "Not hardly. It's called skyball. It's big business around here. We're almost through the season now. The final tournament is due to be held here in a couple of weeks."

"Sports," Morgan groans. "You should have led with this news at orientation, to be honest. I fucking love sports."

Catherine's smile grows broad. "Well, flyball is interesting. Imagine the human sports of soccer and football combined, and anybody with wings is allowed to fly. The Annabelle is usually full of visitors then, the motel too. But it's sort of a last resort."

"The motel? Why?" Wren asks.

Miriam and Catherine exchange a look before Catherine

speaks up. "The motel is run by wraiths, so there's a fairly creepy vibe."

"Wraiths?" Wren presses. "Like ghosts?"

Miriam purses her lips, eyes darting upward as they narrow. "More like spirits of the past. Not a specific person, per se, but sentiment leftover from a time in history. So they're all kinda . . . intense. That's probably a good word for them. The customer service at the motel is severely lacking."

Catherine laughs. "Let's table this discussion for another time, shall we? If you three stay, you'll get plenty of skyball experience when it's time for the finals." She glances around, smiling when I give her two thumbs up.

"Alright. The most complicated thing about magic, when you didn't grow up with it, is simply recognizing its existence. Unrecognized magic can be dangerous, depending on the strength of your gifts. That's why the Keeper thinks your arrival in Ever could be related to the hole in the wards."

I swear my heart pulls a reverse Grinch and shrinks a few sizes. I pray with all my might that the hole isn't my fault, but it's sounding more and more like it is, even though it wasn't purposeful.

Morgan crosses her arms and looks off into the distance, where a group of small fairies flits about. "Would have been nice to hear that detail from him privately before he put us on blast."

I'm surprised when Miriam speaks up.

"I hate to say you have to let things roll off your shoulders with him because I don't want to make excuses for his bluntness. Most of us grew up with him before he was ever identified as a Keeper. He was different before. But taking on the keeper's mantle brings a heavy weight. No matter what sort of monster you were before, it always changes you. All keepers are like he is."

"Assholes?" Morgan laughs, her tone bitter. "Rude and pretentious?"

"Yeah," Miriam laughs. "Sort of!" She looks to Catherine, seemingly for backup.

Catherine sighs. "Keepers have to be very focused, very logical, and it doesn't leave a lot of room for emotion. During keeper training, they undergo a process to rewire their thought patterns. It makes them far more harsh. I know it's hard to believe this, girls, but he has the biggest heart you can imagine. It's just that it's tucked beneath layers and layers of conditioning."

There's an uncomfortable silence where Wren and I look at Morgan, who's pursing her lips and scowling off into the distance.

After a tense moment, she waves her hands above her head as if to shoo away the entire conversation. "Can we puh-lease get to the learning portion of today?"

Wren reaches out to rub Morgan's back, just like our mother used to do. I know Morgan isn't thrilled with the Keeper situation, but now isn't the time to dig into that. Although, I intend to cover the topic completely while I'm getting ready for tonight.

We refocus on Catherine, who unwraps the package in the center of the table to reveal a gigantic white crystal. It's long and sharp and as big around as her palm.

"This crystal was grown with pixie dust, and it's called a divining crystal. We use this sort of crystal to help aggregate and locate power in young witches. We can use it now to strengthen your power enough to make it noticeable to you." She places the crystal back on the red rag and looks at me. "Thea, let's start with you. Pick up the crystal, please, and hold it upright in your palm."

When I reach out and grab it, I find it's even heavier than it looks. It's hard to hold my hands out in front of me with the crystal in them. As I situate the flat bottom in my palm and point the top toward the sky, a zing travels up my left arm.

"Ouch!" I squeak, almost dropping it. "It shocked me."

Catherine smiles a little, more of a smirk. "Good. Now close your eyes and think about the wards."

My left palm quivers slightly from the shock, but I try to tune out the sounds of everyone breathing and instead focus on the wards surrounding and protecting us. I think first of the hole the thralls came through. A sour, musty taste fills my mouth, so vile and strong I scrunch my nose up. I imagine myself flying along the inside of the wards, away from Shepherd's gas station, and deep into the forest. The trees are so dense, it's dark, but there's a niggling sensation in the back of my mind like I'm flying toward something.

There! Up ahead of me, red flames shine from outside the wards. As I fly closer, I see dozens of thralls, their faces screwed up in horror. Human faces, wolf faces, gargoyle faces. They're terrifying, and they're throwing themselves at the ward over and over again. It shimmies and shakes when they hit it, but it holds.

The crystal sends a fresh zing through my arm, so sharp I drop it and lose focus. I'm brought back to the picnic table, where my sisters, Catherine, and Miriam are staring at me expectantly.

"What did you see, child?" Catherine asks quietly.

"Thralls," I gasp, my chest heaving. "Dozens of thralls throwing themselves at the ward, somewhere in the forest near the gas station. Is that real? Did I see something that's happening? Is that part of my power?"

"One moment, my sweet," Catherine chirps, lifting her comm watch. "Call the Keeper."

Moments later, his deep voice echoes out of the small device. For the first time, I'm grateful to hear him. If what I saw is real, he can do something about it.

"Catherine, what's wrong?"

"I'm working with Thea, and she sees thralls attacking the

ward in the forest near Shepherd's station. It's hard to say if it's something from the past or more of a sentiment as she learns her power, but—"

"The sensors don't indicate this in real time," he mutters in a low, irritated tone. There's silence for a moment. "I'll do a visual check with Shepherd."

He clicks off without another word, and Catherine turns back to me.

"When a witch's magic is discovered, there's typically a period where the magic feels more like intuition than an actual controlled force. That's normal, and identifying that sensation of power is the most important in the beginning." She gives me a sorrowful look. "I'm sorry that hurt you, Thea. That means your power is quite strong, which is good! It's important to do this crystal work several times a day until you're able to think of and feel your power without holding the crystal."

"So what about what I just saw?" I have to know more about what just happened. "I was imagining myself examining the wards, and it's like I zoomed forward to see the thralls. Does that mean it's happening right now?" Creepy crawlies slink and scatter down my spine when I think about the thrall from before.

My sisters are stone silent next to us.

"It's hard to say," Catherine hedges. "But it's possible you're seeing real-time insights into what's outside the wards, Thea." She pauses for a moment. "That ability is common for white witches, which is why I called the Keeper. It's why a haven having a white witch is such an advantage. Thralls are attracted to ward energy, that's pretty much all they care about. That and turning other monsters into thralls. So to some degree, some thralls are always attacking wards everywhere. For the most part, they're never able to get through."

I nod along with her explanation, but I'm lost in thought. To think the thralls are attacking the wards right this minute is fucking awful. While we sit here in a beautiful garden, evil is still trying to burrow its way in. And if Catherine is right, it's trying to get in all the damn time.

Wren and Morgan go next. They get shocked too, but Wren's able to feel the roots under the garden, and Morgan's able to sense everyone's emotions. It's weird and exhausting.

Still, we keep at it for hours, practicing over and over again as Catherine lays out a lesson plan for the next week. By the time we finish, I resolve to get ahold of my magic. The reality is, I feel invested in this place and the people we've met, even after a short time.

One person in particular.

CHAPTER TWENTY-FOUR
THEA

ours later, my brain is both exhausted and wired, but it's time to get ready for my date with Shepherd. Wren lies on my bed, and Morgan's tucked up in the window seat with a bowl of cereal. God, she reminds me of our mother sometimes. She used to eat cereal at all sorts of inappropriate times. Cereal is only a breakfast food, in my book.

I haven't done my hair yet, but I need to sort the outfit first. I step out from behind the closet doors and do a little twirl.

"Ooh!" says Morgan, her eyes lighting up as she shakes her spoon at me. "Yes, girl, definitely that dress. Shepherd's gonna rip it off you in two seconds flat."

Wren's green eyes drift down to my combat boots and back up.

"Most excellent. He's gonna combust for sure." She waggles her dark brows at me, sipping at a cup of coffee from Higher Grounds. She licks at their signature green foam and laughs. "I wish I could see Shepherd's face when you show up. He plans to cook, right?"

"Yep." I pop the *p* as I twirl in the mirror.

215

My pale purple dress has thin ruffled straps and a tight bodice, but then it flares out into a poofy knee-length skirt, so it's only really fitted on top. I look like a badass combat Barbie. I dig it.

"Want us to walk you over?" Morgan offers. "I'm kinda curious to see his place."

I snort. "Like hell. You just wanna cockblock me, and I'm not having it."

Morgan cackles. "Okay, but for real, I do want to see it. It can be another day though. Can you tell him I ate all my cookies, and if he'd like to continue pursuing you, I'm gonna need a few more?"

I shake my head at that with a laugh. "You're incorrigible."

"Big Scorpio energy," Morgan agrees. "He said it was important to court Wren and me too. I'm just saying I could do with more snacks. He promised snacks, and there has been a shortage of snacks in the last two days."

"He did promise. We love him. Definitely keep him," Wren agrees.

Well, if there was ever gonna be an opening for this conversation, that was it. I rub at my elbow and settle in the window seat across from Morgan, making sure to catch Wren's attention too.

"I know everything has been crazy since we came to Ever," I begin.

"No shit," Morgan laughs. "Crazy doesn't begin to cover it."

I barrel on before I lose my nerve.

"Ever feels like the beginning of something amazing to me. I think I want to stay past our girls' weekend." I hold my breath after I spit it out. I could go on, but I want to give my sisters a chance to respond.

Wren looks from me to Morgan, and Morgan sets her cereal bowl down in the window and crosses her arms.

"You two are going to make me make this decision, aren't you?"

"You *are* the oldest," Wren offers helpfully, taking another sip of her coffee.

"I think you two are having a far better time than I am, but I obviously would never leave you behind, not after . . ." I watch her beautiful eyes fill with unshed tears.

Sliding closer, I shove my way into her lap and wrap my arms around her neck.

"I know," I whisper into the space between us. "We won't ever be the people we were when Mom and Dad were here, but we can find a new normal, right?"

That's been our constant motto since our folks died. Find the new normal. There will always be a hole in my chest where my parents' memories sit, but life is for the living.

Wren sits behind me and rubs my back when Morgan's tears finally spill over. She sobs for a long time, but we don't let her go until she's run out of tears. When she does, she lays the side of her head against mine and clears her throat.

"If you both want to stay, then I will too. Obviously. But I think we should call Lou. I don't want to be here without her, it doesn't feel right. It's like our fourth sister is missing, and I just, I really want her here."

"Done," Wren and I agree at the same time. Wren continues. "Lou would love this place, and I'm with Thea. This place is fascinating, and there's nothing left in New York for me. I liked my naturalist job just fine, but I don't feel compelled to go back to it."

"And I can't stand the thought of going to the precinct and seeing Dad's empty desk one more time," I admit. "I've been the shittiest detective since he died. I can't focus there."

Morgan listens to our admissions and looks out the window, auburn brows knitted together.

She looks upset, but finally, she turns with a nod. "Let's do it then. I'm down if you both are. We can revisit this convo later if things change, right?"

"Of course," I breathe, not realizing how much I needed to hear that she agreed to stay until she said it. "If you wake up one day and you just can't do this anymore, I'm with you."

"I'd never do that to you," she murmurs. "Not when you and Shepherd seem to be getting serious, and Wren's got the googly eyes for Ohken."

Wren snorts and slaps Morgan on the boob, careful to hold her coffee steady with her other hand.

"What?!" Morgan shouts. "Ouch, bitch. I'm just saying, every time he comes around, you choke on something and can't get a word out. It's unlike you. And honestly, he's got that big daddy energy we all know you love. Don't act like you haven't thought about him like that."

I turn slowly to look at my green-eyed sister, but she sips at the coffee with a haughty look.

"No comment," she eventually manages.

Morgan and I stare at her, inviting her with our eyeballs to say anything else, but she resolutely refuses.

Eventually, I fix my hair and make it out the door with another quick twirl for Catherine and the Annabelle. The inn's front steps happily clatter when I say goodbye. I don't understand her like Catherine does, but I think I'm starting to. She's happy.

Well, that makes two of us, girl, I think to myself. Because despite the thralls and the terror of their attack, I'm not nearly as scared as I probably should be.

I head up Sycamore toward Main and take a left, walking past Higher Grounds and the apothecary. A centaur sweeping the sidewalk across the street waves with a soft smile. Clutching my sweater, I push myself to walk a little faster, then remember I was supposed to let Shepherd know I'm on the way.

I'd sort of like to surprise him, but then I worry he won't be ready or he'll feel caught off guard, so I comm him with my watch. I've kept Dad's watch on, and it makes me happy to see tech from my old life and this new one together.

"Be there in a few minutes, okay?"

"I've been ready for hours, angel," comes the gruff response. "I'll meet you at the door."

Fuck me, why does that sound so hot? I'm practically jogging by the time I get to the end of Main and the road changes to gravel. It only turns into concrete again when I reach Shepherd's street. I stop at the very end and close my eyes, listening to the sounds of the dense upstate forest around me.

It's quiet, but it feels peaceful. Despite not having the crystal with me, I think about the wards. Unlike before, though, I can't see them or fly along them. I don't feel worried, but I don't feel present at their edges either. I stomp my foot in irritation and then head down the street toward Shepherd's house, the last one on the left.

True to his word, he's at the front door, both purple-gray hands holding the doorframe above his head. His handsome face splits into a big grin when I head up the crushed gravel pathway to his door. The beautiful flowers in his front yard sway happily, shimmying the closer I get to him.

Somehow, I understand this. The house thinks I look nice.

"Thank you," I laugh with a little curtsy toward the nearest shrub.

It shivers and shakes, almost like it's laughing with me.

"You make her happy," Shepherd murmurs from the door.

When I look up at him, his grin grows wider. White teeth poke out, and he nips his lower lip as his gaze falls to the ruffles at my shoulder, then down my body to my boots. His expression goes devilish when he reaches the boots.

"I wanna fuck you with those on, angel. What do you think about that?"

Heat floods my core, and cream soaks my panties as I look up at the big gargoyle in front of me.

"I think most dudes are into heels, but if combat boots are your thing, we can make that work."

Shepherd steps out of the doorway, down the one step leading to his home, and slips both hands into his jeans pockets.

"Little witch, I want you in every way I can get you. Boots, no boots, heels, lingerie. I'm a greedy male, and I need all of that."

"Good," I agree. "I want to show you all of that."

Shepherd gives me a heated look and reaches his hand out. I marvel again at his three fingers—three fingers! Reaching out, I stroke my way along his palm and trace each digit all the way to its pointed nail.

"Are you gonna scratch me with these?" I joke, pulling at one tip.

Shepherd laughs, grabs my wrist, and pulls me into his arms. "I'll be careful when I slide my fingers inside you, angel. I promise not to hurt you unless you want a little bit of pain."

I shudder. He shifts his wings, shuffling them behind himself until they're firmly tucked against his back again.

"I need to feed you, Thea," he growls, bending down to brush his lips against mine. "Come on." His hand trails to my fingertips, and he pulls me toward the door.

I'm an absolute slut for the view I get walking behind him. His jeans barely contain his round, bubbly ass. I wanna bite that ass. God, it's such a good ass. Thick, muscular thighs frame that perfect peach, tapering down to equally muscular calves. Per usual, he's shoeless. Long feet end in three claw-tipped toes just like his fingers.

"I don't think I've told you this," I say, staring at the muscles of his ass flex while he walks. "But you've got a great ass."

Shepherd growls, pulls me through the door, and then lifts

me against the wall before I can blink. He wraps my legs around his waist and brings his mouth to hover over mine.

"How dirty can you be with that mouth, little witch? What does looking at my ass do to you?"

I rock my hips against him, desperate for the friction I need to get off. I'm already overwhelmed by the raw sensuality this male exudes. I've never understood the phrase "sex on a stick," but god does he exemplify it.

"You're a needy little thing, I can tell," he breathes.

His lips play against mine, and I moan. He chuckles, a dark, monstrous noise that's lower than a human man could ever emit.

"Screw the food," I gasp. "Please, Shepherd."

"Screw the food?" His voice is teasing.

"Screw the food!" I shout.

His mouth claims mine before I start to beg in earnest. He thrusts his tongue between my lips, sucking at mine as our kiss grows wild. He kisses me like a man starved for touch, starved for affection.

One hand grips my throat. Shepherd's wings flare wide behind him. He embeds his wing claws in the wood above us with a deep *thunk*, and then I'm shielded from the world, lost to the darkness of the cocoon around us. There's only his mouth on mine, his lips nipping at me, his tongue teasing with soft darts and languid strokes. He's a masterful kisser, absolutely masterful.

He breaks the kiss but doesn't go far, his lips still lightly pressed to my mouth.

"Last chance, angel," he growls. "I should feed you, but I think you're right that maybe we need to do something about this need first. I'm giving you the choice, but I know what I want."

I suck his lower lip into my mouth, biting it harder than I

think a human would like. Hard enough that he shudders, then growls.

"Take me to our nest, please."

My request has him moving in moments. He never puts me down, although he does fold those glorious wings away. I whine when he tucks them behind his back, but he laughs.

"You can explore every inch of them in our nest, little witch."

"Good," I laugh. "Wings and horns and a tail are bound to make things more interesting."

"Oh, just wait till you see what I can do with them."

I can barely breathe around the heat of his insinuation.

Moments later, he swings the door open to his room and tosses me in the middle of the nest. I bounce once, then prop myself against the far wall to watch him.

He reaches for the buttons along his shoulder and carefully removes his shirt. Next, he unbuttons his pants, but much to my dismay, he doesn't take them off. Thankfully, his cock head peeks out of the top, swollen and leaking and ready for my mouth.

I shuffle forward across the nest.

"No, angel," Shepherd growls. "You first. Always you first."

"No," I reply playfully, reaching for his zipper to unveil the rest of him. "I haven't gotten a chance to explore yet, and I want to. Can you be patient for me, Shepherd?"

His needy growl deepens. I slide the zipper down, watching the fattest cock I've ever seen fall out of his pants. It's thick and veined with a more pointed head than a human would have. And fuck me, at its root, just below his abdomen, is an extra bit. It's a small, flat plate that pokes out parallel to his dick, the same width as the shaft but only a few inches long.

I stroke it softly, watching his erection bob to meet my hand. "What's this?"

Shepherd gasps. His wings flex and grip the walls as I continue my exploration of this extra bit.

"For you, to rub your clit," he moans. "It can remain outside or slide inside. Fuuuck." He runs both hands through his hair. "It . . . gods, Thea, you feel so good. It . . . it vibrates." His voice breaks as he stares at where I'm touching him.

A vibrating peen shelf? I can dig it. I can dig it a lot. "So, it's sensitive?"

I pull gently at it. His hips jerk in response, precum spilling from him to drip on the edge of the nest.

"Fuuuuck," he pants.

Both hands come to my hair, which he strokes lightly before fisting it in one hand.

I wonder just how wild I can make him before he takes over. Deciding to test my luck, I lean forward and lick the flat piece of skin, and it's more like a bone. I suck it into my mouth, and the effect is instantaneous. Shepherd's hips jerk, and his dick slaps underneath my chin. God, I could come just from playing with him. I've never made a man pant quite like this.

The hand in my hair tightens, a slight burn starting along my scalp.

I want Shepherd uncontrolled, lost to the pleasure.

Reaching down, I grip his cock and take him as far into my mouth as I can, hollowing my cheeks around his velvety smoothness.

The cry that leaves his lips sends a zing straight to my clit.

I suck harder, swirling my tongue around the tip before taking him deep again. Big as he is, I can only get a quarter of his dick in my throat, but I'm nothing if not an overachiever. I will learn to take more if it's the last thing I do.

Shepherd rolls his hips rhythmically, helping me to suck him off. When I look up, his eyes are narrowed, his gaze focused on my mouth and tongue.

"Bite, angel," he commands, sending a fresh wave of heat through me. "Gargoyles love pain. Bite."

I find that hard to fucking believe, but I give him a small test bite, dragging my teeth along the very tip of his cock. He jerks. Cum spills onto my tongue as he begins to fuck my mouth harder.

"Again, angel." His command is clear, so I bite harder.

And then I pick up a regular pace of biting and sucking as he goes almost breathless. I want to watch him explode.

He growls deeply and yanks at my scalp, and then I'm flipped onto my front and dragged to the edge of the bed, face down in the fucking nest.

"I don't come first, little witch. I've already told you that. I know you're determined to tease me and fuck if your mouth isn't perfect. But it'll always be you first, Thea."

I can barely speak around the nest fluff, but I don't need to because he lifts the back of my dress and growls. A sharp cracking sound fills the air, and then pain streaks across my ass cheek as I gasp.

"Did you just fucking spank me?" I shout into the plush fabric.

Shepherd pushes my face harder into the nest with a growl.

"Don't tell me you didn't like it."

He delivers another hard slap, his wing rough on my sensitive skin. But when I open my mouth to protest, the soft nibble of his teeth at my core has a plea falling from my lips instead.

"You're soaked, Thea," Shepherd growls.

Thick fingers prod at my core through my panties, and then he slips the wet fabric aside. As expected, he slides a finger inside me, and god, it's as big around as a human man's cock. At the same time, he closes his warm lips over my clit and tugs gently.

"Oh fuck!" I scream, overwhelmed by the sting on my ass, the finger in my pussy, and the lips on my clit. It's too much—I'm going to come just from this tease. But I don't want to come that fast. I want to draw out this pleasure as long as possible.

I struggle to scooch away from him. I'm not ready for this to be over. But there's a steady, gentle thrust from his finger and constant pressure from his lips. Before I know it, I fall into depthless pleasure, screaming for mercy as I squirt him right in the fucking face. It feels too good for me to even be embarrassed. Liquid floods from me and drips down my quivering thighs as Shepherd continues his slow taking of me.

He growls when I push forward on the bed, boneless from his attention.

"You running away from me, angel?"

I flip onto my back and shimmy out of his grip. He's kneeling at the edge of the nest, his horns dripping my cum, his mouth shiny. His eyes narrow as he climbs onto the bed and hovers over me, his cock bobbing against my stomach.

"I didn't want to come too fast," I gasp. "I'm not complaining, I just didn't want this to be over too soon."

Shepherd laughs and rolls us so I'm on top of him. He wriggles his hips, shifting his pants down. I hear them hit the floor, and then he reaches down to rip my soaked panties right off me. With a rock of his hips, he notches his dick between my soaked pussy lips.

"Mmm, better. Now tell me again why you think I can't drag a dozen orgasms out of you right now?"

"Errr." I look around the room for help that's not coming. "That's just . . . how it is?" I shrug. "I've never been able to orgasm a bunch of times."

This feels silly now that I'm saying it out loud. Maybe monsters have wild monkey sex and I'll be a huge disappointment. I sure as shit hope not, but . . .

Shepherd grabs me by the throat and pulls me down so my breasts brush his broad, naked chest. My dress is in the damn way, and all I want is to rub my nips on his big, cool body.

"None of those males were your mate. None of them took the time to learn about you and your needs. I'll do all of those things, little witch. And you won't leave this nest tonight without at least five orgasms, I promise you that. We'll start small."

"If you say so," I breathe.

There's not a chance in hell I'm gonna come five times, but I'll suspend disbelief. Because Shepherd looks really fucking sure of himself, based on the self-satisfied smirk tipping his lips upward.

"Glad we've settled that," he murmurs, tucking my hair over my shoulder. "Count for me, Thea."

"Count what?"

"Every time you come, you're gonna count for me, angel. One down, at least four to go."

Oh fuck.

CHAPTER TWENTY-FIVE
SHEPHERD

I don't know how human men fuck, but I'm sad for Thea not to have experienced amazing sex her whole life. That's in the past though, and I'm a male on a mission.

I reach up and tug the frilly purple straps off her delicate, freckled shoulders. Goosebumps follow my touch as her cheeks flush pinker.

"Any good male knows the key to seduction is not to go immediately to penetration," I whisper. "Which is why I'll touch every part of you but where you need me to."

"Nooo," she whines, rocking her hips, both thighs squeezing my stomach as she rides me.

Sweet honey drips from her pussy to coat my cock and soak my balls. She feels so fucking good. I'd love nothing more than to pull her inch by inch down onto me, to pleasure her until she's hoarse, but I need her to let go of past expectations first.

I spread my wings wide and grab a wrist in each claw. I pin them behind her back, and using that angle, I push her wrists so she falls forward. Her breasts hover close to my mouth, and I can't help my smile. They're so godsdamned beautiful, filling out the soft fabric of her dress.

I suck at first one, then the other through her dress, loving the way fresh wetness covers me. She's soaking wet for me. I've been worried about our size difference, but now I'm confident we'll fit. There's no way the gods would dangle her in front of me just for her not to fit me in every way. I'm *made* for her. For every part of her.

When I bite the underside of her breast, she jerks and moans, her head falling forward. Long pale hair slips over her shoulder. Reaching up, I pull the front of her dress down to expose her breasts to me. They're small but round, and she's braless.

Perfect. I don't need a single additional layer hiding her from my lips.

Growling, I roll my hips underneath her while I suck her bare, pebbled nipple hard between my lips.

Thea cries out.

With my other hand, I stroke the underside of her other breast, then play gently with it before pinching her. She jerks in my lap. I wonder if she's even aware she's thrusting faster and faster against me. She's getting herself off on my cock, even though she said she couldn't come again.

I'm about to let out a victorious laugh, but then she does come on a scream, her body locking up tight as her tummy muscles contract. I lick her nipples voraciously until she sags against my chest with a huffy groan.

"Two," she moans into my ear. "Lucky break. Three ain't happening."

Using my wing claws to drag her upright and bind her hands behind her back, I shift her with my hands so she rides along the top of my dick and not the underside.

And then I concentrate on directing energy to my cock. A faint vibration starts in my ridge, the flat piece that runs along the top of my dick.

Thea gasps. "I thought you were fucking kidding, oh my fuuu—"

She lets her head drop back as I guide her hips along me. I slide so easily through her soaked, puffy folds. Her thighs quiver under my fingers as I concentrate on rolling her hips. When she reaches the vibrations, I shove her back down my length.

I could come like this, I realize. I could come watching her take her pleasure from me.

She struggles against the grip I have with my wing claws, so I let her go. Her cheeks are bright red, her eyes closed, her pink lips open. I watch in fascination as she plants her hands on my abs and begins fucking my length in earnest. Her thin hips gyrate against mine as I concentrate on amping up the level of the vibration.

"Oh god, I'm com—" She screams my name as wetness spreads in our laps.

The sounds of our fucking are wet and sloppy. She's filling our nest with her scent. Now, even when she's not in it, I'll be able to scent her.

"What number's that?" I question with a smirk. "I've lost count."

She holds up three fingers, her chest heaving, her nipples swollen from my bite.

"I can't even imagine you doing that while inside me," she laughs, swaying over to one side, her head falling back against my wing. She strokes it absentmindedly, and my muscles clench.

Thea gives me a devious look. "I think it's time for me to tease you a little bit, Shepherd. What do you think?"

"Tease away," I growl. "We're almost to five, so I win."

She smirks and then shifts off me, turning to face my cock and straddling me again. I push the ruffles of her dress up over her ass. When she leans over, I'm presented with the perfect view of her sweet pussy. Liquid drips from her, coating her inner thighs. A soft nest of curls sits at the very top above her clit, and then it's all pink, pretty folds.

Reaching up, I rub up the back of both thighs, wanting to explore her from this angle.

I'm unprepared for her mouth around my cock again, one of her hands tugging softly at my balls.

I arch my back and grunt, but it seems to simply spur her on. She goes crazy on my dick, licking and sucking until I'm ready to explode.

Panting, I focus on the vision in front of me, sliding a finger into her pussy to stroke her while she sucks me off.

She can't take much of me into her mouth, but she sucks like a champ, going deeper with every bob of her head.

Orgasm overtakes me in a rush, and I fill her mouth with my seed as her channel contracts around my fingers. She screams around my cock, wetness flooding into my palm as I bellow loudly into the room.

Ecstasy blocks out sight and sound until all I can focus on is the way her mouth feels on me, the way her pussy is clamped and fluttering around my finger. I don't know how long I come for, but when that begins to fade, she keeps sucking, soft, playful swipes of her tongue threatening to start everything all over.

"One," she growls around a mouthful of cock.

"Four," I counter with a laugh, gripping her hips and pulling her backward until I can stick my tongue deep into her slit and lap at her.

Thea cries out and squirms, and then her stomach rumbles, and we both pause. When I move, she whips around to face me.

"Don't you dare tell me we're stopping for food," she teases, pointing one finger at me like I'm getting scolded. "I want that D and I want it now, Shepherd."

Laughing, I haul her underneath me and notch my cock at her entrance, teasing her with the tip.

"I'm so much bigger than you, angel. I need you good and wet to take this cock. Look at it, Thea."

She shifts up onto her elbows and looks down between us, huffing at the frills in the way of her view. She rips her dress up over her head, then watches my cock spear her folds.

"Everything in this damn nest is wet," she counters. "And you told me you weren't worried about fit."

I grip the base of my cock and guide it to her pussy, thrusting a little farther.

Thea cries out and falls back. My cock bobs and flexes. I want nothing more than to drive home, deep inside her right now. The feel of her wet skin against mine is almost too much. I could come without even entering her all the way. Her pussy flutters around my cockhead, pulling me deeper.

On matching groans, I push harder, then withdraw.

Thea whines, grabbing at my hips and rolling hers to meet me.

"I want it, please," she begs, watching me enter her and pull out over and over again.

I use my wings to push her thighs out wide and hold them there. Then, I slide farther and farther, until I'm sunk to the hilt inside her.

Thea pants, her breaths coming faster and faster. I think it's half from pleasure and half from the stretch of me. I still for a moment, then get an idea. Snaking my tail around, I slide it between her ass cheeks and play with her pucker, dipping my spade inside her. It's already soaked in our combined juices, sloppy and slick and ready for her.

She squirms and grunts. "Anal on the first night? Are you serious?"

Chuckling, I curl the sides of my spade so they form a cone and push into her just enough to tease. Thea cries out, and then I slide my dick out of her and back in. I keep it slow. She's tense underneath me.

But as her muscles relax and go limber, I pick up the pace, notching my hips against hers as she grips my cock hard.

I use my spade to play with her ass, and then my mate comes on a scream I'm sure my neighbors can hear. She screams over and over, squirting my cock with her release as she writhes underneath me, clutching at the sheets. Watching her like this sends me over the edge, and I match her sound with my own, thanking the gods who made her for me in my head as I fuck her through a soul-altering orgasm.

Pleasure eventually recedes, and I remove my spade carefully from her ass. I'm not ready to leave her heat though, so I roll gently and pull her on top of me. Thea's coated in a fine sheen of sweat, and we're both covered in cum and sticky release.

"Never would have thought anal without lube was a thing I wanted," she grunts, her face buried in my neck.

"Monsters don't lube," I laugh. "I only know what that is because of the movies. We don't need lube because our precum functions in that way."

She gives me a thumbs-up that makes me laugh even harder.

"You are goofy and perfect. You know that?"

Thea lets out something between a groan and a whimper. I smile and stroke her cheek, bringing my lips close to her ear.

"Time for food, sweet witch. Come on."

CHAPTER TWENTY-SIX
THEA

A week. It's been an amazing week of spending time with my sisters and Shepherd. I'm happier than I've ever been, and the ache in my chest from losing my folks slowly dissipates a little.

Sweating, I look at the view in front of me. Shepherd jogs along the wards, his wings tucked tightly to his back as he trails the Keeper. And then there's me, dripping impossible amounts of sweat as I try to keep up.

"None of this is fair," I shout up to them, wiping sweat away from my forehead. My hand comes away dripping. "You're both fucking huge. I've gotta stop."

Shepherd is the first to turn, giving me a cheeky grin as he jogs back and stops next to me. He takes my hand and guides me to a nearby log, gesturing for me to sit. Up ahead, the Keeper groans, but he turns around and lopes back toward us.

"Thea," he complains. "We all agreed we'd get you into fighting shape so you can patrol with Shepherd or me. And keep up," he tacks on, giving me an irritated look.

"You know what?" I snark, leaning back as I cross my arms

and look up at him. "I've realized why everyone thinks you're such an asshole."

The Keeper huffs, but an amused smile appears on his face. He crosses his arms and begins to tap one foot against the dirt.

"And why is that, Althea?"

I gesture at his outfit. It's always the same—dark turtleneck, black jeans, dark boots.

"You've got this whole 'fuck off, I'm cooler than you' vibe, and combine that with the insane amounts of hair gel holding those blond locks back. It's like someone shoved a whole broom handle up your ass, that's how tight you are."

Shepherd snorts, and the Keeper gives him a cross look, blond brows furrowing. His half smile doesn't disappear though.

"Who could even run in a turtleneck," I complain. "You're a psycho."

A week ago, the Keeper demanded I begin working with both him and Catherine. My ability to sense activity at the wards is growing. More importantly than that, I'm learning to understand him. His sense of humor is drier than the damn Sahara, but it's there. By now, I can understand what Miriam meant when she tried to explain him that day in the garden.

The Keeper drops down to his heels, leaning close to me. Long fingers, covered in dozens of light scars, tug at the edge of his turtleneck. He pulls it down, exposing a gorgeous black and red tattoo that covers his entire neck.

"Family tattoo," he explains. "Vampires of a certain level in our hierarchy are tattooed when we come of age. The tattoo serves a few functions, but the primary one is acting like a name tag to others."

I frown. "And you cover it why?"

The Keeper glances at Shepherd, then back at me.

"The Hearth is run by vampires, Althea. I feel if I let my tattoos show, it makes me appear to be closely aligned to the

Hearth, and I'm not. While they are our ruling body, I have publicly disagreed with many of their decisions over the years. I'm grateful they created the haven system, but that's where any similarity with my political views ends."

"I thought they came and helped after Wesley broke in," I say.

The Keeper blows out a frustrated breath and squints off into the distance before meeting my eyes again. The irritation in his gaze is enough to make me hunch my shoulders.

"The Hearth likes to say they came and helped after Wesley, but it was more like they came and lorded their power over me, Alo, and Shepherd. They left a small contingent of protectors here for about six months, and I think we all breathed a sigh of relief when they left. We avoid interacting with the Hearth at all costs."

"Do I still need to register?" My voice is soft as my focus moves to Shepherd. He's no longer smiling.

The Keeper purses his lips.

"Since you're staying, yes, all three of you will need to register."

We're all silent for a moment before I can gather my thoughts enough to keep talking.

"Will there be a target on my and my sisters' backs once the Hearth learns of us? Is that why you didn't want Moira to do anything on record?"

The Keeper nods his agreement. "Not a target, Althea, but focus to be sure. White and black witches are both rare. They will want a hand in your training, as well as Morgan's."

Ugh.

"And if I don't want that?"

"They will likely insist," he says softly. "Which is why I did not want to register you any sooner than necessary. It made more sense to allow your relationship with Shepherd to unfold naturally, without the Hearth's intervention. I would not wish them upon you both."

Something like kinship or maybe even friendship blooms in my chest. Despite his brusque manner, he's constantly making decisions to benefit Ever's residents. I've seen it over and over in the week I've been working with him.

Fuck, I like him. Morgan is gonna kill me.

And I'm desperate to lighten the mood.

"You know what?" I muse, reaching out to muss his blond hair.

He grumbles but cocks his head to the side to watch me. It's odd to be on the receiving end of his focus since he so often seems distracted.

I run my hands through his hair. He huffs and swats my hand away.

"Althea, do not put your hands on me. Your mate is—"

Shepherd chuckles. "Highly enjoying watching you get fussed over. Leave her be."

The Keeper's frown deepens, the scar bisecting his face pulling his lips to one side.

I use one of my hair ties to pull half of his hair into a teeny ponytail on top of his head.

"Voilá!" I gesture at the ponytail.

Shepherd snorts and doubles over with laughter.

"Listen," I continue as the Keeper rolls his eyes and stands. "This could help your image. It wouldn't kill you to come across a little more friendly."

He growls at me and yanks the hair tie out, snapping it back at me before jerking his head toward the dense forest behind us.

When he says nothing, I elbow him in the side. "Might do you some good to be a little more friendly to Mor while you're at it. Whaddya think?"

He rolls his eyes and takes off at a brisk jog toward the wards.

I look over at Shepherd, who wears a bemused look as he watches me.

"If I wasn't crazy about you already, this pretty much sealed the deal," he laughs. "Gods, the look on his face when you made that little ponytail."

"Looked good though, didn't it?" I say, taking off in the direction the Keeper disappeared in.

I sense Shepherd's gaze on me as I sprint into the forest.

"Looks great," he growls. "Good enough to chase later."

"If you can catch me," I mutter under my breath.

CHAPTER TWENTY-SEVEN
SHEPHERD

It's been a week since the attack, a blissful week. Probably the best week of my life. During the day, Thea spends time with her sisters. They heard back from their aunt Lou and sent her directions asking her to meet them in Ever. I know they're all looking forward to her arrival.

Sometimes Wren and Morgan join us for dinner, and sometimes they hang out with other friends they're making in town. The triplets work hard every day to find their magic, and they're picking it up quickly. Thea's been the fastest, but I think that's because she's spending a significant amount of time around the Keeper and me.

Under me. On top of me.

Gargoyles and white witches are meant to work together. She's growing more powerful by the minute.

I drop to my heels in front of the oven to peek at the lasagna inside. Iggy's perched on the kitchen island behind me.

"Is it almost done, Uncle Shepherd? I'm so hungry."

I hear his tail beat against the wood countertop and stifle a groan. He's asked me fifteen times in the last five minutes.

Alo comes into the kitchen and grabs the lashing tail.

I turn and give Iggy a look. "Ignatius Zion. What did I tell you?"

He rolls his eyes at me. "That the timer would go off when it's done, then it needs to sit for a little while."

"And what else," I urge.

He crosses his arms, matching my stance.

"We can't eat until the girls get here anyway."

"That's right," Alo and I say at the same time.

My pantry door pops open, and a shelf slides out with a bag of beef jerky on it.

Iggy lets out a war whoop and pushes off the island, flying to the pantry to grab the bag.

"You're lucky she likes you, kiddo," I warn.

My house has chased off people before. She can be prickly if she doesn't think you deserve to spend time inside her.

Iggy zooms around the kitchen, clutching the snacks to his chest as Alo and I set the table. When the doorbell rings, Alo lifts one brow.

"She still rings the doorbell? You doing your best in the nest, brother?"

Moments later, I hear the door swing wide, and Thea's soft footsteps pad from the front.

I give Alo a devilish look. "Oh yeah, I'd say I'm giving it my all in the nest, for sure."

Alo's smile deepens. It's broad and genuine, the best smile I've seen from him in years. "I'm happy for you," is all he says before Thea and her sisters enter the kitchen.

Thea throws herself into my arms, her mouth on mine before I can even tell her how stunning she looks in tight-ass jeans and a bright pink fuzzy sweater. Alo greets the girls, and then I hear heavier footsteps through the front door. That would be Ohken. Alo can handle greeting everyone. I need a moment with my girl.

With Thea still wrapped around me, I step out of the kitchen onto the side porch, pressing her up against the wall. I deepen our kiss, gripping her throat as her soft tongue tangles against mine. I suck at it, then I nip it, and then I press her harder into the wall as our kiss grows heated.

She breaks it when Iggy zooms out the back door and shoves his way between us, landing on Thea's shoulder. She grabs his tail and tosses it around her neck like a scarf but winks at me while she does it.

I'm in love. I'm in love with this goofy, brave, gorgeous woman.

It hits me like a ton of bricks as she steps back inside my home with my nephew perched on her shoulder. Pausing in the doorway, I look inside and find myself surprisingly over-whelmed with emotion. Alo's there, pouring Morgan a glass of wine. Ohken and Wren are sitting at the table talking. Physical tension is obvious between them. I'd bet my left wing some-thing is slowly building there.

Thea and I have been taking our relationship slowly, but I'd be a damned liar if I didn't admit that putting my claiming mark on her neck is my goal. We haven't spoken about it, but we're going to soon. The triplets have thrown themselves fully into learning, making friends, and integrating. It's time to talk to my girl about keeping her, permanently.

Stepping inside, I give Iggy a look. "Lasagna's coming out, Iggy. What happens next?"

He looks around my small kitchen, full of family and friends.

"We've gotta wait ten minutes, then we can dig in!" he shouts.

Everyone cheers, making the biggest possible deal out of his pronouncement.

An hour later, we've gorged ourselves on lasagna, and Iggy's passed out over Alo's shoulder from carb and excitement over-load. Thea's hand is on the back of my chair, and she's stroking the edges of my wings. It's driving me wild, and she knows it, but if I've learned anything about her in the past week, it's that she's an insane tease. She wasn't kidding about that.

Ohken smiles at the triplets, swirling mead in a glass. "I heard a rumbling that you've considered your long-term plans, but I haven't wanted to pry. Ever would certainly welcome three permanent residents."

"We're staying for the time being," Morgan hedges, playing at the edges of her napkin.

"Catherine told us we'd have to register with the Hearth," Wren offers. "That sounds intense."

Ohken nods, swirling mead in his glass. "Hearth sounds cozy and homey. They are anything but. You're right to consider all the factors before becoming permanent residents. Still, you three fit so well here." His eyes flick to Wren's. "It would be a shame for you to leave us."

Wren's gaze is firmly planted on Ohken. She looks serious. "Does anyone ever come and go, living in both worlds?"

"It doesn't work that well," I offer gently. "Others have tried it. Spending a day in the human world is equivalent to almost a month here. We've had some residents do it, but it's hard with a family."

Thea squeezes my wing. I take it in a comforting way, but now that this has been brought up, we'll need to talk it through. It sounds like the Hectors are still considering their plans, even though Thea shared with me they'd all agreed to stay for a while.

I just hope she'll decide that the benefits—chief of those being me—are enough to get her to remain in Ever.

CHAPTER TWENTY-EIGHT
THEA

I expect dinner to feel somber after Ohken asks what our long-term plans are. The reality is that we've discussed it at length. None of us would miss our jobs, and once Lou gets our invitation, I know she'll want to come to Ever.

Still, we haven't said we'll stay permanently. It's always been a "we'll stay for the time being" sort of answer.

When I think about what we're giving up and what we're gaining, the answer is obvious. I want to stay here. This world feels like home to me more than New York does. The human world isn't nearly as appealing since losing our folks.

Still, it feels like an all-or-nothing situation. We either all agree to stay or go. I can't imagine staying if they choose not to. But when I think about my sisters leaving Ever, I know I'd worry about them endlessly. I want them to *want* to be here. So far, they do. Honestly, Wren is easy; she'll stay for sure. Morgan is our sticking point. She and the Keeper are barely on speaking terms, and she's struggling the most with her magic. Wren and I are worried she won't be happy here, but I have to believe it'll work out in the end.

When I look to my left, Shepherd's listening to the conversation, but there's a tic in his square, angular jaw. I want to lick that muscle and then bite my way down his neck to his shoulder. His shoulders are so sensitive. Almost all of him is crazy sensitive, and now I'm squirming in my seat because I'm ready for our nest.

Our nest.

"Earth to Thea!" Wren laughs as she snaps her fingers in front of my face.

I meet Ohken's whiskey eyes across the table. He gives me a knowing look and then stands. Jesus, he takes up almost the entire kitchen, he's so big.

"I'm heading home. Wren, I'll see you in the garden in the morning?"

"Naturally," she jokes, biting her lower lip.

She's stopped choking to death when he shows up, but she's so obviously attracted to him, I have to resist the urge to laugh.

Ohken smirks and walks out of the kitchen. Morgan looks over at Alo but jerks her head toward us. "Should we give these crazy kids some space and head back to the Annabelle?"

Alo smiles softly, looking at his brother. I think it's the first time I've ever seen him smile for real. And it is fucking glorious. A smile transforms his surly face, and for the first time, I see similarities between them. Shepherd is always smiling.

Alo shifts Iggy higher up his muscular shoulder and stands carefully, pulling Morgan's chair out for her.

She gives him a thoughtful smile. "Smiling looks good on you, Alo. Maybe you should direct that toward Miriam one of these days, whaddya think?"

He groans. "You too? Why don't you pay attention to your own love life, Ms. Hector?" He gives her a snarky look, but his tone is playful.

"Oh, I think you know why," she says. "I got the raw end of the stick when the gods were handing out monster mates."

I suddenly feel defensive of the Keeper. Over this past week,

I've spent a lot of time with him, and I think I'm starting to understand him on a deeper level. The only thing he cares about is keeping everyone safe, even at the cost of his happiness and safety. He is ready at all points in time to sacrifice for this town. The weight of it is heavy on his shoulders all the time.

It's a weight I find myself wanting to help with.

I don't say anything though, because I don't want to pressure Morgan.

Alo nods toward the door. I hug my sisters and then they crowd around Shepherd and hug him too. Seeing him with them warms my heart. It feels so fucking right.

We walk them to the door together, holding onto one another as we wave goodbye to our family. The moment they turn from us, Shepherd pulls me back inside and into his arms. Pressing me to the wall, he kisses me like he's ravenous, like it wasn't a few hours ago he had his mouth on mine. I groan at the first swipe of his talented tongue.

"Mine," he gruffs. "You're mine, Thea."

~

The following day, I'm grabbing a late afternoon pick-me-up from Higher Grounds when the Keeper walks in with a male I haven't seen yet. He towers over the Keeper, all harsh edges and mountain man vibe. I haven't met any of the shifters in town yet, but I'd bet my ass he is one. He just has that I'm-probably-a-wolf vibe. Maybe it's the sharp teeth poking out from behind thin lips. Maybe it's the way his forearms are coated in soft-looking, dark hair.

Or maybe it's just the way he looks at me and grins like one of those velociraptors in Jurassic Park who was distracting the prey so the others could pounce.

I clear my throat. I've learned a lot about monsters in the

short time we've been here. I give the probably-werewolf a big grin and a sarcastic bow.

"Let me guess," I offer when he and the Keeper block my path. "Shifter. Am I right?"

The male laughs, a deep rumble that hits me right in the gut. His voice is impossibly low when he speaks and holds out his hand.

"Richard. And yes, you're right. I run the pack here in Ever. We're not downtown too often, we live in the forest to the north."

The Keeper ignores our pleasantries, although he does wait until Richard's done shaking my hand before he says anything.

After a tense, quiet moment, he turns to me. "I've got a theory about the wards, Althea. I need your help to test it. Come with us?"

It's phrased like a question, but if I've learned anything about him in the last week, it's that nothing he says is optional. His asking for help is merely a formality. Phrasing it like a question seems like a holdover from his personality before becoming the Keeper.

I sigh and agree, following the males out of Higher Grounds, heading toward a big pickup parked on the street.

"What part is Richard playing in this adventure?" I ask as we get into the car. The Keeper hops into the driver's seat, his head almost touching the ceiling. Richard, on the other hand, is hunched over, his dark salt-and-pepper waves brushing the top of the truck's interior.

I laugh when he lays the seat all the way flat so he can spread out a bit.

"Don't know why I couldn't meet you at the gas station," he grumbles.

I resist the urge to reach out and scratch behind his ears to see if that might make him happy.

Sipping at my coffee, I stare out at Main Street as the Keeper pulls the truck out of its spot and heads toward Shepherd's gas station.

He looks at me in the rearview. "Richard and his pack are my backup. It's never wise to face thralls on your own."

My blood chills. "We're facing thralls? Is Shepherd coming?"

If he's not, I wish I could call him and ask him to. Everything related to the wards involves him, typically.

"I've sent him on a separate errand related to this," the Keeper says cryptically, eyes focused on the road.

"Okay, well then, do you want to fill me in on your theory?" I prompt. I'm not fussed by the brusque way he talks anymore, but the idea of coming face-to-face with thralls is concerning. I don't feel ready in the slightest.

He meets my eyes in the rearview again. "Most thralls act independently, wandering alone and simply attracted to the closest haven's wards. Ward energy is the specific thing that pulls them to us. Where things get tricky is thralls under the sigil of someone. Any monster willing to use dark magic can claim a thrall. That's why we looked for the sigil on the two who attacked before." He sighs and focuses on the road. "Aimless thralls drawn to Ever aren't a big deal, but sigiled thralls under focused direction can be a problem. The only way to stop them is to find who's controlling them and take them down."

"You didn't recognize the sigil, though, right?"

The Keeper shakes his head. "I didn't. But I still have a theory that Wesley is somehow behind this, perhaps even working with others to focus on Ever. I need to capture more thralls and try to verify that."

Dark eyes come to mine again before flicking back to the road.

"Thralls are drawn to ward power, and white witch power functions much like ward power does. I have a hunch that if I take you to the ward, the thralls will be drawn to you."

"Cool, cool," I mumble. "So, I'm the bait. Do I have that right?"

"Something like that," Richard confirms, smiling over his shoulder at me.

That devious smile does nothing to chill my nerves out. If anything, they're amping up higher the farther we get from downtown.

"So, how are we doing this?" I ask as we wind our way through the forest.

The Keeper doesn't bother to look at me this time. "We're taking you outside the wards, Althea."

My heart freezes in my chest. Neither of the males in the front seem the least bit worried about this.

"Is that safe? And won't I lose a ton of time here in Ever?!" I hate that my voice goes tiny and squeaky. It's just that I've seen the thralls up close now.

"We need to know," the Keeper murmurs. "We won't go far from the wards, so you'll still be on Ever time. We'll go just far enough to draw them out if they're in the area."

Richard turns in his seat, as much as he can being so big. "Wesley proudly stamped his sigil on every one of his thralls. Even though you didn't see his sigil on the two who attacked, everything else about the attack reeks of Wesley. That's why we have to know. If it's Wesley, we'll have to get the Hearth involved."

"What if it's not Wesley?"

"That would be better." The Keeper states the obvious. When I give him side-eye in the rearview mirror, he rolls his eyes, but the hint of a smile curves his lips up. "It would be better to deal with almost anyone but Wesley."

"Was that so hard?" I joke. "To give me a full explanation rather than half of one?"

The Keeper scowls.

Richard laughs. "I like you. Please stick around. You give the

Keeper a run for his money, which I'm highly convinced he needs."

"You should meet Morgan then," I offer, catching the Keeper's gaze again.

Every time I bring up Morgan, he scowls and huffs and gets extremely surly. He gets very *busy* with other things when I bring her up. I love needling him.

When nobody offers any further info, I focus out the window. "What, precisely, do you need me to do? Are we going to step outside the wards and start whistling or what?"

"*You'll* step just outside," the Keeper says. "Richard and I will watch and wait for the right moment to capture several at once if we can."

"Wait, wait, wait," I shriek. "You're sending me outside the wards alone? You're not coming?"

"You'll be close enough for us to grab you, Thea," Richard offers. "We would never let you get hurt, I promise. Shepherd would have my head if I did."

"Speaking of which, he should be here," I demand.

We round a corner, and the gas station comes into view. I want Shepherd. I need him here for this. I'm more uncomfortable by the moment.

The Keeper parks and exits, holding my door open. I'm too wound up by this new revelation to thank him for doing something so uncharacteristic.

Richard gets out, the car's suspension groaning under the relief of his weight lifting off it. He rounds the front with graceful, powerful steps.

"Thea, you don't have to do this. We would never force you to. But white witches are protectors of havens. Shit, Hel didn't even have a Keeper for a short time, and a white witch stood in as Keeper until one could be identified. We trust you to help us protect this place, but you're not obligated to do so."

The Keeper's lips are pursed, his arms crossed over his broad chest, but he nods in agreement.

I think about it for a moment, setting my coffee in the truck's center console cup holder.

"I'll do it, but I'm calling Shepherd. It doesn't seem right to do this without him."

"Of course," the Keeper croons.

I lift my wrist and speak Shepherd's name into the comm watch. He doesn't pick up, so I leave a message explaining what we're about to do.

Five awkward minutes later, he hasn't called back.

"Fuck it," I mutter. "Let's just get this over with."

"It'll be fine, Althea," the Keeper says. "Come on. I wouldn't do this if I thought we couldn't keep you safe, I promise."

I'm sure he's trying to make me feel better, but all I can think of is the way the thralls hissed in the street when they attacked. And I'm supposed to go outside town where they'll be drawn right to me? Yeah, okay, sounds like absolute insanity.

Still, the side of my personality that was always proud to be a detective and protect people rears her ugly head, reminding me who I am, reminding me that my father wouldn't have hesitated to do this. Protecting people is something that was instilled into me at a very young age.

I finger his watch as I follow Richard and the Keeper to the edge of the ward. It seems to shimmer and move a little when I get close. I reach out to touch the opaque surface, but it feels hard to me, strong. I know I'll be able to step through it easily since I'm an Ever resident. Instead, I focus on shoring up the ward with my power. It's something the Keeper's had me working on all week, and I'm able to do it for short periods.

I shove against the ward again, but this time it hardens to a solid film and I can't get through.

Good job, me.

"Your power is growing, Thea," the Keeper says.

Richard tacks on his own commentary. "It'll be good to have

a white witch living permanently in Ever."

I snort because I deflect awkward moments with humor. "Just don't let anything happen to me because I'd hate to be dead or enthralled, and I'd really miss gargoyle dick. It's really good dick. Neither of you seems to be into dick, but you can take my word for it."

Richard bursts into laughter, and the Keeper purses his lips together and looks away. I see his shoulders move though.

Gotcha, motherfucker. My first official laugh pulled from the stoic male. I hope it's the first of many.

The Keeper gets serious.

"Althea. The only reason I am not joining you outside is because my magic acts as a repellent to thralls. If I'm there, they won't come. Richard is going to join you outside, but he'll trail behind you and out of sight. Focus on dropping the ward enough to allow both of you through. Do that now."

I gulp. Am I really about to do this?

Richard gives me a reassuring look.

I focus on letting the ward go filmy again, pressing my hand to it. Richard and I are both able to sneak through. He gives me a look and then jogs off into the forest in one direction. It's a weird feeling to be outside the protective barrier. The forest on this side is frigid and wintry.

"Walk in the opposite direction, Althea," comes the Keeper's voice.

When I look through the ward, he's right there, close enough to touch me. My sense of the ward is the same out here as it is inside. Deep in my mind, I picture a huge dome covering all of Ever. It feels thick and strong.

A twig cracks somewhere off to my right, but I start walking, trailing my fingertips along the ward to center myself. The Keeper paces quietly to my left, sticking close. I know Richard is somewhere behind me, but I can't hear or see him. My heartbeat is a steady gallop in my ears. God, I'm desperate for Shepherd to be here. My whole body is one tense muscle. This feels so fucking unsafe.

When I hear a low growl ahead, echoed by a second growl to my right, I know the thralls are close. It's almost like my magic can sense it. They're drawn to me, and I'm prey in their line of sight.

"I'm coming back in," I snap, pressing my hand to the ward. "I can hear them, Keeper."

"Wait," he hisses. "Draw them out, Thea. Please, give it another moment. Richard will not allow them to hurt you."

I'm beginning to understand what fish in a sea of sharks feel like. All around me, the forest is ominous and dark. Another branch breaks in the distance, and sudden movement ahead in the shadows catches my attention. It's so quick, I can barely track it with my eyes.

Oh god, I can't die here today. I'm in love with Shepherd, and I want to have a very long life to love him.

When an ungodly screech rings through the trees, I turn and press both hands to the wards, pushing my way through despite the Keeper's insistence. He reaches for me, sensing my terror.

Except the wards don't budge, and horror turns my skin to ice as my eyes flick to the Keeper's. His expression goes from shocked to worried, and he throws himself against the ward with a furious look.

"Focus, Althea," he snaps, his tone urgent. "Let the wards down enough to come through."

A roar shakes the ground under my feet, and a crashing sound raises the hair on my nape. I'd scream, but I'm far too fucking terrified. The rising sense that I'm being hunted overtakes everything else, and I start pounding on the wards, trying to beat my way through.

But they won't budge.

Not an inch.

I'm trapped outside Ever.

CHAPTER TWENTY-NINE
SHEPHERD

I pull myself out of the mermaid lagoon, shaking water out of my hair. I've spent the last two hours examining the wards underwater with the mermaids' help. Usually, I don't mind the monthly chore because while it's time-consuming, the mermaids are hella funny. They tell me jokes nonstop, and it makes the time pass.

But today, their jokes just make me think of my girl and how she's the funniest person I know. We're getting together for dinner, and I'm going to bring up the claiming topic. I'm so ready, I'm practically vibrating with the need to touch her.

I stalk naked across the rocky beach and grab my comm watch. There's a flashing message. I'll bet it's from her.

Grinning, I command the watch to play the message.

My blood freezes when I catch her tense tone. "Hey, it's me. The Keeper asked for my help with the wards up by your station today. He wants to capture a thrall and see if we can figure out if there's a Wesley connection or not. Richard's here too. I assume you know him? Anyhow, I'd feel better if you were here. Call me back?"

My heart sinks into my gut, churning as I grab my pants and

push off the rocks, bulleting up into the sky. She sent the message almost ten minutes ago. She sounded nervous. If I know anything about Thea in the few weeks since we've been together, it's that she rarely lets anyone see her nerves. That she's showing me without making a joke means it's serious.

I pump my wings hard, flying above the clouds to grab one of the cool breezes that runs near the ceiling of the wards. I use it to spin my way through the thinner air and move faster. I've got to get to her. I don't know how I know something's wrong, but it is.

I direct the watch to comm her, but she comes up with a red out-of-range message.

Oh fuck. That means she's outside the wards.

I've never felt terror like this before. If she goes too far outside the ward, she'll be back on human time and I'll lose her for godsdamned *months*.

Roaring, I skim the edges of the ward ceiling, using aerodynamics to my benefit as I bypass the forest and rush for my station. When I get close enough, I don't immediately see anyone. There's not a fucking sound. I land with a thud, looking around. There's a pickup and footprints. Richard's.

A faint noise echoes along the ward, and its translucent surface shimmers like a wave rippling from somewhere to my left.

I break into a run, sprinting along the shiny surface until I see thralls. I can't even count how many there are, but they're throwing themselves up against the ward, shaking its surface.

Fuck, oh fuck. Where's Thea? And where the fuck are Richard and the godsdamned Keeper? It's then I see them, they're all outside the ward, surrounded by a circle of thralls. That circle gets smaller by the minute.

I bellow from inside the wards, pushing at the pliable surface to shove my way out and get to her. The protective barrier doesn't move like it usually does. I can't push my way out.

"Thea!" I scream for my mate.

Richard and the Keeper move slightly, and I can see her body tucked tightly between theirs. She's pressed flat between them, staring in horror at the circle of thralls.

I bang my fists against the wards, but they don't let down. This has never happened, but it's got to be related to her power. I look up, and my eyes meet my mate's. Hers flutter in relief, and she visibly sags. The wards make a snapping sound, and I fall through and onto my knees.

Barreling through a group of thralls, I slice and stab with my wings. They're close to her, too fucking close. If they manage to bite her, she'll become enthralled too.

Bodies hit the wards and bounce off as I shove my way through the group. In front of me, Thea shouts. The Keeper and Richard are both fighting. I rip a thrall in half and push off the ground, stabbing at two more who leap for her at the same time.

The pounding of footsteps thunders in the air, and the trees burst open. It's the rest of Richard's pack. They attack the thralls, even as some dart away into the dark forest to escape the shifters.

All I can think about is Thea and how she's in danger. White witch power is just as enchanting to thralls as the ward themselves. I've got to get her the fuck out of here.

Richard grunts, knocked to the side by a monster with a dragon-like face. My mate is exposed, her back pressed against the Keeper's as she turns to look at me. Time slows as she blinks once, holding her hands protectively in front of her face because she doesn't have a fucking weapon.

But she has me, and I will always be the weapon between my mate and the darkness.

I leap, knocking into both her and the Keeper. He goes flying, but she's in my arms, wrapping her body around mine. As soon as I've got her, I rocket up into the sky, trying to pull her as far from the thralls as I can.

"Wait!" Thea shouts. "The Keeper and Richard!"

Fuck them. I'm in such a rage because she was in danger that I don't stop, barreling through the ward. But instead of sailing through, we hit the ward with a thud and begin to slide down its milky surface. I beat my wings hard to stop our fall. The sounds of fighting echo up along the ward, amplified by its dome-like shape.

"I think I reinforced it. Fuck I can't focus on this damn power. Give me a sec and I can let us through," Thea says, her tone breathless. "God, can we help the Ke—"

"No," I snarl. "He can take care of his godsdamned self."

We're high above the fight, but a flying thrall could attack us. I glance around for anything threatening her up here, but there's nothing. Just a dark, ominous forest. Just the human world.

I can't ever let her go. If I thought I could, I was a fool. There's no fucking way.

Thea reaches out and places her hand on the ward, closing her eyes. It shimmers again, her hand slipping through. I press immediately through it, breathing in a sigh of relief when we get fully inside the barrier.

My nature demands I neutralize the threat and protect my mate. Thea's safe, but I don't feel better until I land in front of the gas station with her in my arms. Immediately, I whip my wings around her. It's not just intimate for gargoyles to do this, it's a protective stance. And right now, I need to know she's in one piece. I need to examine every inch of her. If a fucking thrall even managed to nick her with its teeth. . .

"Help them, please," she begs, pointing behind me where thralls continue to hit the ward.

Growling, I pull her close. "They can deal on their own. They took you out there. Your message sounded scared, Thea." My voice is rising, and I don't want to yell at her, but I'm so fucking amped up, even now.

Thea wraps her arms around my neck and nudges the tip of my nose with hers. "I'm fine. It was scary, but I'm fine. Please, help them."

Something between a bark and a warning yip comes out of my mouth when I look over her shoulder, parting my wings enough to see the fight is slowing. One thrall is backed against the ward, but three shifters advance on it and rip it to shreds. The Keeper and Richard, that fucker, stand just outside, looking through the opaque ward at us.

"They're done, mate," I murmur, opening my wings.

She shimmies out of my arms and looks around my body. The Keeper stands there, eyeing her. He lifts a fist and knocks at the ward like he's knocking on the front door.

Thea jogs toward him with a laugh—a laugh!—and presses her hand to the barrier as I stalk right behind her. The moment she touches it, it shimmers and her hand moves through easily.

The Keeper salutes her with a wry grin and steps through.

The second he's through, I grab him by the collar and yank him off his feet, snarling in his face. He looks unhurt.

I plan to change that status immediately.

"Is this why you sent me to the grotto today, specifically? So you could dangle my mate in front of the thralls and risk her life?" I'm screaming at one of my oldest friends, but one of his brows inches upward.

He nods. "I knew you'd say no. I was there. Richard's entire pack was there. Put me down, Shepherd."

"I should have been here," I shout. "If she'd been hurt—"

"She wasn't," the Keeper reiterates, gesturing to Thea, who stands patiently by my side.

"She was afraid," I growl. "You scared her by even asking. She wanted me to be here, and you should have waited."

Richard and his second stride through the wards then, dragging parts of thrall bodies. Thea must have let the barrier down enough to allow it.

Richard tosses one down at my feet. "Look at that, Shepherd, that sigil."

I set the Keeper down and drop to one knee, looking at the severed leg at my feet. And there it fucking is. Wesley's sigil. Something I haven't seen in almost four decades.

"I knew it," the Keeper hisses. "I knew it was that fucking asshole. So he must be working with someone. All these thralls were focused and working as a cohesive group."

"Holy shit," Thea deadpans. "You cuss?"

The Keeper narrows his eyes at her but stops at a growl from me. I'm fucking pissed. It was a breach of trust not to include me in this.

I stand and wrap one arm around my mate, giving Richard and the fucking Keeper a look. "You two can clean this up. Consider Thea and me out of pocket for the rest of the night. You've lost my trust, pulling this bullshit. Might want to think about how to earn it back." I look down at the thrall. "Something tells me you're gonna need my help."

The Keeper nods. "I'll report it to the Hearth of course. It'll go on my record, Shepherd. This decision was not without consequence."

I grit my teeth about that. All havens hate involving the Hearth unless they have to. But two attacks in just as many weeks? And now Wesley's back? The Hearth has to know.

But the Keeper and Richard can deal with that. Right now, I'm taking my mate back to my place. I'm going to fuck her long and hard in our nest and then stuff her full of snacks. And then I'm going to ask her to stay with me because if I know one thing for sure, it's that I'm not willing to let go of Thea Hector. Not now, not ever.

~

T he flight back to my house is quiet. Thea's lost in thought. My tail is curled around her waist, and her legs are intertwined with mine. Both of my arms are around her, my face buried in her hair.

I love you, I think to myself. *And I'm telling you the minute we get home.*

When I land on my walkway, the cottage's front windows slam open and shut excitedly.

Thea takes a few steps forward and pats the front door. "Good to see you too, friend."

My heart clenches in my chest at the way the cottage responds to her.

Like she belongs here.

I flip her gently around and press her to the front door with my body. My wings come up over us, partially cocooning us. I leave just enough light to see the tender expression on her face.

"I love you," I whisper. "I know it's soon, but I'm so deep, Thea. Tonight scared the shit out of me."

Tears fill her gorgeous blue eyes. I lift my hand to wipe them gently away when they begin to spill down her cheeks. She handled tonight with remarkable bravery, considering the danger she was in. A true white witch. A protector, just like her father.

I have to wonder if there will be emotional fallout from it though. It sounds like things didn't exactly go according to plan, and I want to kill Richard and the Keeper a little.

Thea reaches for me, hopping up into my arms. I sigh with relief as her legs go around my waist.

Her lips come to mine. "Take me to our nest, mate. Show me how much you love me." Her tone is demanding, almost bossy.

My girl wants to play. She wants to make me work to hear those words back.

I can do that.

Swinging the door in, I stride through. The house shuts it herself, the lock quietly slipping into place as I carry my mate through the living room and up the stairs at the back. When we make it to the nest, I toss her in, relishing the way her tits bounce under her shirt.

Thea kicks her shoes off and tosses them out of the nest. I grab her ankle and pull her to the very edge, using the rounded cushion to prop her hips higher up. Unzipping her jeans, I pull them off her thighs, grinning when it turns out she's not wearing underwear.

"Did you have big plans for our date tonight, angel?" I bend down and press my nose to her mound, breathing in her woodsy, natural scent.

"Before I got dragged out of the wards like bait, I thought I might tease my big, gargoyle mate a little bit."

"Yeah? Tell me more," I demand, rubbing my horns along her thighs. Pleasure streaks along them.

Thea shudders and rocks her hips, bringing her pussy close to my mouth. She deserves teasing, all the teasing.

My tail lashes from side to side as I watch and wait. Thea reaches down and grabs it, bringing my spade to her mouth. She licks up the middle of it. I grunt at the pleasure that pops down my spine. My horns are throbbing with the need to fuck her. She sucks at the tip of my tail, nipping playfully.

"I want you to tie me up, Shepherd," she demands. Blunt teeth close on my tail spade and tug.

A needy whine leaves my mouth.

"Do you want to see what I'm doing to you, angel? Or should it be a surprise?"

Thea props herself up on her elbows and grins. "Surprise for two hundred, please."

Thank god we get the occasional *Jeopardy* rerun in from the outside or I'd never know that reference.

The door to my closet swings open, and a drawer pops out. I

yank my tail out of my mate's hand and drag it down her body as I turn to the closet, grabbing a length of rope and a blindfold. I rub the pointed tip over her clit, teasing along the outer edges of her pussy before turning and depositing my tools on the edge of the nest.

"On your stomach."

She obeys, ripping her shirt off and flipping over, her ass propped up perfectly by the raised edge of the nest, toes hovering above the ground. She looks over her shoulder with a big grin. "I love you too, you know." She waggles her ass as my knees buckle under the weight of her words.

She loves me.

"Say it again," I command, reaching out to grip her ass cheeks in my hand.

"I love you . . . fuuuuck," she cries out as I lick a strip up her slit, all the way to that sweet pucker.

I haven't had her back there yet, not with my cock. I want that tonight, but I need to get her ready.

I suck and nip along both labia, circling her clit with my tongue in rhythmic, smooth moves until she's thrusting her hips back, trying to get me right where she wants me.

Her cries grow louder, her breathing stuttered. But right before she can come, I pull back and grab her hands, pressing them to her lower back. Thea whines. I reach over and grab a length of pliable rope. Wrapping it around her wrists, I tie them at her lower back, admiring the way the muscles of her back stretch and flex under smooth, soft skin.

I lean over her and nip at her beautiful shoulders and down the center of her back. Thea moans softly, stepping up onto her tiptoes to press her ass right against my cock. She whines at finding it still hidden behind my pants. I'm hard for her, though; I'm always hard for her.

"You want that big, monster cock, don't you . . ." I purr into her ear, running both hands up the backs of her legs.

When she whines and squirms, I laugh devilishly.

"Tell me you'll never put yourself at risk like that again, angel, because if you do, I'll tan this ass with my belt until you can't sit."

"God!" Thea cries out. "I promise I'll at least warn you better next ti—ouch!"

My hand slaps her ass hard enough to leave a red mark. My dick throbs in my pants at seeing my handprint on her smooth skin.

"Not good enough, mate," I murmur. "Try again."

My second slap causes her to jerk against the side of the bed. Her breathing is quick and shallow as she squirms to get away from me.

"Never again," she shouts. "I promise!"

My third and fourth spanks have her gasping for relief. Even so, her slit drips that sweet honey for me. I massage her skin before landing a fifth slap on the side of her ass. God, I'm so hot from this, I can barely stand it.

Shoving my pants down to my ankles, I grip my cock and slide it between her thighs, coating myself in slick wetness.

"Shepherd, please," Thea whines. Her head is turned to the side, her cheeks red.

I pull my cock out from between her thighs and slap her ass with it. Then I tuck it between those pretty ass cheeks and rub, loving the way my dark length looks next to her skin.

"Mate," she groans. "Please."

"Please what?" I grunt out, shoving my cock back between her thighs so I can rub it on her swollen clit.

"Don't make me wait, please." She's breathless and she's right.

I was going to torture and edge her for scaring the shit out of me tonight, but it turns out all I want is to claim her and cover her with my scent. I want to take her inside the cocoon of my wings, the only sound the sloppy fucking between us.

I don't untie her though, because she was still naughty. Grabbing her carefully by the wrists, I spin her and cradle her in my wings. She wriggles happily, propping one foot on the edge of the nest, opening herself to me.

"This is all yours, Shepherd," she whispers. "I want you to claim me. I want to stay. I know it's soon too, but it's all I want."

Those are the words I've been dying to hear since I met her, but right now, I can't seem to summon the appropriate response.

"Are you sure?" I ask it on a growl, my cock notched at the entrance to her pussy.

I don't wait for an answer as I jerk my hips and sink deep inside her. Her breasts bounce, and she gasps, her head falling back against my wings.

"Yes," she moans. "Absolutely sure."

"Good," I snarl, picking up a steady pace that has her pussy clenching around me. "I'll bite you and you'll bite me, understand?"

She grunts as my hips piston steadily but slowly between her thighs. "I have to bite you?"

I nod and grin, watching my cock disappear inside her. "Wherever you want, angel. Neck and shoulder are the most common."

"Where do you want me to bite you?" she cries out, her stomach muscles clenching with exertion.

"Wherever feels right. I want you to choose," I growl, moving my wings so her body is pressed against mine.

The hard points of her nipples dig into my chest, her eyes glittering in the low light. Thea's body jerks with every thrust of my hips. She gives me a cocky smile, then lets her head fall back against the barrier of my wings.

"I'm yours," she whispers, tits bouncing as my thrusts grow harder.

A vein throbs in the side of her neck. Leaning forward, I kiss it, then pull her skin with my teeth. Thea whines and grinds her hips against mine, panting. I move to another spot, kissing and biting my way down her neck to the hollow at the base of her throat. Her skin pebbles under my touch, her cries growing louder as we edge toward relief.

I'm losing control of my ability to stay steady. I'm about to claim her, and I want it to be wild. Unleashing, I growl and bite my way along her shoulder and collarbone to the spot where it meets her delicate neck.

Thea's a writhing, begging mess in my arms. I kiss her neck once, then I bare my fangs and sink them deep into the muscle. She bucks and screams, and then that scream morphs into a wail of pleasure as ecstasy hits us both. Waves of pleasure batter me until all I can see are stars and all I can taste is her sweet blood on my tongue.

Suddenly, I hate that I can't feel her hands on me. Reaching around her back, I slice the rope. Her arms come to my chest, scratching and clawing. I feel like a godsdamned caveman right now, biting her. It's so primal, so hot. Groaning, I come again, lining her pussy with my seed.

Releasing the bite, I howl out my pleasure. Thea's scream matches mine as she squirts, her release covering my cock and sliding sticky and wet down my balls. I'm dripping with her.

I unfurl my wings just enough to see the bite on her neck. Four big puncture wounds bleed slightly. Leaning forward, I lick the blood away. She'll heal fast because she's mine.

My mate's chest heaves with aftershocks, but she eyes mine like a predator. My dick throbs inside her, and she grunts.

"Give me your neck, Shepherd," my mate commands, her voice sultry.

I unfurl my wings and reach out, gripping the ceiling with my claws. Thea strokes her way along both wings, laughing when I shudder and growl. Her soft lips come to my chest, and then she nips and bites, toying with me.

Anticipation has me hard inside her, my hips moving slowly as I start to fuck her again.

"You're fucking sloppy for me, angel." My voice is broken gravel as I throw my head back, letting her bite her way up my neck.

Gods, I'm dying to know what spot she'll choose. Because when she does this, my heartbeat will start, and then she'll be mine forever.

Thea growls like an animal, licking at a spot just below my ear. I gasp at the pleasure that builds in my system, my balls pulling up tight against my body. Her lips are nothing more than a light, teasing flutter against my skin. I roll my hips, rubbing against her clit with every thrust, her channel clenching tightly around me.

"I'm gonna come so hard when you bite me," I growl, closing my eyes to savor the feel of her lips as she explores me. But then she lets out a low groan, her channel tightening around me. She's close.

Thea goes wild, biting her way from my shoulder back up to that spot under my ear. When that bite grows harder and breaks the skin, a dam breaks somewhere inside me. All that connection, all that gorgeous intent, floods through me as orgasm erupts between us.

She screams into the bite, her pussy milking me as I howl and roar her name. Every muscle in my body is clenched tight. She bites harder. A new bond snaps into place between us, a stronger sense of her.

Something bursts inside my chest, great, rolling waves of pleasure sending my eyes rolling back in the sockets.

Thwomp.

Thwomp.

Thwomp.

Thea gasps and groans, her ear pressed to my chest.

I let go of my hold on the ceiling and fall into bed, threading our legs together.

Blue eyes shine brightly in the fading light.

"Your heart," Thea murmurs, rubbing at my chest. She presses her ear flat to my skin.

I can feel my body pumping blood. I can feel the beat of my own heart speed up slightly to match hers. The sensation of a heartbeat is so new, so unusual. After a long minute, it syncs perfectly, beating in time with hers.

Satisfaction and pride flood the bond we share now.

"You're mine, little witch." I smile, leaning down to rub my horns gently over her heart. It feels so good to touch her with them. "And I'm yours," I whisper, bringing my lips to hers.

I pull her on top of me, rolling onto my back with a grin.

She smiles, thrumming her fingers along the bite at my neck. "Let's do that again, mate."

CHAPTER THIRTY
THEA

I wake in the morning surprisingly settled. I should be unsettled given the events of yesterday. Thank god Shepherd missed the part where I couldn't control my magic. The wards turned into huge barriers. I couldn't get in and the Keeper couldn't get out. It was dicey for a sec until Richard came out of nowhere. His showing up allowed me to focus, and the Keeper was by my side in a moment.

Surrounded by thralls, I wasn't terrified even then. I was focused and pissed. And I could sense that same sentiment from the Keeper and Richard. It was clear to me—I'm meant to protect this place. My power can be used to keep Ever safe, but I've got to learn what I'm doing so I can keep myself safe too.

I roll over in our nest. God, how does it smell so good after a night of supreme fuckery? So many fluids should be all over the bedding right now, but somehow it smells good and there aren't any sticky spots. I'm pondering that when the door opens, and Shepherd strides through with a plate full of croissants in one hand and two cups of coffee in the other.

The cottage shuts the door quietly behind him. I shuffle onto my knees to help him with the coffee and the croissants.

"You are the best with snacks," I laugh, biting into one to find gooey chocolate dripping from inside.

I roll my eyes in pleasure and flop carefully into the pillows, devouring the croissant as I look over at my mate. .

My mate.

It's really something, to think he's mine forever and ever. I can feel his heartbeat connected to mine. It's the best warm hug I could ever hope for.

Shepherd's dark lips curl into a satisfied smirk, his eyes dropping to my neck.

"That's gonna scar, isn't it?" I huff, trying to look down and see it, but he placed it close enough to my neck that I can't see it.

"Mhm," he snarks. "Mine will too."

"Not hardly," I snort. "I barely broke the skin."

"It's all about intent, angel," he says with a grin, leaning over to take a huge bite out of my croissant.

He moans around a mouthful of chocolate, and hearing that noise makes me want to repeat last night.

Still, I'm protective of my croissant. I tuck it on the side of the nest with my coffee. Then I crawl on top of my big mate and kiss his chest. He sips his coffee and watches me.

"I made croissants for your sisters too. Wren already threatened to come get them if we don't show up for witchy lessons on time."

"I made pretty good strides yesterday," I huff. "You missed the worst, scary bit, but the short version is I reinforced the wards with my magic. It was hard to focus, but I did it."

"Oh, I know," Shepherd growls, his tone bitter. "I took a trip up to the Keeper's castle early this morning to have a word. He put you in danger, and I won't stand for that. To be honest, I'm shocked he did it."

"I'm not upset," I say gently. "I understand, and we accomplished the outcome we were aiming for."

"Never again," Shepherd purrs, his tone brooking no argument. He's mad.

I understand. "I'll do what I have to to protect this place, mate, same as you," I warn.

A little bit of chocolate is on his lower lip, and I'm having trouble concentrating on the serious topic when he needs a good, hard nibble.

"I don't want you putting yourself at risk like that, please. For the sake of my sanity, let's don't do that again."

"I can't promise that," I say, finally getting serious. "But I can promise to make sure you know what's going on, okay?"

Shepherd growls and looks away. That streak of chocolate begs for my tongue.

Shoving myself right into his face, I suck the chocolate off his plump, swollen lower lip. I attacked him like an animal last night, and he's covered in small scrapes.

"Move in with me tonight," he demands when we part. "I want you here."

On cue, the closet opens, and I notice all the clothes are shoved to one side. Three drawers on the right-hand side open and close like piano keys. The cottage seems to be laughing.

Oh, I don't think that'll be a hardship at all.

"Yes. As long as you don't stop cooking for Morgan and Wren. They'd miss our dinners."

"Never," Shepherd agrees. "They're my family too, you know . . ." A smirk hovers at the edges of his lips. "I need you at least once before we go to work, angel."

"Good," I laugh, sliding down his big body toward his cock. It bobs against his stomach.

Groaning, I circle the tip with my tongue. "I'll start."

∾

Two hours later—and half an hour late—we show up at the garden. Wren's already there, chatting with Ohken, Miriam, and Catherine about the moonflower vines. I can't hear them, but I don't miss the way the big troll is focused on my sister, even when Catherine starts to speak.

Amusement fills the new bond I share with Shepherd. He explained it as us having a sense of one another's emotions. It'll continue to grow stronger the longer we're mated. Eventually, we'll be able to direct emotions toward one another. I can't wait.

Wren's green eyes light up when she sees us arriving, but they narrow just as quickly. She crosses her arms.

"I've been waiting on those croissants for half an hour, you big lunk."

I laugh and hold a basket out. "My fault. We were busy talking about moving my stuff to the cottage, among other things." I shove my hair to the side, showing off the bite.

Wren gasps, Catherine chuckles, and Ohken growls out a congratulations, shaking Shepherd's hand.

"The croissants are finally here?" Morgan strides through the garden gate behind us with Alo and Iggy. Iggy zooms off his father's shoulder and flies for mine, landing lightly with his tail around my neck. The moment his spade lies on my chest, I realize I can sense his emotion too. He's elated—and starving. And focused on the croissants.

Shepherd must sense my surprise.

"It's a whole family thing," he whispers into my ear.

I can practically feel my devil horns growing. If I can sense emotion, maybe I can play matchmaker a little bit between Miriam and Alo. Even now, she's staring at him with such open longing.

I hand Iggy a croissant, and then Wren takes the basket and offers one to the rest of our group.

Morgan joins us, grabbing a croissant from the basket. She bumps my hip with hers.

"I heard through the grapevine you had a little trouble yesterday with my lover boy?"

"That's one way to put it," I huff. "I went outside the wards and got attacked, but the Keeper and Richard came to my rescue, and here we are."

Morgan crosses her arms and scowls at me. "I swear to god, I'm going to murder him next time I see him." She takes an aggressive bite of her croissant.

I look at Wren, who's chuckling into her coffee and exchanging knowing looks with Ohken.

Catherine smiles at me before opening her arms wide.

"Shall we begin, girls?"

I don't think I've ever been happier in my life. Happily Ever after?

Yeah, I think so.

Wanna know what happens when Shepherd and Thea take snacks into the bedroom? Sign up for my newsletter at www. annafury.com to access the spicy bonus epilogue where all that (and more) transpires.

If you can't wait to see how Ohken offers to "teach" Wren, preorder Tangling With Trolls to find out!

TANGLING WITH TROLLS
SYNOPSIS

A month ago, I had no idea that monsters lived in hidden towns. Surprise! The tiny New-England town of Ever is a haven for them. Vampires run the coffee shop. The werewolf bikers will fix your car. They've got a gargoyle police force. I can sort of wrap my mind around that.

But then I meet Ohken Stonesmith, bridge troll and all-around badass. He's way older than me, crazy confident, and he owns the town's only flower shop. In short—he's perfect.

The second surprise? I'm a green witch! But when I struggle to use my newly-discovered magic, Ohken offers to teach me, even though his methods aren't exactly conventional. He's a big fan of teasing, withholding and making me crazy enough to get out of my own head—he worships my body the way every plus-sized girl dreams of. As our lessons grow more heated, I realize I'm falling for not only this wacky little town, but also the quiet male who's becoming my biggest cheerleader.

Unfortunately, not all monsters want to live in peace. When evil sneaks past the town's protective wards, I want to help. The only thing is, I keep blowing things up instead of fixing them. I've got to get control of my power fast, or this little town—and my budding romance with Ohken—will be in deep trouble.

CHAPTER ONE

WREN

I stare out the window of my mermaid-themed room at the Annabelle Inn, looking at the empty stone perch where a gargoyle sometimes sits. Alo told me he sits there in stone form when he needs a minute away from his rambunctious three year old son, Iggy.

I wonder where they are today? Probably up at Miriam's Sweets on Main getting candy, or maybe at Scoops getting ice cream. Sometimes I wonder if they go so much because of Iggy, or if Alo's just coming around to the idea of Miriam being head over heels for him.

They'll sort out their love story, if they're meant to have one. Or not.

That used to be my mother's favorite advice—*it'll either work out or it won't*. Which isn't advice at all, but more like a statement of the obvious. Thinking about her sends a stabbing sensation through my stomach, my heart clenching in my chest.

I miss her so much.

I look down at the journal resting on my thighs, wondering what my mother would think of the turn my life has taken.

I can almost imagine the conversation now. If cell phones worked here in Ever, and time didn't pass at the speed of molasses, I'd call her.

Hey Mom, me and the girls took a road trip, discovered a hidden monster town, and now Thea's dating a gargoyle!

She'd look shocked, and then she'd cackle, and then she'd make me my favorite caramel latte and we'd talk it out.

We can't talk it out anymore, though, so I'll journal it instead. It's what my therapist recommended after Mom and Dad died.

Thea and Morgan are handling our parents' deaths in different ways, and it's okay to grieve however you need to. I can hear Morgan working out through the Annabelle's thin walls.

Reaching over to the window, I stroke the glass softly and grin. "Let Morgan know I'm up?"

The house creaks and groans, and the window in front of me opens and shuts three times. The Inn's telling me she'll help me out.

Two seconds later, there's a loud crack and a thud, and Morgan shrieks.

"Annabelle! What gives?!"

I laugh, and the window next to my leg vibrates a little bit. The Annabelle is laughing along with me.

Houses laugh here in Ever, Massachussetts. It's not weird, it's totally fine. No matter that two weeks ago I had no idea there was a town where monsters hid from humans and houses came alive to choose their owners.

I hear footsteps stomping up the hallway, and then my bedroom door, which is painted with iridescent scales, flies open and hits the wall.

CHAPTER ONE

The Annabelle's pipes creak in warning.

My triplet, Morgan, stomps in with her long arms crossed. Auburn hair is piled high on her head and she's sweaty as fuck. She's gorgeous, though, even when she's pretending to be mad.

"Wren Elizabeth Hector, did you send the Annabelle to trip me?"

I snort. "Trip you? Hardly. I simply asked her to tell you I was up."

Morgan narrows her green eyes at me then kicks my door shut and looks up at the ceiling. It's painted with a stunning scene of mermaids frolicking on a beach. I follow her gaze up and sigh. "Isn't she lovely?"

"Isn't she wonderfullll..." Morgan mutters, crossing the room to flop down on the bench seat across from me.

The reading nook windows flutter open and closed quickly in greeting. Morgan reaches out and strokes the thick paned glass affectionately. Her eyes drop to my journal.

"I haven't seen you journal in a few weeks." Her voice is soft and thoughtful as green eyes flick up to mine.

I give her a saucy look. "Two weeks ago we were living in New York with normal jobs, totally unaware that Ever existed. Two weeks ago, Thea wasn't mated to a goddamn gargoyle. And two weeks ago? I didn't know all three of us were witches."

Morgan puffs air out of her lips and sits forward, picking at one of my Converse laces.

"Do you miss the outside world? I mean when our weekend here is done, do you think you might wanna go back even though Thea's staying?"

It's on the tip of my tongue to say 'hell no', because Ever and its monstrous inhabitants are fucking fascinating to me. But I miss my job as a botanist. And to say I'm not great at being a witch is the understatement of the century.

When I hesitate to answer, Morgan frowns. "That's what I thought." She crosses her arms after she unties and reties my shoelaces. "I know we all agreed we'd stay once she and Shepherd got together, but I feel like my opinion on that changes by the day."

I give her a grim look. "Would that have anything to do with the Keeper?"

Morgan stands and scowls. "He's part of it for sure, but more than anything I don't really feel like I have a place here."

I stand and tuck my journal behind a pillow in the window seat. Even the Annabelle is quiet after Morgan's pronouncement. Pulling my triplet in for a hug, I squeeze her crazy hard.

"We might find places here and we might not, and it's okay either way, right?"

"Yeah," she grumbles onto the side of my head.

"Plus we've basically got the best brother in law ever, and that's worth something too, right? Wouldn't you miss being constantly inundated with snacks?"

Morgan lifts her head at that and smiles. "I do fucking love Shepherd."

"He makes the best baked goods," I agree.

Morgan chuckles a little, her low mood disappearing a little bit. "I guess the whole gargoyle mating tradition of feeding his mate's family has worked out pretty well for us. I swear he shows up every day with some kind of food."

As if on cue, the doorbell rings, and the floor beneath our feet shifts. The Annabelle shoves us toward the door to my room, and the door itself opens politely. Morgan wraps her arm around my waist and we head out into the plush, carpeted hallway. Beautiful paintings of lush gardens and happy gargoyles and enchanting mermaids line the halls. They're all done in the same style. I think it must be Catherine, the Inn's lovely owner, but I haven't actually seen her paint yet.

Downstairs, a big shadow covers the entire front, glass-paned door.

Shepherd.

He peers in, grinning broadly at us with our triplet Thea standing in front of him with her face pressed to the glass. She's goofy as fuck on the best of days, but I think he's brought that personality characteristic out even more.

Morgan opens the door with a wry grin. "Ya know, I think Thea is already hooked like a prize fish, you don't have to keep feeding us every day." There's no actual chiding in her tone though, she adores Shepherd. Best I can tell, everyone in this damn town adores Shepherd.

Thea strides inside and hands Morgan a box. I can already smell freshly-baked cookies. When Shepherd ducks in after her, dark purple horns nearly hitting the doorway, I grumble.

"I've probably gained ten pounds since you started courting Thea. Any chance you know how to make healthy snacks?" I've always been the fat sister, and I'm fine as hell with that. I'm gorgeous and I know it. But since we met Shepherd, my diet seems to consist of 90% cookies and 10% his great grandmother's lasagna recipe.

Which is bangin', by the way.

He's wearing a plain white tee and jeans like every other day, his long tail wrapped around Thea's waist. The spade-shaped tip lies flat against her stomach. His enormous wings are tucked up behind his back like a cape, so he looks like a badass gargoyle hero from that 80's show I used to love.

Which he is.

I do find it a little interesting that my sister, the former detective, is now mated to a man whose job it is to protect this town. Like calls to like, I suppose.

"Are we ready for witchy woo lessons?" Thea claps excitedly, her long, blond braid swinging freely.

"Yeah!" I deadpan. "Can't wait to blow up more shit in the garden that literally powers the wards that keep the town safe. Goodie!"

Shepherd and Thea give me matching looks of warning.

He's the first to speak, though. "Wren, you've known, you were a witch for all of three weeks. Discovering this is a monster town was a huge shock. Be kind to yourself and eat more cookies, it'll help."

I snort at that. Morgan and Thea both grab my arm, and then we leave the Annabelle's cozy front entryway and head outside. Our view never fails to amaze me. Right across the street from the inn is the community garden. It's surrounded by a seven foot tall hedge, but as soon as you step through the open gate, it's like being in the secret garden from my favorite childhood classic.

A long A-frame support runs the length of the garden to my right. Giant gourds hang down in rows on the inside of the frame. It almost looks like a hallway dripping with pumpkins. That's where the town's pixies live when they're in small form. Which makes me wonder if Miriam is joining us today. She's become one of my closest friends since we arrived her.

As if on cue, a tiny green glow exits a hole in one of the gourds. It expands from being a mere dot until there's a quick flash, and Miriam stands there in her human-sized form. She's slight like Thea, but a little bit taller, almost my height. Her green pixie cut sticks up in the front like always, and it matches the green and pink dragonfly-esque wings fluttering at her back.

She eyes the box of cookies I'm carrying and claps her hands, trotting over to me excitedly. Without asking she rips open the top of the box and grabs a chocolate chip cookie, shoving it into her mouth. Her green eyes roll back into her head as she moans.

"By all means," I deadpan.

Miriam slaps my shoulder. "You love me. You'd never deny me snacks. That's why we're soulfriends."

That does pull a real smile to my face. The first time I met Miriam she pronounced me her 'soulfriend', and it's honestly just been our thing ever since. I think it miffs Morgan a little bit that she didn't get included in the title.

Unfortunately, Morgan has gotten the shit end of the stick about everything since we arrived in Ever. She's got the weirdest monster situationship. She's got the hardest witch power to master. And the Annabelle picks on her relentlessly, almost like she's trying to drive her out.

Oh.

Maybe she is. The houses in Ever do pick their inhabitants, after all. That thought hadn't occurred to me until now, but I make a mental note to talk to Catherine about it. The Inn seemed fine with all of us until we decided to stay. Hmm.

"Catherine's at the table," Miram chokes out around a mouthful of cookie, jerking her head toward the round table in the far corner of the garden. It's where we do most of our witch lessons.

"Ugh," I groan. "I suck so bad at this." My eyes flash to the edge of the table which is still burnt from my last attempt to control my green magic.

"Yeah, you really should be growing things as opposed to blowing them up," Miriam chirps helpfully. "But you'll get it."

"Thanks," I grunt as I snap the top of my cookie box closed. "No more for you Miriam."

She gives me a salty look and sticks out her tongue, reaching out with one veined, green wing to slap me on the back of the head.

Before I can holler about it, she pushes off the ground and flies up into the air, zipping up over the gourd structure.

I sigh and follow her. My sisters and Shepherd are already seated at the big, round table. I shoot Shepherd a pointed look. "Staying for today's show?"

He grins back at me, a dimple appearing on one side of his dark gray lips. "Wouldn't miss it for the world, sis."

Thea nudges him in the side and gives me a quick nod of solidarity.

Next to Shepherd, a cough draws my attention.

Catherine, the Annabelle Inn's owner and our current hostess, smiles at me. Salt and pepper waves hang in an elegant half updo framing her round face. Her smile is genuine, and just like every other day, she's wearing a beautiful wrap dress that accentuates her buxom, hourglass figure.

God, she's more put together in her sixties than I've ever been. She's elegant as fuck. And nice. She's the sexy grandmother I never knew I needed in my life.

Her lips purse and she looks over at Shepherd. "Friend, I think it might be easier if you don't stay and observe today. Would you mind giving the triplets some space, please?" She bats her eyes exaggeratedly.

He groans and sticks his tongue out at me. "No fun. I wanted to help put out another fire."

"Rude," Miriam snorts, grabbing my box of cookies and opening it back up to steal another.

"Hey," Shepherd starts, pointing his finger at each of us in turn. "I brought her that box of cookies you know. The Hector triplets are mine now. Shouldn't I get to be here for the downs as well as the ups?"

"Honey," Thea says with a laugh. "Get outta here."

I watch Shepherd purse his lips, but he leans over and nuzzles Thea's cheek, growling playfully. He looks up to wink at me and then stands. I'm pretty sure we all stare at his ass as he crouches down and then rockets up into the sky, spreading his wings wide as he grabs an air current and shoots toward Main Street.

Thea sighs and grabs one of my cookies, shoving the whole thing in her mouth.

When he's gone, Catherine sets a giant, tall purple crystal in the center of the table. I hate this damn thing. Thea immediately grabs it, smiling when the crystal glows a bright purple, lit from within by a billion tiny dots. I watch in awe like I always do. Morgan sits stone-faced next to me. Thea grabbed ahold of her magic from day one, it seemed, and she's getting better by leaps and bounds.

"Excellent, Thea!" Catherine chirps. "I don't think you'll even need the crystal soon."

Thea beams, then gives Morgan and me a baleful glance. "I was able to envision the wards yesterday for a few moments before it faded. I'm definitely starting to be able to focus on my power. I'm thankful, just in case something happens to the wards again." Her smile falls, and the table grows silent. Ever's cute as shit, but it's got its cons—most notably the soul-sucking thralls who constantly try to burrow through the wards to attack us.

You know, normal small town monster things.

Catherine looks over at me, gesturing at the crystal. "I don't know that Ohken will be able to join us this morning for training, but he said I should tell you to come find him later if you'd like to practice outside the garden." She doesn't grin super huge, but I know she wants to. It's a well known fact I think the town's one-and-only troll is hot as hell. I'm pretty sure he knows it too, and while he's very flirtatious, he's never made a move.

And I am not the girl to put the moves on a man who's not interested. Plus, I've got bigger fish to fry. Like figuring out how to grow things in this garden with my magic, instead of burning them to the ground.

Thea sets the crystal back in the center of the table. I grab it and close my eyes, focusing on the garden itself. Like always, I can sense the earthworms under the dirt and follow the myriad network of plant roots. I can always do that part, but then my focus changes, and the crystal zings my hand so hard, I drop it to the table with a yelp.

Catherine gestures to the crystal with an expectant look. She's always so encouraging and never makes me feel bad that I didn't pick up magic quickly like Thea.

Grimacing, I reach out for the crystal again.

BOOKS BY ANNA FURY (MY OTHER PEN NAME)

DARK FANTASY SHIFTER OMEGAVERSE

Temple Maze Series

NOIRE | JET | TENEBRIS

DYSTOPIAN OMEGAVERSE

Alpha Compound Series

THE ALPHA AWAKENS | WAKE UP, ALPHA | WIDE AWAKE | SLEEPWALK | AWAKE AT LAST

Northern Rejects Series

ROCK HARD REJECT | HEARTLESS HEATHEN | PRETTY LITTLE SINNER

Scan the QR code to access all my books, socials, current deals and more!

@annafuryauthor
liinks.co/annafuryauthor

ABOUT THE AUTHOR

Hazel Mack is the sweet alter-ego of Anna Fury, a North Carolina native fluent in snark and sarcasm, tiki decor, and an aficionado of phallic plants. Visit her on Instagram for a glimpse of the sexiest wiener wallpaper you've ever seen. #ifyouknowyouknow

She writes any time she has a free minute—walking the dog, in the shower, ON THE TOILET. The voices in her head wait for no one. When she's not furiously hen-pecking at her computer, she loves to hike and bike and get out in nature.

She currently lives in Raleigh, North Carolina, with her Mr. Right, a tiny tornado, and a lovely old dog. Hazel LOVES to connect with readers, so visit her on social or email her at author@annafury.com.

Printed in Great Britain
by Amazon

33038713R00163